"EVERYBODY THAT GOT HIT WAS SHOT FROM A DISTANCE, RIGHT?"

Unable to figure out where Grissom was going with this, Sara took the ride. "That seems to be the consensus."

"Shot from the front," Grissom said, gesturing to himself, "or side."

"Right. That was the line of fire."

"Mostly hit with nine-millimeter rounds, correct?"

"Mostly, or something bigger. From the shell casings and bullets we've harvested, I think a couple of the shooters had .357s."

Nodding, Grissom said, "So, if we begin with everybody shot with nine mils or larger, and from a distance . . . how do we explain Nick Valpo being shot up close and personal . . . from *behind* . . . and with a small-caliber weapon?"

Now she frowned in thought. "Somebody took advantage of the melee . . . and committed a murder in the middle of a gunfight?"

"Yes," Grissom said. "B   urder, exactly."

"No?"

His eyes tensed

CSI:
CRIME SCENE INVESTIGATION™

SNAKE EYES
a novel

Max Allan Collins

Based on the hit CBS series "CSI: Crime Scene Investigation" produced by CBS PRODUCTIONS, a business unit of CBS Broadcasting Inc., and ALLIANCE ATLANTIS PRODUCTIONS, INC.

Executive Producers: Jerry Bruckheimer, Carol Mendelsohn, Anthony E. Zuiker, Ann Donahue, Naren Shankar, Cynthia Chvatal, William Petersen, Danny Cannon, Jonathan Littman

Series created by: Anthony E. Zuiker

POCKET STAR BOOKS
New York   London   Toronto   Sydney

An *Original* Publication of POCKET BOOKS

A Pocket Star Book published by
POCKET BOOKS, a division of Simon & Schuster, Inc.
1230 Avenue of the Americas, New York, NY 10020

ISBN-13: 978-0-7434-9665-0
ISBN-10:   0-7434-9665-5

This Pocket Books paperback edition September 2006

10 9 8 7 6 5 4 3 2 1

POCKET STAR BOOKS and colophon are registered
trademarks of Simon & Schuster, Inc.

Cover design by Patrick Kang
Photograph by John Lamb/Getty Images

Manufactured in the United States of America

For information about special discounts for bulk purchases,
please contact Simon & Schuster Special Sales at
1-800-456-6798 or business@simonandschuster.com.

AUTHOR'S NOTE

From the beginning, as an author of novels based on *CSI: Crime Scene Investigation*, I have followed the lead of the gifted creative team behind the show. As such, these novels have tended to lag behind the continuity of the television series.

This story takes place some time after the previous novel, *Killing Game* (2005), during the period when the CSI team had been split into two shifts . . . and just prior to the dramatic events that would bring this family of investigators back together.

I would also like to acknowledge my assistant on this work, forensics researcher/co-plotter **Matthew V. Clemens.**

Further acknowledgments appear at the conclusion of this novel.

M.A.C.

For the real CSIs of the LVMPD—
who sparked the idea of this novel

"It is completely unimportant.
That is why it is so interesting."

—Agatha Christie's Hercule Poirot

"There is nothing like
first-hand evidence."

—Sir Arthur Conan Doyle's Sherlock Holmes

"I knew it was a fight for life,
and I drew in defense of my brothers
and Doc Holliday."

—Wyatt Earp at the OK Corral inquest

THE MYTH OF THE GOLD RUSH has captivated the world since America's first post–Lewis and Clark westward move—when mountain men, prospectors, settlers, and gunfighters set out to explore a vast, unknown landscape in search of vast, unknown treasure.

Over the passage of time, that concept has changed only slightly: the gold rush rushes on, but the destinations have shifted—instead of Sutter's Mill or Deadwood or Tombstone, names like Romanov, The Sphere, or Platinum King await fortune-seekers.

Yes, the rush is still on, and those who wish to strike it rich—as always—find a way to make their journeys. No longer do wagon trains bump and bounce over the Oregon Trail, nor do horses sprint over the Great Plains; modern-day prospectors arrive at McCarran by way of airlines. In the wilds of Vegas, riders on mustangs have been replaced by those in Mustangs—not to mention Cherokee and Wrangler Jeeps, Eldorado Caddies, and Dodge Durangos, today's west echoing yesterday's.

Little has changed, however, about what the hopeful expect to find upon arriving in Las Vegas. Sin City—at least in the imaginations of travelers—still has more in common with the Old West towns of Deadwood and Tombstone than the chamber of commerce might care to admit. In their day, those wild and wooly boomtowns were regarded as wide open in a manner not unlike today's Las Vegas. Sex, gambling, booze, and the day's top entertainers could be found in both the notorious South Dakota mining camp and that infamous silver-mining boomtown in Arizona. And, no matter how family-friendly the chamber might paint it, a similar naughty playground awaits tourists in the Nevada desert . . . and not just in Vegas.

Fifty miles down Highway 95, south of Las Vegas (but still in Clark County), planted in Piute Valley, rests Boot Hill, Nevada—a hamlet of 5,654 (prior to the event at the Four Kings Hotel & Casino, that is) with even more in common with the wild boomtowns of the Old West.

Where Deadwood had Wild Bill Hickock and Tombstone boasted Wyatt Earp and Doc Holliday, Boot Hill traded on being the only western town in America to which all three of these gunfighters had, at one time or another, individually found their way. None stayed as long as six months, all traveling on to bigger and wilder adventures; but this bump in the desert road held a rare historical honor as the only place where every one of these Wild West superstars had stopped and stayed for a time and, before leaving the dusty gold camp, taken the trouble of reducing the population of Boot Hill while adding to the population of boot hill.

Perhaps not the greatest thing to build a town's reputation on—three famous gunfighters killing three unknown miscreants—but it had worked. Over the years, tourists had found their way to the off-the-beaten-path hamlet with its dubious place in the history of the Old West—guidebooks, unkindly if accurately, often referred to Boot Hill as "the poor man's Tombstone."

In the late '80s—1980s, that is—the tourist business had dried up, and Boot Hill found itself slinking toward a fate it had once narrowly avoided: becoming that commonplace historical footnote of the Old West, the ghost town. Boot Hill was shrinking by the day—at its peak, over ten thousand residents had made livings from the tourist and gambling trade. By 1991, the town's six casinos had dwindled to two; the only businesses to survive: one grocery, two gas stations, a bank, three restaurants, and a lightbulb factory.

Then the town invested municipal funds in the dot-com boom of the later '90s, and things started to turn around. The city fathers took that money and reinvested it in drawing tourists back—a museum; monthly reenactments of their famous gunfights; statues of Earp, Holliday, and Hickock in the park; even a strip mall—creating a small oasis on the road to that mirage of wealth, Las Vegas.

No one can yet say whether the incident at the Four Kings will prove a boon or deterrent to the future of Boot Hill, though certainly the poor man's Tombstone has finally found its OK Corral gunfight. The crime scene investigators of the LVPD, however, are neither sociologists nor prognosticators, and the only history that interests them most is the recent history inherent in a crime scene.

In Boot Hill, at the Four Kings, after the living are sorted from the dead, the CSIs' job was to sift the sands of evidence not for gilt, but the guilty. . . .

one said, just as she had been for most of the la

1

HERE IT WAS APRIL FOOL'S DAY, and Vanessa Delware was still in Boot Hill—some joke.

The petite, pretty brunette barely seemed old enough to enter the Four Kings Hotel & Casino, let alone be a seasoned dealer. Even with her shoulder-length hair tucked up in a businesslike bun, and black plastic-rimmed glasses that made her large blue eyes look even bigger, she might have been a high school kid, though she was in fact twenty-one, her tightly packed little body swimming in the white frilly shirt with red bow tie, and black tuxedo slacks.

At least dealers didn't have to wear the skimpy outfits the barmaids did, not that that stopped drunks from grabbing at her and making salacious remarks. If this were Vegas, that sort of thing wouldn't have been tolerated. And anyway, Vegas promised a better class of groper.

Yet, here she still was in Boot Hill, working second shift, just as she had been for most of the last year. But Vanessa had vowed long ago that she would get out of Boot Hill—growing up in a little bump in the road had been bad enough and contributed to the poor decision she'd made, putting out for a cute boy whose body piercings were many but whose prospects had been zero.

Pregnant at twenty, local girl Vanessa had found herself abandoned by her boyfriend—*ex*-boyfriend, the loser—and barely tolerated by her mother, who'd had enough trouble making her own ends meet since divorcing *her* loser husband when Vanessa was fifteen. Cody Jacks, a family friend who worked part-time at the Four Kings, had pulled some strings and helped Vanessa get the job. The casino was glad to train her—a pretty young dealer was a nice draw (nicer draw than most card players otherwise got).

She'd taken this small opportunity to heart and vowed to make her life as a single mother succeed.

The plan had been formulated in the hospital. She and Cyndi, her infant daughter, would be in Vegas by next Thanksgiving . . . which became next Christmas, then Valentine's Day, and now here it was April *Fool's* Day and she was still tossing cards in Boot Hill, not in a glitzy casino along the Strip.

Of course, working here, sort of apprenticing here, had been part of the plan (even a cute girl couldn't walk in off the street and get hired in a top casino without credentials, without skills). But *staying* this long *hadn't* been.

Oh, she made decent money, really good tips some nights, but always there were bills and more bills (babies were *expensive*), and she just could not seem to get enough saved for her and Cyndi to make that mere fifty-mile move up the highway.

She hated her situation; she felt stranded in the midst of her own life. Vegas was the promised land, so very close and yet always just out of reach. . . .

Usually around this time of day, the casino was empty, most tourists either having an early dinner or in their rooms resting before the night's attack on the gaming tables. Around her blackjack station, bells tinkled, whistles blew, and the slots made their various obnoxious noises over the piped-in country-western music, the whoosh of the air-conditioning, and the chatter of the gamblers who were scattered around the casino's convention center–size floor. The cacophony barely registered with Vanessa, who had long ago learned to tune it out. She concentrated on the cards . . . and the people.

Unlike on most days at a slow time like this, Vanessa found herself with three gamblers seated at every other chair of the seven places at her table. To her left, a fortyish fat man in denim shorts and a souvenir T-shirt ("Go to Boot Hill and Live!") constantly had to be reminded about the hand signals used in the game to aid security cameras in following the action. At center sat a younger guy, mid-thirties with a nice build and an okay face; beyond him, a busty middle-aged woman with weary features and dyed blond hair was clad in a beige sweater and tan skirt.

All three were losing—only the guy in the center seemed to have any idea how to play—and they were all chain-smoking. Vanessa knew she shouldn't be annoyed by that—heavy smokers were an occupational hazard—but why couldn't they have plopped down across the aisle at Laura's table? Laura smoked even more than *they* did!

No, they had to gather around Vanessa's table, constantly belching fumes in her direction; and what with the way they were losing, she had absolutely *no* tip to look forward to.

Even if she was the dealer, Vanessa felt like the *real* loser, on a day like this. . . .

"Hit me," the guy on the left said, hands on the table's edge.

"Sir . . . your hand signal?" she reminded him for what felt like the hundredth time (though the guy had been playing barely ten minutes).

The guy gave her a "sorry" shrug, made the proper gesture, and she hit his fifteen with a queen and busted him out of another five dollars, which she swept away as if it had never existed.

The younger center-seated guy offered up a sympathetic smile and tapped the table for a hit on his thirteen. She fed him a three, his smile got broader, then he tapped the table again and she busted his sixteen with a seven. His smile quickly disappeared, his body not far behind as he spun off the stool and stalked off.

The weary woman down at the end took a drag on her cigarette and decided to stand on her fifteen after watching what had happened to her compatriots. Flipping her hand, Vanessa showed a seventeen and sucked up the chips from the woman, just as she had with the other two.

Scanning the room slowly, she mindlessly dealt another round to the two losers. Even though she gave them an empty smile with each card, she was paying them only the barest attention now as her eyes caught a group across the casino, a regiment of leather-clad bikers emptying from the three elevators—the Predators.

Here for the annual Boot Hill Biker Blowout, the Predators had been spending one week a year in town for as far back as Vanessa could remember. Many retailers had ceased to see the advantage of having several-hundred-plus rowdy bikers around, even if they *were* pumping money into the local economy. She'd on more than one occasion overheard some merchants bitching that the Biker Blowout was turning their "fair city" into Boot Hell.

Hypocritical jerks, Vanessa thought. The city fathers gladly accepted the bikers' money, only to constantly complain about the gangs and the sort of trouble they brought with them.

"'Nother card, honey?" the bottle blonde asked, sighing smoke in Vanessa's direction.

"Sorry," Vanessa said, and managed a smile and a card for each: the heavyset T-shirt guy a seven to go with his nine, the woman mumbling an obscenity as Vanessa dealt her a five to go with her eight.

T-shirt Guy studied his hand for a long moment, said, "Stay," then at the last minute remembered to wave his hand for the benefit of the camera.

As she dropped the last card on the bottle blonde's hand, Vanessa saw the group of maybe twenty Predators moving across the casino floor in her general direction. After a moment, the woman motioned for a hit and Vanessa dropped a queen on her hand and busted the woman out.

The bottle blonde seemed just about to say something when the Predators started fanning out around the table. She and T-shirt Guy seemed to suddenly have somewhere else to be, and gathered up what was left of their chips and scurried away.

With proprietary swaggers, the four Predators sat down at Vanessa's table. The two in the middle she recognized as Nick Valpo—the Predator leader himself—and his second-in-command, Jake Hanson.

Vanessa had known guys like these all her life— hell, her baby's father would have fit in with the Predators. And she didn't mind them—really. One at a time, they could be fine. They could be nice.

In groups, however, they could be . . . a handful. Particularly when they had eyes glistening with the dullness of drink.

Of the half-dozen security men in the casino at this hour—late afternoon, fairly light security staffing, a few more in the video room—the only one Vanessa's eyes sought out was Cody.

A Boot Hill police officer, Cody Jacks moonlighted at the Four Kings, as did virtually every cop on the force. Cody was a big, tough, dependable bruiser whom she could count on to keep the peace.

Finally, she spotted him over near the slots, his eyes glued to her table, even though he was mostly out of sight. He wore the silly red sport coat of the male floor employees—black slacks, white shirt with a black string tie. Already she felt comforted, knowing he was looking out for her.

Tall, with lupine gray eyes, Jacks may not have been the hardbody he was twenty years ago (why hadn't her mother married *him*?), but he still provided an imposing figure. Sure, his hair had grayed at the temples, and his waistband hung farther south than it used to.

But Cody Jacks could still lay down the law; and that feeling calmed Vanessa.

Not that she was really worried about Valpo, Hanson, or any of the other Predators, for that matter. All the years the Blowout had been going down, the motorcycle gang had never started any *real* trouble in either of Boot Hill's casinos or any of its several saloons.

Oh, yeah, of course, some fights here, some drunken partying there, a couple of broken slot machines; but stuff like that happened in a gambling town whether a motorcycle gang was around or not.

Her concern—and no doubt Cody's, too—was the Rusty Spokes, another motorcycle gang that had been regularly attending the Biker Blowout for the last couple of years.

A Phoenix outfit that seemed to go out of its way not to get along with the Predators, the Spokes had infringed a little more on the Predators' turf all week, at every turn.

Tensions were running high.

The Predators were staying at the Four Kings, technically, but not really—their rooms were strictly for partying; the gang kept its HQ at a campground on the south edge of town.

The Spokes, meanwhile, had taken up residence at the Gold Vault, the casino motel directly across the street from the Four Kings. A certain antagonism between the two casinos underscored the rivalry between the motorcycle crews.

Fistfights and worse had been going on all week. Around the casino, rumor had it that the Rusty Spokes planned to force a showdown with the

Predators and had designated Boot Hill to host the action.

While Vanessa would have liked to dismiss the rumor as paranoid b.s., she knew it made a sick sort of sense. After all, Phoenix had too big a police force to risk a showdown, and the Predators seemed to have no fixed home, bouncing between dozens of small towns in California, Nevada, and Arizona. Both groups knew that Police Chief Jorge Lopez had only a small force in Boot Hill, and that the nearest Highway Patrol substations in Jean (to the northwest) and Laughlin (to the southeast) were both over thirty miles away.

The only real police force of any size was the Las Vegas Police Department, the nation's ninth largest . . . but that, as Vanessa knew only too well, was a world away, fifty miles from Boot Hill.

Two nights ago (and this was no rumor) Chief Lopez and three of his officers had broken up what appeared about to turn into a nasty knife fight between the two factions (her coworker Laura had said, "It's a real powder keg, I tell ya, Vannie . . . and it's *lit*!").

She'd talked to Cody about it just before her shift started.

"Should be cool," the older man said. "Jorge put the fear of God in 'em. Past twenty-four hours, Spokes and Predators been avoidin' each other like the plague."

"Really?"

Cody nodded. "Tomorrow, Blowout's over, and these fellas'll be on the road back home. Like the song says, 'head out on the highway, lookin' for adventure.'"

And, across the room, Cody was giving Vanessa a reassuring smile. She gave him a little nod, then turned her attention to the Predators at the table.

The first one on the left, long brown hair swept straight back, wore worn jeans, a white T-shirt under an Army shirt with the sleeves ripped off, and that same smart-ass smirk that Vanessa had seen on a hundred bullies. Though thinner and younger, he reminded her of that weird-hair guy from *The Sopranos*, the one in Springsteen's band.

On his left sat the head Predator, Nick Valpo. Nearly fifty, the shirtless Valpo sported a black cotton vest, his skin frog-belly white, belying how much time he spent on his hog tearing across the desert. Two tattoos nestled in the hairy thatch on his chest— over the right breast, a dagger pierced a heart, blood drops trailing down his torso (allegedly one for every man he had killed), and center-chest a caricature of himself with the words "Ride Or Die" emblazoned beneath it peered from between dark curls.

Like his underling, Valpo wore his hair combed straight back, which emphasized his widow's peak, showing shiny skull where some balding betrayed his age. A black goatee, three or four inches long, looked like an odd sponge hanging from the leader's chin—a clownish effect that was nonetheless intimidating, perhaps due to Valpo's seemingly black, burning eyes.

To Vanessa, the Predator leader looked like Charles Manson on crank; on the other hand, during the several times he'd sat at her table this week, he'd been nice, even sweet to her, and not in a coming-on-to-her way.

Next to Valpo, his chief lieutenant, Jake Hanson, provided a contrast to his buddies, his jeans relatively new, white T-shirt cleaner, and an unbuttoned blue-and-white short-sleeved shirt, not a ratty vest. Hanson had soft blue eyes that reminded Vanessa of a mountain stream. The others were definitely bikers, but Jake Hanson might have been a rock star.

The final Predator of the quartet wore his dark greasy hair parted crookedly near the middle and had a skinny black beard and mustache, possibly intended to make him look older, though the effect was the opposite. He might have been a high school thespian who'd glued on a beard for a role. Vanessa probably should have carded the kid, but why push it with this bunch? Like Cody said, tomorrow they'd be going, going, gone.

"What're you waitin' for?" the bearded kid asked irritably. "Deal, bitch!"

Valpo shook his head, eyes narrowed, and gave her a warm, apologetic smile. "Vanessa, he's young. Be patient with his young ass. . . . Dicky, shut the hell up and treat her like the lady she so obviously is."

Vanessa nodded her nervous thanks to Valpo and dealt. The first guy busted and Valpo got a blackjack.

"Surprise, surprise," Dicky said from the far end.

Holding his breath for a long moment, Valpo seemed to be concentrating on something somewhere in the distance; then his eyes found Dicky's and held them, snake and mouse.

"Dicky, I swear to Christ, if you don't shut it, I'm gonna take you outside and beat the ever-livin' piss out of you myself till your manners improve."

"Ah, come on, dude—"

"Dude. I don't care if your mom's my cousin or not. Be nice to the dealer. Try to remember you're indoors."

Hanson held on nineteen and Dicky managed to start out with nine and still find a way to bust.

"Daaaamn!" Dicky yelped.

Vanessa turned over an eighteen. "Paying a black-jack and a winner." Her eyes caught the blue-eyed Hanson's, and when she passed over his winnings their hands brushed for an instant.

God, he is cute, she thought. *Who does he remind me of?*

"I can't believe this crap," Dicky groused. "Is there any other kinda luck but bad luck in this town?"

Valpo shot him a glare and Dicky went silent. "Here's a thought, sunshine—don't hit on seventeen and maybe you won't lose every damn time."

"You think I don't know how to play cards?" Dicky challenged. "I know how to play cards."

Laughing, Valpo said, "I *know* you *can't* play cards. You can barely play with yourself . . . Dicky bird."

Dicky reddened, but Hanson and the other guy joined Valpo's laughter and nothing was left but for Dicky to take it: he was the kid, Valpo the man.

Vanessa was working not to join in the laughter when she looked toward the front door and beheld an unsettling sight.

Twenty or so Rusty Spokes were rolling into the casino like a bad wind.

That put a chill up Vanessa's spine, and her eyes immediately darted around looking for Cody, for *any* security guy. . . .

She caught Cody, already moving toward the door. But as she turned to see what the Spokes were going to do, guns—as if from nowhere—seemed to appear in all of the intruders' hands. Revolvers, shotguns, rifles . . . was that a *machine* gun? Jesus!

The first shot was fired before Vanessa could utter a sound.

Her mind managed to form the thought, *What about the damn metal detectors?*

But that was as far as she got before Jake Hanson leapt over the table and swept her into his arms. They rolled to the floor and Vanessa looked up just as bullets from the machine gun ripped into her table, tossing splinters like a dealer flipping cards.

Instinctively, she turned her head away and found herself staring into the blue eyes of Jake Hanson, who still held her. His face seemed peaceful even as hell exploded around them.

Mouth to her ear, as if kissing it, he yelled, "Are you okay?"

That's what it took for her to hear the words over the din of the gunfire.

She nodded. He released her from his grip, and the fear hit her harder—she had felt safe, somehow, cocooned in his arms. He flashed a smile, winked, rolled away, rose to a crouch, and moved off.

The smell of shooting filled the air, making her choke. Gun smoke and stirred dust and wood fragments clouded the room and, cowering behind and flush against the bullet-riddled blackjack table, Vanessa felt like this might go on forever—already it seemed like forever since she had turned to see the Rusty Spokes entering the casino and those guns materializing and yet still the guns clattered, some of the Predators now returning fire.

How in God's name had this many guns made it past the metal detectors?

Around her, other patrons, the ones on the floor in fear, those not part of either gang, still had the wherewithal to gather up chips spilled around them by the battle. Nothing could kill greed.

Or anyway, nothing as inconsequential as a fire-fight in the middle of a casino.

She did not avert her eyes, much as she wanted to—she was not ready to shut the world out and just wait and hope and pray she would open her eyes without a bullet finding her first. The violence, the carnage, the destruction had the same hypnotic effect as being in a car crash and having the world go into slow motion. The heavyset guy in the Boot Hill T-shirt took a bullet in the chest and scarlet showered from the ripped logo as he keeled over backward, smacking his head on the corner of a slot machine as he went, which made Vanessa wince even though she knew the man might be dead before his head came anywhere near the machine. . . .

To her right came an explosive sound—*a grenade?*—and her eyes shot in that direction of their own volition. On the floor, in an aisle, a man twitched and danced, blood spurting from a hole in his right pants leg where his limb had been severed by the blast—shotgun, not grenade. He was screaming, but she could not hear him, or anyway discern distinctly the screaming out of the overall din. But she could tell he was bleeding to death, and she averted her eyes, finally taking control of them.

She could feel the wet warmth of tears on her cheeks and wondered, as if from a distance, why she was crying when she was not among the injured, one of the lucky ones in this unlucky casino.

Farther to her right, Jake Hanson was ducking behind a craps table, jamming a fresh clip into a huge black pistol. He then rose and fired several rounds in the direction of the Spokes and ducked down again.

To her left, maybe twenty feet away, the Predators' leader knelt behind a video poker machine. Every few seconds, he would peek out, squeeze off a couple shots, then dodge back behind the machine. When he turned toward her, he saw her watching him and flashed her a grin as if he was having a great time.

The insanity in that smile gave Vanessa an urge to jump up and run screaming from the room; but survival instinct overrode that. She kept her head down and did not move. As for Valpo, he still had that maniacal grin pasted on, though his wide eyes spoke of hysteria and fear.

Valpo leaned out from behind his cover, raised his pistol, and a crimson flower bloomed in his right shoulder, the gun springing from his grasp and bouncing out of reach under a table across an aisle where bullets zinged and pinged.

As Valpo fell sideways, back behind the poker machine, Vanessa finally picked out a sound other than general gunfire—*sirens*.

Whether they were near or far she could not tell, but help was clearly coming, the wailing getting louder by the second.

As if wanting to strike back before the local law arrived to stop their fun, Valpo scrabbled after the pistol, shots chewing up the carpeting and shaking machines till their coins rattled, bullets all around him as he dove for the weapon.

Just as Valpo got to the pistol, a ghostly figure moved through the smoke and dust and running people and came up behind the Predator leader, aiming a handgun at the back of the man's head. . . .

Vanessa saw the flash from the barrel more than she actually heard the sound.

She jumped, a full-body twitch, just as Valpo's body did much the same, the pistol dropping from his dead hand.

Vanessa felt herself screaming, but could not hear it. The shooter now turned to face her, lowered the gun toward her. The scream died in her throat and she followed the line of the gun barrel to the madman's eyes burning through her.

Her mouth dry now, she struggled to cry out, but no sound would come.

Vanessa suddenly felt that distanced, slow-motion sensation again. Almost serene, she prayed in the church of her mind that someone would take care of her daughter.

She knew she would not live through the next minute, let alone her shift. The house always wins, they say, but this time a dealer could lose.

Then, just as suddenly, the killer lowered the pistol and gave Vanessa a smile so gentle and sad that she knew she'd been reprieved, she knew she would see Cyndi again, after all.

"I'll never tell," she said, and averted her gaze, but guns were still firing, and no one heard her, not even herself.

Something slammed into her.

The breath left Vanessa's body and she felt herself toppling to one side—it was as if she'd been struck a blow.

But she had, indeed, been shot.

Her eyes went back to the killer, who turned away now, not meeting her wide-eyed amazement at his having reneged on the reprieve, shooting her after all, and she tried to inhale, but a rope must have been constricting her neck. The more she struggled, the less oxygen she seemed able to gulp down. Her side ached like she had a really bad bruise, but beyond that, all through her body, flowed a red hotness like swallowing a whiskey shot too fast . . . only the burning ran horizontally through her and warmed much more intensely.

Each breath was a greater struggle now.

Surprisingly, no real pain—the broken leg she got when she fell off a garage roof at twelve hurt a lot worse than this, way worse. Okay, she'd been shot, but wasn't sure it was so bad. You can recover from gunshot wounds—her ex-boyfriend had. Her baby's father. Her baby . . .

If only she could breathe. She was sure that would help. Somebody must have hit the air conditioner with a stray bullet, because it seemed to be running full tilt now, getting colder by the second. For a moment she caught the killer walking away and wondered if she'd have kept her promise, if it had been heard, if she'd been allowed to live.

Oh hell, she thought, *I hope it's not Mom who raises Cyndi*, and then even the coldness was gone.

2

CATHERINE WILLOWS WOULD HAVE RATHER kept a dental appointment than go to this meeting.

Maybe that's why she was cutting it so close—the 4:30 was at the other end of CSI headquarters, and she'd have to hustle to make it. She jogged up the hallway, her red hair trailing behind her trim dancer's frame.

Assistant Lab Director Conrad Ecklie, her boss, was a stickler about punctuality, beyond which this was not just *any* appointment: Ecklie, Sheriff Burdick, and graveyard-shift supervisor Gil Grissom were having a rare staff meeting to discuss inter-shift cooperation.

Everyone even remotely associated with the Vegas Crime Lab knew of the animosity between Ecklie and Grissom—which was remarkable in and of itself, because rarely had either man spoken a cross word to the other. Professionalism was something both men valued, as was public decorum, though Catherine considered the two to share the social skills of a dill pickle.

And, of course, she had worked the night shift herself for several years and had been Grissom's right hand until her promotion to supervisor of swing.

So she had a history with and loyalty for Gil; but Ecklie was the one who'd promoted her and for whom she worked on a daily basis—so those ties weighed on her, as well. She was not anxious to become the net in a tennis match between two strong-willed, passive-aggressive men.

And it wasn't like she didn't have anything *else* to do! Her shift was already shorthanded, due to Warrick taking a vacation day, plus two investigators with court dates and another investigator calling in sick. Basically, she had Nick Stokes, Sofia Curtis (borrowed from Grissom's shift), and herself. Oh yes, and a great big city called Las Vegas cooking up all sorts of crimes to solve. . . .

As she approached the glass-enclosed conference room, Catherine could see the others already inside.

A tight-eyed Ecklie—slender; balding; with alert hawkish features; his gray suit, white shirt, and blue tie immaculate (a sure sign his time in an actual lab was limited)—had taken the chair at the head of the table and left the corridor blinds open. A placid Grissom sat to Ecklie's right, facing her as she slowed to a walk near the door. At the other end of the table, a quietly unreadable Sheriff Burdick sat, a cup of coffee in one hand, his forehead in the other.

Allowing herself one deep breath, Catherine slipped into the conference room.

Ecklie glanced at his watch and then at her, but to his credit said nothing. A manila folder lay on the table in front of him like a restaurant place mat. She did not dislike this man, though in her night-shift "days" he had been the object of much coworker griping; now her personal experience indicated Ecklie to be fair and smart.

But his blind spot was Grissom, much as Grissom's was Ecklie—a classic crime-lab case of bureaucrat versus scientist. If she had a dollar for every conflict like this in every crime lab in the nation, she could retire tomorrow. . . .

Sheriff Burdick, his own suit almost as perfect as Ecklie's, gave Catherine a polite smile as she sat. Thinning brown hair clipped short, the sheriff had a quietly rugged way about him, with a certain gentleness in his calm brown eyes that drew voters' confidence, especially (the pollsters said) the female voters.

Catherine had long since proved immune to those eyes, but she respected this man, who backed the crime lab all the way. He seemed less prone to the politics of his recent predecessors.

Across from her, Grissom looked haggard—tiredness was a given for CSIs, and for a driven workaholic like Gil, a constant. But this was different. His hair, especially his beard, seemed grayer than she remembered, and his eyes looked puffy, like he hadn't been getting his usual, already limited hours of sleep.

Despite this, a tiny, barely perceptible smile lurked on his lips. Dressed in his customary black shirt and slacks, Gil Grissom, weary or not, somehow seemed in better spirits than either of the other men.

"Catherine," he said as she pulled her chair up. "Thanks for joining us."

Catherine said nothing, smiling, nodding, then waiting for Ecklie to start the meeting.

Only she soon realized it had already started, and the sheriff was driving the bus. . . .

Burdick's gaze focused on Grissom. "I just have one more thing to get off my chest. Gil, you don't make Conrad's job—or anyone else's, for that matter—any easier by pushing the political and public-relations ramifications of a case to the side."

Grissom could only nod.

"Just because you have the ability to remain objective, don't mistake the world for sharing it. Understood?"

"Yes, sir," Grissom said.

"And Conrad, you'll make an effort to treat Grissom in a fair and impartial manner. Understood?"

"Understood, Sheriff."

"You're two of the best. If you ever got on the same page, do you have any idea how much we could accomplish?"

Catherine supressed a smile. These two strong men—the scientist and the bureaucrat—were sitting with their heads slightly lowered, like two kids a principal had put in their respective places.

"All right. Let's move on." Burdick turned to Catherine. "Can't *you* make these two get along?"

She smiled and shrugged. "How would you say I'm doing so far, sir?"

After a chuckle and shake of his head, Burdick was about to move forward on the meeting agenda, when Nick Stokes burst into the room.

"Yes?" the sheriff said, surprised at the intrusion.

"Sorry," Nick said. "I know I'm interrupting, and I apologize—but we have a big one. Real trouble."

A buff former Texas A&M football player with close-cropped dark hair, piercing dark eyes, and a heroic jaw, Nick was normally the epitome of cool—he did *not* excite easily. But right now, as he approached Grissom, planting himself between Gil and Conrad, the broad-shouldered CSI seemed pretty worked up.

That worried Catherine.

"What kind of trouble?" Burdick asked, resuming his position at the table.

"We got a major shoot-out between two motorcycle gangs, the Predators and the Spokes—that annual Biker Blowout at Boot Hill?"

"Damn," Catherine said.

"You haven't heard the really good part—it went down *inside* the Four Kings Casino."

Burdick put a hand to his head as if checking for a fever.

"Dead?" Grissom asked. "Wounded?"

Nick said, "I don't have all the facts yet, this is straight from Dispatch; but, yes, Gris, there are dead and there are wounded. Not just bikers but civilians—casino employees, tourists . . . sounds like they pretty much trashed the place. D-Day indoors."

"And that's our crime scene," Ecklie said gravely.

"All right," Burdick said, heading for the exit. When he got there, he turned and issued orders. "I'm going to call the governor—he's probably a heartbeat away from sending in the National Guard. Conrad, you get the crime scene team organized and on its way."

"Right now," Ecklie said, nodding.

Catherine stepped forward. "We need the media kept out for at least twenty-four hours. We'll have an extensive crime scene and a volatile situation with those two biker gangs."

"We can handle our end of that," Burdick said, "and I'll talk to the Highway Patrol . . . but anything you can do to encourage the local people to keep the lid on will tell the tale."

Burdick left and the others turned to Ecklie.

"If it'll help," Grissom said to Ecklie, "I'll go—Catherine's shift is shorthanded."

"Good idea, Gil," Ecklie said.

The graciousness seemed strained, Catherine thought, but at least Ecklie was trying.

"This is a unique situation," Ecklie was saying. "Possible mass injuries and deaths to rival a plane crash. And as Catherine says, a high-profile case that'll attract media attention. I need my best people, so I appreciate your offer, Gil. You'll go."

"Good," Grissom said.

"I want Stokes, Sofia, and Catherine there, too," Ecklie said. "Gil, call in Sidle from your shift."

"No problem."

"Catherine, you'll be in charge."

She sneaked a glance at Grissom, but he seemed to accept this as a matter of whose shift was on duty and not an Ecklie put-down.

Ecklie was saying, "Catherine, call Brown in for me, would you? His vacation day is canceled. Gil, better get Sanders in here early, too."

Grissom frowned. "Conrad, I don't think we need him. Somebody has to hold down the fort."

"I agree. My intention is that Sanders will work with Brown, here in the city. Better divide up the calls—Gil, I'll ring Sidle for you."

Warrick Brown, Sara Sidle, and Greg Sanders were fellow LVPD crime scene investigators—Warrick on

Catherine's team, Sara and Greg from Grissom's shift.

They all started moving at once, cell phones coming out, speed dialers in play, and gravitated to different corners of the room so they could hear themselves, leaving Nick standing alone by the door, the messenger who'd started all this having nothing to do at the moment.

Five minutes later, the little group huddled around Nick again.

"Sara will be here in twenty minutes," Ecklie said.

Grissom added, "Greg's on his way, too."

"Warrick will be here in ten," Catherine said. "Nick, get the trucks loaded. Gil, you want to collect Sofia?"

Nodding, Grissom went out the door in search of his team member. Nick followed him out, leaving Catherine alone in the conference room with Ecklie.

The assistant lab director put a hand on her shoulder. "Wrap this up quick, Catherine. This could be a real problem."

"Sounds like it already *is* a problem," she said, finding the remark odd.

His eyes narrowed. "Aside from any injuries and loss of life, the potential for disaster here is imminent. If CNN gets a story about a gunfight in a casino—with motorcycle gangs!—the public won't care whether it's Boot Hill or Fremont Street. Once they hear *Nevada*, the tourists will stay away in droves."

Catherine was glad Grissom hadn't heard that. She had a tolerance for political views like this one, where the lives of human beings seemed secondary in importance to tourism concerns, but the goodwill the politician and scientist had shared in the wake of the sheriff's reprimand would likely have been short-lived had Gil been privy to that PR speech.

Twenty minutes later, two dark, sleek SUVs pulled out of the CSI parking lot, dashboard-mounted emergency lights flashing as they made their way east on Charleston Boulevard to Decatur Boulevard, then north to Highway 95 and the long looping trip south to Boot Hill.

Nick drove one SUV with Catherine in the passenger seat. Sara Sidle—the striking brunette's hair tucked up under a CSI ballcap—was at the wheel of the other, Grissom in the passenger seat and blond Sofia Curtis in the back.

On the highway, Nick barreled along but could have made better time if people got out of the way. Not particularly wanting to die prematurely of a heart attack, Catherine had, over the course of her years on the job, trained herself not to yell at motorists who refused to pull over when they saw the alternating red and blue flashing lights.

Drivers always seemed to move over for ambulances and fire trucks, but most went brain-dead when it came time to pull over for the cops. Why that was, she had no idea; but it was one of the little-known truths of the job.

They were maybe halfway into the forty-five-minute trip when they got a radio call from Burdick.

"Jorge Lopez is the police chief out there," Burdick's voice told them. *"A good man. You shouldn't have any problem with him cooperating."*

"What about the Guard?" Catherine asked.

"I don't have to tell you about the shortage of personnel," the sheriff said.

Sixty percent of the Nevada National Guard was deployed overseas.

"By the time the governor gets you any help," Burdick was saying over the radio, *"you probably won't need it. Half a dozen state troopers are there or en route, but you know they're scattered to hell and gone, too."*

"What about our people?"

"We're spread too thin, too," Burdick said. *"It's mostly going to be you guys and the locals. But, as I say, Chief Lopez is terrific, and he has strong people. We'll maintain media blackout as long as possible. Good luck."*

The sheriff signed off.

Nick flicked a glance at Catherine. "Yeah—good luck to us."

The two black vehicles rocketed down the highway, Nick barely keeping the speedometer below one hundred. Once away from the metropolitan area, traffic thinned, though the highway was not deserted: they passed eighteen-wheelers, a few cars, and at one point, just south of Searchlight, both SUVs slid to the right lane to let a Nevada Highway Patrol car buzz by.

The state cop was definitely not holding his speed under a hundred. . . .

"Nice to know the Patrol'll beat us there."

Nick grinned. "Not by much."

"From Primm Substation, Jean Substation, maybe."

Nick said, "You'd think a bunch of the Highway Patrol guys from Laughlin'll make it over there quickly."

"If not," Catherine said, "no telling *what's* going on in Boot Hill. Those two gangs might still be going hot and heavy."

"Instead of a crime scene, we could be driving into a battlefield."

"D-Day, you said before. Maybe you were right, Nicky."

He grimaced. "Yeah, well in this case, I don't particularly hope to be. . . ."

They passed the wide spot in the road known as Cal Nev Ari—little more than a casino and a stop sign. The latter Nick blew through.

Catherine was on the radio now, trying to get a sit. report from Dispatch.

"*Lots of cross traffic on the Highway Patrol channel,*" the dispatcher said. "*Sounds like things have calmed down a little, but hard to tell.*"

"Thanks," Catherine said. "That's better news than it could've been. 3CSI out."

She replaced the microphone in its holder and sat back. "Gonna be a *looooong* shift, Nick."

"Think the bikers've all split town?" Nick asked.

She shrugged. "We'll know soon enough, but the cops are most likely way outnumbered by bikers. Be hard to round them all up."

"And *keep* them rounded up. Normally, the perps would head for the hills."

"Normally, Nicky? Based on all the other biker gang shoot-outs in casinos we've worked?"

He laughed at that.

But neither one of them really saw anything funny about what they were heading into. . . .

About halfway between Cal Nev Ari and the intersection with Highway 163 that led to Laughlin, Nick took a right onto a two-lane blacktop road.

The desert world this far outside Vegas looked more like a moonscape than Earth—rocks, sand, and the occasional plucky green plant doing its best to hang on in this harsh environment, where the summer temperature would regularly reach 120 or higher, at which point even the snakes looked to cop some shade. With all the hills and valleys out here, Boot Hill wasn't readily visible from Highway 95; but before long, going down the two-lane, the outlines of the town's buildings could be made out in the distance against the background of the mountains to the west and south.

Driving in from the east, still a couple of miles away, the onset of twilight began to give the poor man's Tombstone a surrealistic cast—from here, the place looked to Catherine like a miniature movie set from a Godzilla movie, maybe.

Nearing the town, Boot Hill gained scale, of course, but the movie-set feeling would not let Catherine go. Blue Highway Patrol cars, red lights flashing, sat at angles blocking the road; no one was being allowed in or out of town. Well, they never were in a science-fiction film, right?

Nick slowed as he neared the roadblock and a Highway Patrolman with a shotgun at his side waved for Nick to stop. Catherine counted three more Highway Patrolmen on the scene: two were on the opposite side of the road, one on either side of their car, preventing anyone from leaving to the east. As the shotgun-toting Patrolman came toward the Denalis, his partner remained on the other side of the vehicle, which would provide cover should anything go wrong at the checkpoint.

Normally, the flashing lights would have gotten the CSIs a wave-through. But with two motorcycle gangs shooting up a casino, "normal" was not an operative term, and Catherine didn't blame these guys for being cautious.

The Patrolman nearing Nick's window was a burly guy whose frame had probably been plenty muscular twenty years ago (maybe even ten); but now, the man had gone soft around the middle. His face, however, hadn't gone soft at all; under a sand-colored crewcut, he had on seriously dark sunglasses and a surly frown.

"Las Vegas Crime Lab," Nick said, showing the Patrolman his ID.

"We need all the help we can get," the officer said, his voice friendly though the frown remained.

Leaning toward the driver's side, Catherine asked, "How bad?"

The Patrolman seemed to notice her for the first time; he bent down a little more. "Shooting seems to be over, at least for now. But everybody within ten miles of here is pretty edgy."

"Town under control?"

"Good guys in charge," the Patrolman said. "For now, anyway."

"Possible it could go the other way?"

A tiny shrug from the big officer. "Lots of tension . . . and there's nowhere big enough to lock up everybody on both sides. We're way outnumbered. Chief Lopez has the town locked down."

"How many officers does he have?"

The Patrolman said, "Counting his detectives, eight . . . ten, when two more off-duty guys are rounded up."

"And you state boys?"

"Four of us here. Four more at the west end of town,

even though that blacktop peters out at the edge of the mountains."

Nick said, "Well, there's five of us."

For the first time, a glimmer of a smile crossed the Patrolman's face. "You Vegas CSIs pack heat, don't you?"

"We do," Catherine said, and Nick was nodding.

"Good to hear. Every little bit helps."

Nick asked, "Where's the casino?"

The Patrolman pointed. "There's two of 'em, right across the street from each other. Allen Street. You start into town, go two blocks, then left—that's Allen. The casinos are in the first block."

Catherine said, "Thanks, Officer."

"No problem." He backed away from their window and waved to his partner, who jumped in the car and backed it out of the way. When the Patrol car was on the shoulder, the patrolman motioned the SUVs through and they rolled cautiously into Boot Hill.

The town seemed to have finally embraced its inner ghost town. Deserted streets gave the impression that the whole population had gone on vacation. Occasionally a venetian blind or curtain would shudder, the only sign that the inhabitants had all sought refuge indoors. The Denalis moved west on the extreme north edge of town. As they passed the first street, Catherine looked down the corridor of buildings and parked cars. The only movement was a patrol car, two blocks down, slowly rolling in their direction.

"Cue the tumbleweed," Nick said.

Allen Street, the next block west, had more action. Here three squad cars and a Blazer (the latter with the words POLICE CHIEF stenciled on the doors) were all parked at odd angles, one car blocking the street, its driver's door standing wide open. Also on the street were two ambulances, their back doors open, their gurneys gone. All of the vehicles had their light bars going. The officers and EMTs, though, were nowhere in sight.

Two casinos, neither big enough to displace the smallest Vegas Strip hotel, squatted on opposite sides of the street, two broad-shouldered gunfighters getting ready to shoot it out. The Gold Vault occupied the east side, just south of a two-story building with a sign proclaiming it THE OLD WEST MUSEUM & GIFT EMPORIUM. Six stories with a parking garage to the south, the Gold Vault appeared to be doing well enough.

Across the street, the Four Kings seemed to be faring even better. Eight stories and taking up twice its rival's space, the Four Kings could damn near have made the grade in downtown Vegas.

They piled out of the Denalis and unloaded their gear. Even though it was early spring, in the shadow of the mountains with a purple dusk settling, the town held heat like a skillet. Whether it was the temperature or the weather or the different kind of heat that generated all this violence, Catherine could not hazard a guess. She only knew that for this time of year, Nevada was unnaturally hot.

Boot Hill, Nevada, anyway.

The five Vegas CSIs joined up behind Catherine and Nick's vehicle. They were red in the blush of a big neon sign of a fanned-out poker hand revealing four kings and an obscured kicker. Underneath, smaller signs advertised an all-you-can-eat buffet and this week's entertainment, a one-hit wonder band from the early '70s that maybe had one original member.

"No police in sight," Grissom said. "You know what that means."

Catherine nodded and frowned. "They're tromping through our crime scene."

"*Your* crime scene," Grissom reminded her, and his tiny smile held not one hint of condescension. "How do you want to play this?"

"Let's see our cards first, and then decide."

"That's a good policy."

Crime scene kits in hand, they strode toward the row of six glass doors at the Four Kings. Catherine could hear more sirens in the distance.

One of the six front doors had shattered, glass scattered across the sidewalk like broken, punched-out teeth. The team picked the door farthest from that and entered. The air-conditioning hit them like a refreshing breeze.

What they beheld was anything but refreshing.

"God in heaven," Sofia said softly, shaking her head.

"This wasn't a gunfight," Nick said, wincing. "This was a goddamn war zone."

Around them only the five remaining glass doors looked like they were part of a casino. The rest of the huge room was like nothing Catherine had ever seen. She'd worked her share of shoot-outs in the past—gang violence was not unknown on her Vegas beat—but none of those had amassed anything remotely like this sort of destruction.

The stench of cordite permeated the air, as did dust motes, and bodies were cast about the floor like discarded refuse among the knocked-over and broken, bullet-riddled slot machines; chips, glass shards, and bloodstains mingled on the patterned carpet.

Four EMTs from the two ambulances were scattered

around the room, each attending to his or her own patient. Professionally soothing conversation and occasional moans and cries pierced an otherwise ominous
silence, the eerie aftermath of tragedy in which Catherine could almost hear the echo of gunfire. Three Boot
Hill police officers were providing first aid for a trio of
victims, and a wide berth was given to two bodies, obviously dead.

In a snack bar off to the right—where cartoony cut-
out images of cowboys, Indians, and gunfighters jovially
rode the walls—four more uniformed officers and two
detectives were taking statements from a shell-shocked
group . . . probably patrons of the casino during the
shoot-out.

Near the entrance to the snack bar stood three men:
a beefy guy, about fifty, wearing black slacks, a white
shirt, and a red suit jacket with the Four Kings logo over
the left breast; a fortyish fellow wearing a charcoal suit
that accentuated a pasty complexion; and a tall, thin
Hispanic man with slicked-back black hair and a hawk
nose, police badge on a chain around his neck over a
blue button-down shirt tucked into worn jeans.

When the three saw the CSI team, the Hispanic man
headed over and the other two followed his lead.
Catherine and Grissom were in front, colleagues fanned
out behind. Catherine watched the leader trying to figure out which of them was in charge—but at least times
had changed enough that the assumption that the man
was the boss wasn't made . . . at least, not out loud.

Unable to make up his mind, the cop took a spot in
front of and between Catherine and Grissom.

He extended a hand in their general direction. "I'm
Police Chief Jorge Lopez."

Grissom's hand started to come up automatically, but Catherine took a slight step forward and accepted the chief's clasp. "Catherine Willows, Las Vegas Crime Lab. We've heard nothing but good things about you, Chief. This is Gil Grissom, Sara Sidle, Nick Stokes, and Sofia Curtis."

They all nodded in turn and Lopez gave them a group nod.

Finally letting go of Catherine's hand, he asked, "You're the supervisor, I take it."

She nodded. "Supervisor in charge. Dr. Grissom here is also a supervisor—we've combined elements of two shifts in anticipation of a big job."

An eyebrow rose. "You anticipated right, Ms. Willows." He turned slightly so she had a better view of the two men behind him. "This is Sergeant Cody Jacks— one of mine, also works part-time here, like a lot of my fellas. He saw this thing go down. And this is Henry Cippolina, chief of security and floor manager of the casino."

She shook hands with both men.

"Looks like Custer's last stand," Grissom said grimly.

Lopez's dark eyes, behind wire-frame glasses, were hooded, his expression grave. "Twenty-three years on the job, never seen anything could touch this. Thank God, only two deaths so far . . ."

"Small miracle in and of itself," Grissom said.

". . . but three more are critical, and five others are going to need serious medical attention. There's also quite a few with splinters, glass cuts, assorted bumps, bruises."

Grissom said, "When panic sets in, people run blindly."

Catherine said, "Which means even the luckiest survivors'll have at least superficial injuries. . . . How many shot?"

Lopez's sigh bore the weight of the world. "Ten we know of . . . Christ knows how many others. Both gangs cleared out and, except for the one dead Predator"—he pointed toward a male lying facedown on the floor, the back of the man's head very bloody—"they took their wounded with them, if there were any."

"We're going to need to clear the people from this room," Catherine said, "the living ones, that is. We're limited in what we can do till then."

Lopez held his hands out. "We're treating the wounded as fast as we can, and our officers are getting statements in the snack bar—really the only part of the casino that took little or no damage—to avoid having the witnesses traipsing through your crime scene."

Cippolina then spoke for the first time, his voice a shade higher and louder than it should have been, his hands trembling at his sides. "How long do you think we'll be shut down?"

Grissom blinked. "What? You plan to reopen?"

"No, no, no—I mean . . . before we can start cleaning up that mess."

"That's not a 'mess' out there, Mr. Cippolina. That's evidence."

Catherine slipped gently between Grissom and the casino man. "This is going to take quite some time, Mr. Cippolina," she said. "It's a huge scene and we won't finish until we're satisfied that we have collected every scrap that might matter."

"Which means?"

From the corner of her eye, she saw Grissom tense; but he said nothing.

"We'll work as fast as we can, Mr. Cippolina, but this is not fast work. We'll do our best not to have your casino shut down one more minute than it has to be."

The casino's floor manager still frowned, but he said nothing more. The unspoken tension between him and Grissom was not lost on Catherine, however, nor did she think it was lost on Lopez, who seemed not to miss much of anything.

The chief put a hand on the shoulder of the man beside him. "Sergeant Jacks is the lead detective on this case—I'd appreciate it if you'd keep him apprised of your findings."

"Mr. Jacks, aren't you a witness?" Grissom asked.

Jacks's voice was deep and resonant. "I was here—saw a lot of what happened, but not all of it. Gave my statement to Adam Bell. I can stand down, if you think I should."

"Dr. Grissom, we're lucky Cody was on the scene," Lopez said. "He's got the detective slot right now."

"Detective 'slot'?"

"We have three sergeants who rotate on a six-month basis in the one detective post on the force. Adam Bell, another one of our sergeants, for example, is interviewing witnesses right now. We're a small department—only have one detective going at a time."

Catherine looked toward the uniformed officers in the snack bar. One had sergeant's stripes on his sleeve. He and a plainclothes officer were in the midst of interviews on the far side of the restaurant. "If you only have one detective slot going at a time"—Catherine gestured with her head toward the snack bar—"how can you have two detectives interviewing over there?"

Giving her a tiny smile, Lopez said, "The bald guy is Troy Hamilton."

Catherine studied the man from a distance. Forties, paunchy, and so darkly tan he might have spent every waking moment outdoors, Hamilton was talking to an African-American woman of maybe twenty-five.

Lopez said, "Troy retired a year ago—bad back. But because of the size and nature of this crime, I called him to come help with interviews."

"Good thinking on your part," she said. "And generous of him."

Looking at Cody Jacks, Grissom said, "Speaking of seeing what happened, is there video?"

Cippolina was the one to answer, though. "Too much."

Grissom almost smiled. "My kind of problem."

Catherine took Sofia aside. "Collect all the videotapes and take them back to the lab. We can get by with one truck here, and our own facility will be better suited to the task."

Sofia nodded. "I'll pick up some Visine and get right on it."

Turning to Cippolina, Sofia asked, "Could you show me to Video Surveillance?"

"This way," he said, and led her to the left and up a corridor.

Sheriff Lopez said, "We can't lose sight that there were crimes committed here besides murder—attempted murder, assault with a deadly weapon, rioting, destruction of property, and on and on."

"Our evidence processing will cover all that," Grissom replied. "Video tapes alone—"

"I appreciate that," Lopez interrupted, "but my handful of men and my five jail cells won't cut it."

Catherine said, "Well, we can have the state police handle that—their investigation division can come in and grill our gangs."

Then Catherine surveyed the ravaged casino. The other CSIs gathered around her and did the same as if viewing a battlefield after the fray.

"Let's each take a quarter," Catherine said, pointing, "and work from the outside in. Take lots of pictures—don't be shy; we don't know what might be important later."

Grissom took the quarter with the biker body, and Nick and Sara got the two far quarters, while Catherine assigned herself the nearest quarter with the other corpse.

Getting out her camera, Catherine moved slowly through the detritus of the crime, careful not to disturb anything.

She bent over the body.

The woman was young, early twenties, brunette—a dealer, judging by her clothing. A name tag introduced Catherine to Vanessa Delware.

Lining the woman's body up in the viewfinder, Catherine wondered idly what her story was.

3

WARRICK BROWN WAS PISSED OFF.

This was not a common state of mind for the tall African-American with the piercing green eyes. Not that shades of inner anger from disgust to rage were uncommon on the emotional rainbow of this man, whose demeanor was generally so low-key. But "pissed off" was something Warrick rarely got.

Today was different.

Warrick Brown was a dedicated professional, a CSI devoted to his work, who routinely went above and beyond the call of duty and had logged more overtime hours than anybody in the department. Couldn't he even have one goddamn solitary day (and night) for himself?

He hadn't shared this feeling with anyone else in the office, but as he sat in the locker room in one of his best ensembles—brown cashmere sweater, brown jeans, and brand-new sneakers—he was genuinely, definitely, decidedly, well and truly *pissed off*.

I'm supposed to be having dinner tonight, he told his sympathetic inner self, *with the most beautiful woman in town—and the* town *is* Vegas! How could Catherine do this to him?

The woman in question, a nurse with only one day off a week, had finally acquiesced to Warrick's appeals and agreed to go out with him—tonight.

He'd been halfway out his door for the evening when Catherine summoned him. After calling and getting an understanding but clearly disappointed response from his date, he'd gone straight to HQ, since he kept a spare set of clothes in his locker and could change there. But now, sitting on a bench staring at the interior of his locker, he was realizing that he did not have a spare pair of shoes here, which meant the brand-new sneakers would be going out into the field with him tonight. And who knew *what* kinds of crime scenes awaited?

Case in point—Frank the Perv, a deviant so far off the path that Warrick refused to ever use the guy's real last name, even in the privacy of his own brain. When called upon to investigate Frank the Perv as a sex offender, Warrick had entered the man's house to discover that Frank kept an extensive collection of jars of his own feces, urine, and semen. ("Everybody needs a hobby," Grissom had remarked.) The shoes worn into that house for that investigation had ended up in a Dumpster when Warrick refused to wear them again after wandering through Frank the Perv's love nest.

Warrick had changed pants and was just pulling on a tan T-shirt when Greg Sanders came into the locker room.

"Looks like it's you and me tonight, 'Rick," Greg said.

Shorter than Warrick but similarly lanky, Greg had finally tamed the unruly thatch of brown hair, blond-highlighted within an inch of its life, and—since moving out of the DNA lab into the field as a CSI—dressed more professionally now, or at least conservatively (tonight, blue polo shirt and black Levi's).

"Who called you in? Catherine?"

"Yeah."

"She tell you what's up?"

"No—just said we were shorthanded and I was needed. Man, I almost didn't answer my cell. This is supposed to be a vacation day for me—the night I had planned, aw . . . don't even wanna talk about it."

"Bummer," Greg said, and filled him in on the Boot Hill shoot-out.

As the realities of his job came into focus through the young CSI's words, Warrick felt a twinge of shame for having been petty about the broken date. Hell yes, he deserved his day off and this date; damn right, he wanted it right now more than a new car or a raise. But with something this serious, not some bureaucratic screwup, a genuine emergency?

After all, somebody had to hold down the fort.

And suddenly he really didn't mind at all.

Gears shifted within him, and he was cool and ready to work.

"We've got a call," Greg said, holding up a sheet of paper with an address scribbled on it. "Apparent suicide."

"Where?"

"Sweeney Avenue." Greg rattled off the house number.

"Let's roll." Warrick shut his locker and they were moving. "Where exactly is that on Sweeney?"

"Just west of Maryland Parkway."

They went out to their SUV, Warrick climbing into the driver's seat, Greg dutifully walking around to the passenger side.

As he drove west on Charleston, Warrick hit the flashing lights.

He glanced at his young partner. Before the night-shift team had been split up, Warrick had mentored the young CSI, and falling back into that role felt natural.

Warrick asked, "So . . . what do we know?"

Greg got out his small notebook but didn't refer to it in the dark SUV. "The vic, Kelly Ames, apparently locked herself in the garage with the car running. A friend thought it was weird when Kelly didn't show up for work, then weirder still when she didn't an-swer her phone. So the friend called nine-one-one. Officer found the body and called the vic's husband, Charles Ames, to come home from work."

Turning off Charleston onto Park Paseo, Warrick asked, "Officer on the scene?"

"Weber," Greg answered.

Warrick jogged left on Eighth Street, which would intersect with Sweeney. Jackson Weber, a swing-shift beat cop for most of his twenty years, was a good man with solid instincts.

Taking a left on Sweeney, Warrick didn't need to check the number on the house because emergency vehicles out front, their light bars flashing, identified it. A squad car, an unmarked vehicle, and a coroner's wagon lined the street in front as well.

A one-story stucco with a two-car garage tacked onto the left, the house was decades old but well tended. After pulling to a stop facing the squad car, Warrick jerked the gearshift into park and climbed out. As he did, Greg seemed to sprint to the rear; he already had the doors open and was pulling out his crime scene case when Warrick arrived back there.

"Moving fast is good," Warrick said.

Greg eyed him. "But . . . ?"

"Haste makes waste at a crime scene."

They were just getting ready to walk up the driveway when Captain Jim Brass emerged onto the front porch, then wandered down to meet them. A dogged detective with a world-weary mien and eyes that somehow seemed sad and sharp at once, Brass—in a crisp powder-blue suit with a dark blue tie snugly in place—was the one detective that Warrick always wanted at his side, whether at a crime scene or heading down a dark alley.

"Aren't these vacation days relaxing?" Brass said with a faint, knowing smile. "Think she'll give you a second chance?"

"They reelected Bush, didn't they?" Warrick said. "What have we got?"

Brass, like Greg, had a small notebook in hand; and, like Greg, he did not refer to it. "Kelly Ames. Twenty-four, suicide. Still in the garage."

Frowning, Warrick noted, "Garage door's open."

Brass shook his head. "Officer Weber said she was definitely dead when he arrived, and there was no reason to disturb the scene with attempts to revive the vic . . . but he opened the overhead door to clear the garage of carbon monoxide. Hard for you fellas to do your thing, otherwise."

"What else's been done?" Warrick asked.

"That's it," Brass said with a shrug. "Scene's undisturbed."

"Where's Weber?"

Brass gestured with a head nod. "In the house with Mr. Ames."

Warrick led the three of them up the driveway, where a navy blue Toyota Rav4 was parked. The left side of the garage was empty; on the other side beckoned the rear end of a gray Honda Accord, maybe seven years old.

When they got to the garage door, Warrick and Greg both set their crime scene cases down as Brass looked on. As they got down to business, Warrick noticed that the Accord was a four-door, no kid's seat. No kids' toys in the garage either.

"A childless couple?" Warrick asked.

Brass said, "Yeah—husband I haven't really interviewed in depth. He's reeling. Typical reaction—can't believe she'd do this, happily married, no problems. Met at UNLV. Both graduates. I'll get more."

Brass headed off to do that.

"Greg," Warrick said, "camera."

But then Warrick noticed that Greg was already on one knee, opening the case that held his thirty-five-millimeter camera with flash attachment.

A lot of police departments were going digital, but Vegas had not completely turned that corner yet.

Though digital was unquestionably faster and cheaper, with no need to develop hundreds of rolls of film, digital photos still were not admissible in court in some venues, viewed as too easy to doctor.

While Warrick went up the driver's side, Greg took the passenger's. Before either touched anything, Greg took several photos of the vehicle from every angle. The car windows were down, the engine turned off, probably by Weber when he showed up. Through the driver's window, Warrick saw the young woman leaning forward in her seat, her forehead resting against the steering wheel. Long brown hair hung down, obscuring her face from view. She wore an orange T-shirt and—when he looked in through the open window—Warrick noted purple shorts and white tennis shoes.

Something about the color combination of the shirt and shorts struck him as odd; but then, suicide always struck him as odd. He understood how things could pile up on you so much that you'd consider killing yourself—he'd been there, till he licked his gambling jones, anyway—but some of the methods chosen over the years by perp/vics had made him realize that this was one "crime" he could never entirely understand. After all, he had once been called to a suicide where the man had not only killed himself but shot his pet ferret and taken a ball-peen hammer to his cat.

Some suicides were ritualized, some were simple, some included a note, some didn't. In this case, a white business-size envelope waited on the dashboard.

Warrick wished Catherine were here—he would have liked to have asked her about that odd combination of clothes. He tried to think of a time when he'd seen a reasonably attractive woman wearing purple and orange. Most didn't wear such a jarring color combo, he decided.

Of course, most women didn't kill themselves, either. Maybe they were the first two pieces of clothing she grabbed; maybe the explanation was just that simple. Perhaps the combination of colors meant something significant to her or her husband (school colors? wedding?); no way to immediately tell.

"Did you get a picture of that envelope?" Warrick asked.

"I got *four* pictures of it," Greg said.

Wearing latex gloves, Warrick picked the envelope off the dashboard.

Unsealed. Flap merely tucked inside.

He carefully extracted the flap and found a tri-folded piece of paper inside, which he also removed. When he had the note unfolded, he held the sheet flat on the hood of the car while Greg photographed it, then he read the typed note.

> Charlie,
> I'm so sorry but I just can't take it anymore. The pain was too much to bear. I hope you can understand and forgive me. I will always love you,
>   Kelly

In the movies, on TV, the typewritten suicide note is always a sure sign that someone is trying to cover up a murder. In real life, Warrick knew, this was not always the case. Some people just did not write out their suicide notes by hand. Often such notes these days were typed on computers, and the suicide just grabbed the paper out of the printer (or left it there) and didn't bother signing it.

Hell, only a little more than half of all suicides even bothered to *write* a note. . . .

Carefully, he bagged the sheet of paper.

This one still felt odd, though—peak ages for women to commit suicide were between forty-five and fifty-four, with another large at-risk group over seventy-five.

Kelly Ames appeared to be in her mid-twenties.

Although women attempted suicide twice as often as men, their male counterparts were successful four times more often. High school graduates and those with some college were more likely than high school dropouts to kill themselves, but Kelly had graduated from UNLV. Warrick also knew suicide was more common among women who were single, recently separated, divorced, or widowed. Kelly Ames was happily married—supposedly, anyway.

Although poisoning, including drug overdose, had long been the leading method of suicide among women, guns now held the top spot, in fact used in sixty percent of all suicides.

For this case, the statistics were all against Kelly Ames committing suicide.

What did all that mean?

At this point, nothing. Statistics were numbers, and victims like Kelly were human beings. But Warrick knew he would be watching this one carefully, making sure that nobody was just going through the motions. That this suicide was not by the numbers did not make it murder; it meant the investigators needed to *not* work by the numbers and to be painstakingly thorough.

"What next?" Greg asked.

"Check the backseat—I'll take the front, starting with the passenger side."

"You got it."

"Then we'll process the body together."

Greg jumped to work, going over the backseat with care. Warrick did the same with the passenger seat in front, and when they were done, all they had were two cigarette butts from the ashtray in the front and a gum wrapper that Greg had dug out from under the driver's seat.

Nonetheless, Warrick was pleased with Greg's processing—that the body was keeping them company did not seem to bother the young CSI, neither spooking nor intimidating him. For a former lab rat like Greg, this was no small accomplishment.

"All right," Warrick said. "Let's do the vic. Who's here from the coroner?"

"David."

"Find him and get him over here."

"On it," Greg said, and disappeared.

Rigor had set in, so Warrick had to be careful prying the dead woman's fingers from the steering wheel.

By the time Warrick had managed that, Greg was back with assistant coroner David Phillips in tow. His dark, curly hair receding, the boyish Phillips took a position on the driver's side, next to Warrick. He pushed his black, wire-frame glasses up on his nose, then jammed both hands into the pockets of his dark blue lab coat. Normally Phillips had a wide, easy-going smile, but not when he was working.

"Where shall I start?" Phillips asked Warrick.

"Time of death?"

"Judging from the progression of rigor—midday. Maybe noon or so."

"Where was the husband then?"

"According to Brass, Mr. Ames says he was on his way to work. Brass called him at his job; guy's a second-shift supervisor."

Leaning the victim back in the seat, Warrick examined the woman's face. Her eyes were closed, her face was peaceful. High cheekbones; small, sharp chin; full, pink lips; no lipstick. What she did not have was the extremely red skin that comes with carbon monoxide poisoning.

"Pretty lady," Warrick said to no one in particular. "Something's not right about this."

"She *is* awfully young," Greg said, not seeing what Warrick had seen.

Warrick cut to the chase. "David, why isn't her skin red?"

Phillips shrugged. "That doesn't happen one hundred percent of the time with carbon monoxide death."

Warrick thought he saw a shadow under the tousled brown hair and he pulled out his mini Maglite and examined the victim's neck. . . .

A dark spot about the size of a dime.

But whether this was a bruise or even dirt or possibly makeup, he could not tell. Before he took it to the next step, he asked the coroner's assistant, "Is that a bruise?"

Phillips leaned in through the back driver's-side door, moving Warrick's hand slightly to get more light on the darkness on the woman's throat.

"Could be," Phillips said. "Can't tell for sure . . . yet."

Warrick grabbed a breath, told himself not to push. "The autopsy will tell us about that, and the lack of redness. Got anything else for us, Dave?"

Phillips shook his head. "No. Check with me later, at the lab."

Moving the light farther around the throat of the vic, Warrick could not find any more marks, bruises or otherwise; but when he got to the back of the woman's neck, he said, "Hey, guys! Have a look at this."

Phillips leaned in closer and Greg came in through the passenger-side rear door, camera at the ready.

"What?" Greg asked.

Warrick used his flashlight to highlight the tag on the back of Kelly Ames's shirt.

"It's on inside out," he announced.

Greg snapped a picture.

"It could mean," Warrick said, "she didn't dress herself."

"Or it could mean," Greg offered, "she just threw the first thing on because she was distracted and distraught—what kind of state of mind would she be in if the top of her priority list was coming out here to start the car and take one last ride with the garage door shut?"

"That's a well-reasoned possibility," Warrick admitted. "Okay, David, your guys can take her out of here."

Phillips was handling that when Greg asked Warrick what was next.

"I need to talk to the husband. Let's clear up some questions of evidence. Come on."

Entering the house through the attached garage door, Warrick found himself in a tiny mudroom with a washer and dryer. Beyond that lay a galley kitchen and then a small dining area with a round table and four chairs, two of which were now occupied, one by Brass and the other by, presumably, Charles Ames.

A scrawny guy with blond hair, big blue eyes, and a wispy beard, a hollow-eyed Ames sat across the table from Brass. In the living room, near the front door, Sergeant Jackson Weber stood tall, his blond crewcut and matching mustache perfect down to each hair. His face was impassive, his gray eyes unreadable, his presence comforting for investigators, intimidating for anybody else.

"We're sorry for your loss, Mr. Ames," Warrick said as he and Greg moved through the small dining area and took up positions, standing on either side of Brass.

Ames said, "Thank you," but there was no inflection to the words at all.

Warrick introduced himself and Greg, and Ames said, "Call me Charlie."

"We were just getting ready to start the interview," Brass said.

Warrick nodded and, as procedure and courtesy dictated, let the detective carry the ball.

"Some of these questions will make you uncomfortable," Brass said. "But in situations like this, Mr. Ames, they have to be asked. And sooner is better than later."

Ames nodded, saying nothing.

"Have you and Kelly been having any trouble lately?"

Ames shook his head.

"Has she been despondent about anything?"

"Not that I can think of. Everything's been pretty good between us, always."

"Mr. Ames," Brass said, "taking one's own life is always done for a reason—it may not seem logical or even sane to the survivors, but there's always a reason."

"I know, I know," Ames said, a little agitated. "But I can't *give* you a reason. I didn't see this coming at all!"

"Nothing going on in your marriage," Brass gently probed, "that you want to get in front of . . . and tell us about? Just so we don't get the wrong idea, later."

"No!" Ames said. "What do you mean, wrong idea?"

Brass said nothing.

"I told you, Captain—told you, we were happy. She was my best friend . . . I loved her. . . ."

The man's head lowered, chin to his chest. Warrick looked for tears. Didn't spot any.

Brass was asking, "Any friends she might have confided in, Mr. Ames?"

"Maybe Megan—Megan Voetberg. Her best friend. They work together." He frowned. "Didn't you tell me she was the one who called you people?"

"Yes," Brass said. "Any others?"

"Hell, I don't know," Ames said, and shook his head. "Megan could give you a better idea than me, if there are other girlfriends of Kelly's who she might've opened up to. But honestly, we didn't keep secrets, we talked to each other, not like some couples. . . . Captain, I understand this is important, but . . . but . . . I'm not really doing very well right now. Can we wrap this up?"

The tremble in the voice, the pain in the face. But still no tears.

Warrick said, "Just a couple more questions, Mr. Ames."

The man nodded wearily. The color had drained from his face and his lank blond hair lay limp against his forehead. Dry eyes or not, Charlie Ames looked so depressed, he might not have been far from following his wife's example.

"Did your wife use a computer at her job?"

Ames winced, trying to make sense of the question. "Yes, I'm sure she did—she's a postal worker. Yes, sure. She keys in zip codes and stuff, over at the encoding station. She worked nights."

"Did that put a strain on your marriage, working different shifts?"

The husband shook his head. "No—I mean, I can see how you'd think that, but she just got the job. It was like a . . . probationary deal. If Kelly worked out, they'd give her a raise after six months and eventually a chance to go to days."

"When would that have come?"

"Another month."

Warrick had one more question. "Is there a computer in the house?"

"Yeah. Why?"

"We'll need to take it with us."

"Take it with . . . Why in hell?"

"It's evidence, sir."

"Evidence?" Ames asked incredulously. "Kelly

dies in our garage, and our *computer* is evidence?"

Warrick said, "Technically, a suicide is a homicide, Mr. Ames—and we investigate that as thoroughly as we would a murder."

Suddenly Ames seemed a little unsteady. "Guys— I need that PC for my job."

"What do you do?" Brass asked, even though Weber had probably already told him, from when the Patrolman had called Ames at work.

Returning his attention to Brass, obviously relieved not to be responding to Warrick, Ames said, "I'm second-shift production supervisor for Cactus Plastics."

"What does your home computer have to do with that?"

"Sometimes I type up production reports and the like. Almost everybody works partly out of their homes these days, Captain."

Warrick said, "We'll get it back to you as fast as possible, sir. We have no desire to inconvenience you."

Ames's frown dug deep lines in his forehead. "I still don't get it—why do you *need* it? I mean, I want to cooperate, but—"

"Your wife's suicide note seems to have been written on a computer. We'll need your printer, too. Knowing whether she wrote that note on her work computer, or here at home, might be instructive as to her state of mind."

Greg gave Warrick a sideways look, knowing that Warrick was, like any magician, using misdirection.

Ames thought about it. "It's in the spare bedroom. First door on the left . . . but I better get it back from you people! You gotta sign for it!"

Brass said, "We wouldn't have it any other way."

While Weber and Brass stayed with Ames, Warrick and Greg checked out the spare bedroom: single bed coming out from the wall on the right; long, low bookshelves filled with paperbacks running below the window on the wall opposite the door; and a student desk on the left wall with a monitor, two speakers, mouse with pad, and a keyboard on a pull-out shelf under the desktop. The computer tower itself sat on the floor against the right side; on a separate stand perched an inkjet printer.

Greg took pictures of the whole setup, then he and Warrick tore the machine down, taking the tower and the printer with them, leaving the rest. When they had everything loaded in the SUV, they came back into the house.

"Again, Mr. Ames," Brass said. "We're very sorry for your loss."

Ames said nothing and did not rise as the detective and CSIs filed out.

On the front stoop, Officer Weber asked, "You fellas need anything else?"

Brass shook his head. "Nice job, by the way."

"Yeah," Warrick added. "I appreciate your not disturbing the crime scene."

"I got reamed by your buddy Grissom, once, a hundred years ago," Weber said with a grin, "and I've been real damn particular ever since."

Weber headed to his cruiser, climbed in, and rolled off. David, his guys, and the body were gone already, too.

Turning to Warrick, Brass asked, "What was all

that stuff in the house about taking the computer and finding out why Mrs. Ames killed herself?"

"It's about," Warrick said, glancing toward the house, "Kelly Ames not killing herself."

"This is a murder?"

"I can't go there . . . yet. Signs are it might be."

"Share with the class," Brass said, crossing his arms.

Warrick took only a few moments to collect his thoughts, then went into full oral report mode.

"Okay," Brass said. "Where does that take us next?"

"To the post office."

Brass closed his eyes. He seemed just about ready to drift into a nap when he said, "You really think the U.S. government mail service is going to let us take one of their computers without a court order?"

"Hell no," Warrick said with a shake of his head and a wide smile. "But we *will* be able to talk to Megan Voetberg. Then if there's nothing on the home computer, maybe we can find something on the work computer."

"Something," Brass said. "I hate these damn fishing expeditions."

"Hey, like I said to the husband—Kelly had to write her suicide note somewhere. Or should I say, somebody had to write it, somewhere."

Brass managed a rumpled grin. "Good point. Let's go to the post office and talk to this Megan Voetberg."

"Greg," Warrick said. "You drive—I have a phone call to make."

As they wove through the city after dark, Warrick withdrew his cell phone and made a quick call to a freelance computer expert, Tomas Nuñez, who had helped the CSIs on numerous cases in recent years.

"*Hola*," Nuñez said, his voice seeming to come from some very deep place inside.

"Tomas, Warrick Brown. Busy?"

"Never too busy for my friends."

Greg was puttering through the light traffic. Greg's excessive caution unnerved Warrick, much as Warrick's own loose yet speed-of-light way behind the wheel unnerved everybody else at CSI.

"Tomas, I've got a computer that may have some vital material on it."

"Where and when?"

"Crime lab. Say an hour?"

"No problem."

Warrick looked through the windshield; Greg was stopping for a light that had just turned yellow. "Better make it an hour-fifteen, Tomas."

Nuñez said, "Sure thing, Warrick. *Adios*."

They broke the connection and when Warrick looked up, Greg was frowning at him. "Should I have run that yellow? Say it—you think I drive like a schoolgirl!"

"High school girls in this town," Warrick responded dryly, "get seventy-three percent of the speeding tickets in their age group."

Greg was still parsing Warrick's remark when they got to the postal encoding station, where Brass was leaning against his car.

"You two take the scenic route?" he asked.

Greg's chin came up, just a little. "I drove the speed limit and obeyed the traffic signals."

"Imagine how impressed I am," Brass said. He made a sweeping "after you" hand gesture. "Shall we?"

Unlike a normal post office, no customer business was conducted within—this was strictly a glorified sorting house. A low brick building with a parking lot out front, the encoding station sat in a strip mall on the aptly named Industrial Way. Maybe fifteen cars filled the slots of the lot, the lights of the station the only ones on in the entire area.

"You been inside yet?" Warrick asked, as they headed toward the facility.

Brass nodded.

"Did you mention the computer?"

"No, but I did talk to Megan Voetberg. She's got a break coming up . . ."—Brass tilted his watch toward one of the lights that illuminated the parking area—". . . in about two minutes . . . and she'll be out to talk to us then."

Warrick smiled at Greg and said, "Hey, bro—nice timing."

Greg grinned and said, "Shut up."

Exactly two minutes later, as if she had been using a stopwatch, a young, thin, dark-complected woman with straight black hair and exotic brown eyes swivelled through the door and came out to join them. She wore hip-hugging jeans and a tight white T-shirt emblazoned with a Chinese take-out container smiling and playing guitar. Above the crazy little caricature were the words THANK YOU and below it WEEZER.

Three coworkers trailed out behind the woman, moving to a picnic table at the far end of the building.

"Captain Brass?" she asked tentatively, walking up. She had a soft, almost soothing voice.

"Megan Voetberg," Brass said, "this is Warrick Brown and Greg Sanders from the crime lab."

She nodded and glanced toward the table of coworkers.

Taking the hint, Brass said, "Maybe we should move around the corner?"

Again, she nodded. Even in the dim light, Warrick could tell the woman was trembling.

"I thought you people only did crime scenes and lab stuff," she said as they walked.

Warrick, falling in next to her, said, "Not all evidence of a crime is at the scene of that crime. Your friend, Kelly, working at this station, for example, brings us here."

They eased around the corner between the building and its twin, fifty feet down the parking lot. The light was even dimmer here, the flick of her lighter causing a tiny flashfire as she lit a cigarette.

As an afterthought, she said, "Hey, do you mind?"

They all shook their heads.

"We're sorry for your loss," Warrick said.

"Thanks," she said. She took a deep drag, shaking more as she exhaled. "I can't believe . . . believe Kelly's dead, really dead."

They said nothing.

She frowned as if something smelled bad. "*Suicide?*"

"That's what we're trying to determine," Brass said.

She scuffed a shoe at an invisible piece of dirt. "Guys—Kelly did *not* kill herself."

"Why do you say that?" Warrick asked.

Megan shrugged. "Not the suicidal type. All there is to it."

Brass asked, "Then she wasn't depressed, or despondent?"

The young woman considered that for a long moment. "Depressed, probably. Who isn't sometimes? . . . Despondent? What *is* that, really?"

"Depressed," Greg said, "is being in low spirits. Despondency is the same thing, only worse—no hope."

They all gave him a long look.

Greg stared back. "Sorry. But they are different."

Megan said, "Then she *definitely* wasn't despondent . . . even though she was a little depressed. You wanna know mostly what Kelly was? Mostly Kelly was pissed."

"About what?" Brass asked. He nodded toward the postal building. "Her job?"

"No! No. Hell, no. What do you think? Her stupid husband! She wasn't going postal pissed; but, maaaan, she was getting there."

Brass's eyes tensed. "Why was she unhappy with Charlie?"

Megan's look was incredulous. "Duh. What's the usual reason? Because the jerk was having an *affair*."

Warrick exchanged glances with Brass.

"She knew that for sure?" Brass asked. "She had proof?"

Taking a long drag on her smoke, Megan considered that momentarily. "Not smoking-dick-type proof, no. But she was pretty goddamn sure . . . Kelly was *convinced* she knew who it was."

"Who?"

"She didn't tell me. Not the name, anyway." She dropped her cigarette and snuffed it out under her shoe. "Just some slut Charlie worked with. Hey, my break is over, you mind? . . . You guys can call me at home if you want more—not that I have anything."

They took her contact info, then thanked her and watched as she and her coworkers went back inside at the end of their break.

"So Kelly did have a reason to commit suicide," Brass said when the three of them were alone.

Warrick nodded. "Right, and maybe she hated her cheating hubby so much she set him up to take the fall for her 'murder.'"

"Yeah," Brass said with a sardonic laugh. "That could happen. You been doing this how long?"

"Twelve years."

"You ever see that happen before?"

"Couple of times . . ."

Brass frowned at Warrick, as if to say, *Say what?*

". . . on TV."

Letting out a single laugh, Brass said, "Then you *don't* think that's what happened here."

"No way."

"Then why even go there?"

Warrick shrugged. "Because Grissom taught me to never overlook any possibility—no matter how crazy it seems."

Brass frowned. "Then what *do* you think happened here?"

"I think Charlie Ames killed his wife," Warrick said. "And you know what else I think?"

Greg asked, "That we're going to prove it?"

"Damn straight," Warrick said, grinning.

He held out his open hand, and Greg seemed confused as to whether to shake it, or give him a high-five, or . . .

"Car keys, Greg."

Greg handed them over.

4

FIRST THEY'D USED UP ALL THEIR PLASTIC A-frame evidence markers.

Then, following Grissom's advice, they'd fashioned more, using two decks of cards—turning the numbers outward—and even that had not been enough.

Finally, they resorted to masking tape and a black marker.

And when they were done, over one hundred and fifty bullet holes had been marked and photographed inside the Four Kings Casino.

Sara Sidle didn't know if they had brought enough bullet trajectory rods to mark the scene. She guessed she would soon find out.

With Nick's help, Sara set up the DeltaSphere-3000 3D Scene Scanner. One of the newest tools in law enforcement's crime-fighting arsenal, the 3D scanner had been secured by Ecklie for the lab, on loan from the device's manufacturer, 3rdTech. The

DeltaSphere was like a yacht: if you had to ask how much it cost, you couldn't afford it. But 3rdTech had provided it in hopes of a sale, and Ecklie hoped they would "donate" it to the LVPD in exchange for a glowing recommendation from the ninth largest police force in the United States.

Sara figured that by the end of the trial, both sides would leave disappointed. In the meantime, she and Nick would have a pricey new toy to play with.

Sitting atop a tripod stronger but no larger than a photographer's, the DeltaSphere looked like a silver briefcase with a four-inch black square in its top border that housed the scanner's lens and laser. Weighing in at a shade over twenty pounds, the device would give them a 3D color scan of the crime scene in less than fifteen minutes.

When finished, the scan would be loaded into a computer and give the team a 3D rendering of the crime scene with as much detail as a drawing that would have taken hours to complete. As Sara watched the machine cast its laser around the room, the red, pencil-thin beam slithering over every centimeter of the crime scene, she couldn't help but think how much time this machine would save them if it was just half as good as advertised. She had seen Nick use it at another crime scene and knew that the DeltaSphere was everything it claimed to be, and a bag of chips.

Once the scanner had done its thing, they had marked and photographed over one hundred shell casings, then bagged and tagged those casings (the bullets they could find), and hundreds of other things that might or might not be important evidence. They had shot so many rolls of film that the casino had donated three money bags just to hold them. And Sofia had loaded close to one hundred videotapes into several boxes that were now on a two-wheel cart near the door, along with the film and other evidence.

The wounded had been rushed to hospitals in Laughlin. The *seriously* wounded—those who could make the flight—rode the medevac chopper to Vegas.

To Sara Sidle's surprise, the investigators still only had two deaths on their hands—one male, one female. Henry Cippolina, the Four Kings's floor manager, had identified the female as Vanessa Delware, a twenty-one-year-old dealer and single mom. Both Chief Lopez and Sergeant Jacks had ID'd the male casualty as Predators leader Nick Valpo, the kind of corpse that could spark not just more trouble but grow the past battle into a future war.

Though a couple of the injured hailed from one gang or the other, the largest percentage of wounded were your garden-variety innocent bystanders—staff, tourists, casino regulars, even one poor schlub who'd wandered in off the street for a drink, all simply in the wrong place at the wrong time.

Grissom approached Sara with a tiny thoughtful frown. He said, "Something odd."

"Odd?"

"After all," Grissom said, "everything here seems pretty straightforward."

She arched an eyebrow. "*Riiiiight*—for a biker firefight that broke out in a casino."

He did not acknowledge her sarcasm, still frowning thoughtfully, looking out on the torn-up landscape of the casino. "Everybody that got hit was shot from a distance, right?"

Unable to figure out where Grissom was going with this, Sara took the ride. "That seems to be the consensus."

"Shot from the front," Grissom said, gesturing to himself, "or side."

"Right. That was the line of fire."

"Mostly hit with nine-millimeter rounds, correct?"

"Mostly, or something bigger. From the shell casings and bullets we've harvested, I think a couple of the shooters had three-fifty-sevens."

Nodding, Grissom said, "So, if we begin with everybody shot with nine mils or larger, and from a distance . . . how do we explain Nick Valpo being shot up close and personal . . . from *behind* . . . and with a small-caliber weapon?"

Now she frowned in thought. "Somebody took advantage of the melee . . . and committed a murder in the middle of a gunfight?"

"Yes," Grissom said, pleased with her. "But not a murder, exactly."

"No?"

His eyes tensed. "An execution."

Sara considered that for a moment. "Small-caliber, you say—what kind of gun?"

"We may have the shell casing among all those we gathered. But we won't know for sure until we see the autopsy results. Judging by the wound, though . . . something small—a twenty-two or maybe twenty-five."

Sara blinked. "That's a purse gun. What self-respecting biker carries a twenty-two?"

Grissom shrugged. "A gun that size would make a good backup piece. In a boot, maybe. . . . Come with me."

She followed Grissom to Nick Valpo's body. Near a large bullet-scarred column, one of many scattered about the room, Valpo lay facedown on the floor, left hand on a pile of glass from a shattered slot machine, right hand reaching into an aisle for his Glock, just out of reach.

Sara knelt over him.

The entrance wound in the back of Valpo's head was just a small, round hole with gunshot residue making a dark targetlike circle around it. Another larger dark blossom opened from the right shoulder of Valpo's black vest—an exit wound.

"He got hit," Sara said, "went down, then someone came up behind him and finished the job."

"Yes," Grissom said.

"Videotapes should tell us the story on that one." She looked across the aisle at the deceased dealer lying on the floor, the dead woman's eyes staring at nothing but locked in Sara's direction. "If she wasn't already dead, the dealer saw the whole thing. . . . She won't be taking the witness stand now, though."

Grissom's eyes narrowed. "No—but if she was shot because of what she saw, the caliber of the bullet inside her *will* testify."

He led Sara over to the woman's body and they had a look at an entrance wound similar to the one on the Predator's remains.

"No powder burns," Sara said. "Shot from a distance. But that doesn't look large enough to've been made by a nine mil—though too big to've been made by a 357."

"I'd agree," Grissom said. "This will be a key autopsy."

They stood back and watched in respectful silence as the paramedics put a sheet over the dealer's body and loaded it onto a gurney. Catherine came over to join them.

"A young one," Catherine said quietly.

Sara said, "With a baby. Single mom."

"Not young," Grissom said flatly. "You don't get older than deceased."

The two women looked at him, wondering at the seeming coldness of the comment; but Grissom's grave expression belied that.

The gurney rolled out, and Chief Lopez edged around it, coming in. Sara had not seen him leave, but for a crime scene that should be secured, people were sure wandering in and out, almost as if the casino was open for business.

Lopez crossed to them, looking like he'd aged a year for every hour the CSI team had spent in Boot Hill.

"Nice kid," the chief said sorrowfully.

"You knew her?" Grissom asked.

"Boot Hill isn't a very big town. You get to know a lot of people. At least she has a mom who can look after the baby."

Catherine asked, "How's it going, getting control of the town?"

"It's about to get harder," Lopez said with a sigh, thumbs in belt loops. "One of the biker casualties just became a fatality—a Spokes member died from his wounds before he even made it to the hospital."

A few ominous moments of silence followed, or at least near silence—omnipresent was the sound of glass crunching underfoot.

"'Revenge is a kind of wild justice,'" Grissom said, "'which the more man's nature runs to, the more ought law to weed it out.'"

Sara said, "Shakespeare?"

"Francis Bacon. Chief, were you able to line up any more help?"

"The governor sent us two dozen more Highway Patrolmen," Lopez said, with a that's-something-anyway shrug. "Got ten of 'em tryin' to keep the Rusty Spokes rustled up in the Gold Vault, across the street."

"And the rest?"

"Tryin' to round up the Predators and keep them from laying *siege* to the Gold Vault."

Catherine blew out a breath, as if trying to put out candles on a birthday cake. "This doesn't sound promising."

"Sure it does," Grissom said. "We just don't like what it promises."

Lopez said, "I've got a police force of twelve plus me, two dozen Highway Patrolmen, and then there's you folks."

Patting the holstered weapon at her hip, Catherine said, "If you need us to walk away from the crime scene and lend support, you give us the word. We're all law enforcement here."

Sara gave Grissom a sideways look to see how he liked the sound of that; apparently he liked it fine.

Lopez was saying, "That gives us a little over forty

crimes committed here, questioning all concerned is called for—and the state police investigators will swell our ranks soon enough, and help on that score."

Flashing a sad grin, Lopez said, "Afraid the point is moot, friends. We've got five, count them, *five* two-person cells. There are in excess of two hundred biker guests in Boot Hill right now." He waved vaguely in the direction of the street. "If we can keep the Rusty Spokes holed up in the Gold Vault, we're halfway home. We're trying to keep the Predators' camp under control, too, of course; but they're not confined to a building, so that proposition is a little trickier."

"Let me ask the key, as-yet-unasked question," Grissom said.

They all turned to him.

Grissom's eyes were slits. "Doesn't the Four Kings have metal detectors at the door?"

Running a hand over his face as if that would wipe away the exhaustion, Lopez said, "Yeah. Of course. I don't have to tell you that's standard nowadays."

Now Grissom's head tilted to one side, eyes still narrow, and he said, "That raises the obvious question then, doesn't it? How did so much hardware wind up inside the casino?"

The chief gave a huge sigh and shook his head. "I frankly just don't know the answer to that one. We're looking into it, and it's important now, Dr. Grissom, no question. But understand that for the last few hours, we've all been more concerned about the *aftermath* of guns getting in than *how* guns got in."

Grissom nodded. "That's fair."

Cody Jacks, his red jacket still showing spots of dried blood and small pieces of glass that glinted when the light hit them right, joined the ever-growing group. His tie was loosened and the top two buttons of his white shirt were undone.

"Guess this is one time you guys aren't exactly short on evidence," he said.

Catherine said, "There's enough that it'll take days to sort it all out."

Nick said, "So, Mr. Jacks—you were here when all the fun went down, we understand."

"Make it 'Cody,' and yeah, I was." Jacks pointed to some shot-up slot machines not far away. "Right over there."

"Dangerous place to find yourself," Grissom said.

"No shit. I hit the deck and started crawling like a baby—tryin' to find somewhere where I could return fire."

Grissom asked, "You had a gun?"

Jacks nodded and pulled back the red jacket to reveal a Glock 19, a nine-millimeter pistol with a fifteen-round magazine. "I work floor security—we're *supposed* to have the only guns in the casino."

"How many rounds did you get off?" asked Nick.

"I'm not proud of this, but . . . not a one. By the time I felt safe enough to pop my head up, the shooting had stopped. And to tell you the truth, it would've been risky in any case, with all the chaos, patrons and staff running around."

"Makes sense, I guess," Nick said.

But Jacks seemed to take Nick's innocent remark wrong, puffing up to his full height.

"You weren't here, son," he said, ears reddening.

"Me, I saw combat in Desert Storm, and lemme tell ya—that was small change compared to this, forty or more guys all firing at the same time, none any too worried about taking aim or even which way their weapons were pointed."

Nick held up his hands in surrender. "I wasn't questioning your bravery, Sergeant."

"If I could have fired, I would have. I had friends in here I would give my life to've helped—that little girl, that blackjack dealer? I got her her job."

Nick flicked a look at Catherine as if to say, *What's this guy's problem, anyway?*

But Sara thought she knew: survivor's guilt.

Jacks was going on, "Truth is, I figured most of the people in the joint would be dead. It's a good thing none of those assholes can shoot straight or this would have been a goddamn slaughterhouse."

"You're right, Sergeant," Grissom said. "Many of the people here were luckier than anybody in a casino has any right to be—at least one hundred and fifty rounds were fired."

Jacks shook his head. "Felt like forever, Dr. Grissom, that's for damn sure. But I'll bet you both my jobs that when you look at the time stamp on the video, whole shooting match didn't last a minute."

"Neither did the OK Corral shoot-out," Grissom replied.

Catherine said, "Why don't you give Chief Lopez's guys a hand, Nicky, and see if you can figure out what's up with the Case of the Mysteriously Malfunctioning Metal Detectors?"

Nick nodded and moved off toward the front of the casino.

"For that matter," Grissom said, "why didn't those metal detectors go off when *we* came in?"

Again they all turned to him.

Grissom had made a good, obvious point that no one had previously commented upon.

"I hadn't really thought about it," Lopez said, "but you're *right*, Doc."

Both Catherine and Sara exchanged glances and stifled smiles: nobody had ever called Grissom "Doc" before.

But Grissom didn't seem to mind. After all, this was Boot Hill, wasn't it?

Lopez was saying, "Those damn detectors should have been howling all night."

Catherine said, "We'll figure it out."

Lopez ran his hand over his face again. "This is going to give Byron Ivers and the rest of that crowd all the ammo they're gonna need."

Sara considered the bullet-riddled casino around them and wondered about Lopez's choice of the word *ammo*.

"And who is Byron Ivers?" Catherine asked.

Jacks said, "He's one of the assholes . . ."

Lopez shot the sergeant a withering look.

". . . I'm sorry . . . *concerned citizens*," Jacks continued, "who bitch about the Biker Blowout every year."

Lopez said, "It's a constant argument here—the merchants who consider the event bad for the town's reputation, and others who appreciate the business the Blowout brings in."

"The anti-Blowout group," Grissom said, "would seem to have a pretty good case now."

The chief said, "Maybe, but nothing remotely like this has ever happened before, Doc. Generally, the bikers were rowdy but behaved. A good segment of the population here thinks it's important that the town continue to host the event, since basically it supports some businesses for the next six months."

"Sounds like a real love-hate relationship," Sara said.

Lopez nodded. "Not a lot has changed here since the days of the Old West. Same thing happened back in Tombstone."

"Tombstone?" Catherine asked.

"Yes," Grissom said, jumping in. "The city fathers there had the same problem. The cowboys who spent their paychecks in town supplied a large part of the economy, but those same cowboys, including the Clantons, McLowerys, Frank Stillwell, and the others, were the very ones that were tearing down Tombstone, making it impossible for the city fathers to lure families in and build a respectable community."

Cody Jacks said, "One family came—the Earps."

"True," Grissom said with a small smile. "They came to represent the town and eventually it got to the point where they had to make a stand . . . and the cowboys lost."

Suddenly Sara understood why Grissom had the history of Tombstone on his mind.

Sofia came up, planting herself in front of Catherine. "I'm heading back to Vegas," she said. "Anything else we need to take?"

"I think that's everything," Catherine said, eyes narrow with thought. "For now, anyway. I'm sure we'll be collecting more evidence throughout the night."

"I'll take the stuff to the lab," Sofia said, "then I'll get to work with Archie sorting through the video-tapes."

Catherine gave her a quick nod. "Let us know as soon as you have something."

They said goodbyes and all watched Sofia pick her way through the mess on the floor and go out the door even as the paramedics came in with another gurney—this one for Nick Valpo. The group moved to one side as the paramedics loaded the body and hauled it away.

The next thing Sara knew, Grissom was hovering over where the body had been, his eyes scouring the floor amid the broken glass, scattered chips, shred-ded gaming tables, and other flotsam left over from the battle.

"Grissom," she asked, "now what?"

He froze, his eyes coming up to meet hers. "Valpo was right there," he said, pointing to the spot where the body had been.

"Yeah, so?"

"That means the killer had to be right about where I'm standing."

She glanced at where the body had lain, her memory going back to the near contact wound of the head shot that had killed Valpo.

Grissom's eyes met Sara's and a reconstruction played in the theaters of both their minds.

The killer is in the casino. He or she is watching Valpo, waiting for their chance, or waiting for the Rusty Spokes to start the gun battle, depending on whether this is all part of a plan or just a lucky break for a murderer.

The firefight erupts.

Bullets fly, everywhere. The killer is either already close or gets close to Valpo. He or she wants this badly enough to be at personal risk in order to assassinate the gang leader—both in public view and in the line of fire.

Valpo takes a hit to the shoulder and goes down. His killer senses the opportunity and moves even closer, the small pistol seeming to fly to the back of the Predator's head, the trigger practically pulling itself. A flash of light from the muzzle, and half a second later, a sharp crack barely makes a dent in the cacophony of the gunfight going on around it.

Flopping once, Valpo goes still. The deed is done and the killer relishes the exquisite feeling of accomplishment, an electric jolt of victory—Nick Valpo is dead.

"Okay," Sara sighed. "You're standing in the right place."

"If I shot Valpo with an automatic," Grissom said, "the shell casing should be around here somewhere. I looked for it when the body was here but came up empty. A second try can't hurt."

Being careful to avoid standing in Grissom's light, Sara joined the search, combing the floor for a metal casing little bigger than a fingernail.

In the meantime, Catherine moved off to search a slightly wider area, in case the thing might have been kicked or knocked away somehow. She also checked where the female dealer had died, since a similar casing might have been produced if the vics had shared a killer.

Lopez and Jacks seemed just about to walk away when Nick hustled up.

"Not rocket science," he said with a crooked grin,

"figuring out why those metal detectors didn't work."

Sliding back a few steps to the group, Catherine asked, "Why's that?"

"Batteries are dead."

They all looked at each other, dumbfounded.

"Batteries?" Chief Lopez asked incredulously.

"The Four Kings, it seems, did *not* spend top dollar on their security equipment," Nick said. "After all, from a management point of view, how often is there going to be a shoot-out in your casino, anyway?"

Lopez was shaking his head in disbelief. "Dead batteries made this possible?"

"As a police chief," Nick said, "this shouldn't surprise you. What industry spends the least on video surveillance equipment?"

The chief did not hesitate. "Banking."

"Same theory here," Nick said. "Don't spend too much money on what you'll never really need. There's nothing wrong with the detector itself—it's a model I'm familiar with. Battery life, on a normal day? Upwards of nine or ten hours. Somebody needs to regularly change the batteries, which is no big deal—except in this instance, they didn't do it."

Without moving his feet, Grissom asked, "How does every metal detector in a casino have its batteries go dead at the same time?"

Nick said, "Who's to say they did? Who knows how long they've been dead? Anyway, if they did have one staffer in charge of the whole perimeter, and changing all the batteries at once, all of 'em going dead at about the same time is possible."

Lopez snapped into action. "Cody, find Henry, now. Tell him to get his ass over here now."

"What if he doesn't—"

"What part of *now* don't you get, Cody?"

Looking a little wounded, Jacks lumbered off in search of the casino's security chief.

While they waited, Grissom and Sara resumed the search for a possible shell casing.

"A lot of places have battery-operated metal detectors," Nick said to Lopez. "For one thing, during a power outage, they'll still work."

Lopez nodded, but obviously still seethed.

Nick went on: "I would've expected them to stagger the times more between each individual detector, just to avoid this very thing. You have six detectors, like the front doors here? Then you have three that have their batteries switched from midnight to noon, and the other three that get changed between noon and midnight, so you've always got at least three working."

Grissom looked up long enough to say, "This is sounding more like conspiracy than simple bad planning."

"You think?" Lopez asked, with no trace of sarcasm.

Shrugging, Grissom said, "If not conspiracy, how did both gangs know that the metal detectors would be out at this precise time?"

"Or worse yet," Catherine said, "that they've been off all *week*?"

Sara was shining her flashlight on a spot near Grissom's right foot.

"Right *there*," she said.

Grissom bent down and picked up a small brass shell casing that had been obscured not only by the shadow of Valpo's pant leg, but by a small pile of chips that had provided the casing a small cave to hide in.

"Nice eye, Sara," Grissom said. "A twenty-two."

He plopped it into an evidence bag and sealed it.

Catherine said, "Too bad we couldn't have found it before Sofia left."

"At least we've got it," Grissom said, and put the bag in his pocket. "Chief, you know anybody who carries a twenty-two automatic?"

"Pretty common piece," Lopez said. "Could be townie, tourist, or biker."

"Nonetheless," Grissom said, undaunted, "it's a start."

Sara began working the area where the dealer had died, and soon said, "Bingo!"

And Grissom bagged a second twenty-two shell, saying, "So the execution was witnessed, and the witness was executed."

Cody Jacks sauntered up, Henry Cippolina at his side.

"Henry," Lopez said with a terrible smile, reaching out to put his arm around the security chief's shoulder. "Who's in charge of changing the batteries in the metal detectors?"

Cippolina looked confused. "Maintenance department, Chief—why?"

"Because all the batteries, in the metal detectors?"

"Yeah?"

"Are dead."

The already pasty Cippolina somehow went a shade whiter. "Oh, shit."

"Can I quote you on that, Henry? . . . Now, whose job would it be to make sure the maintenance department has actually changed the batteries?"

"I usually have one of my security guys check them," Cippolina said.

"And who would have had that responsibility tonight?"

Cippolina rubbed the fingers of his left hand across his forehead, as if he might squeeze the information out. After a moment he said, "Tom Price."

"Where's Tom now?"

Cippolina and Cody Jacks were both craning their necks around to look for the security guard.

"Well," Cippolina said, "he *should* be here."

"Snack bar?" Catherine offered.

They all turned in that direction.

"Maybe," Jacks said, "but he should have been among the first to give statements, so he could get back out here and help keep order."

Grissom asked, "Remember seeing him, Sergeant?"

"Hey, I'm not in charge of him. Right now I feel lucky to know where my *own* ass is."

The group headed over to the snack bar, Cippolina and Jacks slowly scanning the place for their lost security guard. The snack bar was full, probably far more crowded than during its busiest rush, people filling every seat—counter, tables, booths.

Everybody looked exhausted, sweaty, and scared. A few had broken down and ordered something to eat, but most just nursed half-full cups of cold coffee, the only waitress now leaning against the counter, her trailing mascara an obvious sign she had been crying. The smell of cordite had been replaced by the familiar if pungent aroma of fried fish, french fries, burgers, stale sweat, cigarette smoke, and fear.

An older woman touched Lopez's hand as they passed. "Chief Lopez, are those terrible bikers going to come back?"

Lopez patted the woman's hand and shook his head. "No, Mrs. Hill, they're not coming back."

As they moved on, Lopez told them, "Mrs. Hill is a regular. Lives over on the west side."

Catherine asked, "You spotted this fella Price yet?"

"No," Jacks answered.

Cippolina added, "I don't know where in hell he coulda got to."

Sara was right behind Lopez when the chief called over his two investigators, Adam Bell and Troy Hamilton. Bell, blond and in his mid-thirties, sported tiny laugh lines around light blue eyes; he wore a Boot Hill PD windbreaker over a white shirt and jeans. Hamilton's outfit was the same, except his shirt was blue; he weighed maybe fifty pounds more than Bell, was about ten years older, and his hair had gone gunmetal gray.

"Either of you boys seen Tom Price?" Lopez asked.

Bell and Hamilton looked at each other, then shook their heads in unison.

"Was he even *working* today?" Bell asked.

Scratching his neck, Jacks said, "I do remember seeing him around three, come to think of it . . . beginning of shift?"

Lopez heaved another of his trademark heavy sighs. "Nobody's seen him *since* then?"

Bell shrugged, Hamilton shook his head.

As the local cops spoke, Sara noticed a man in a

cheap tuxedo, possibly a pit boss, rising at the far end of the snack bar and making his way toward the far exit.

"Sir," she called to him, but he either pretended not to hear her or actually had not.

"*Sir,*" she called, loudly this time, the group around her all snapping their heads in his direction.

The guy looked back and now seemed to be deciding whether to stop or make a run for it.

"Keith!" Cippolina said.

The guy froze.

"Mr. Draper," Jacks shouted in his cop voice, "get your ass back over here. Pronto."

But Draper hesitated.

Jacks took an ominous step in the man's direction, the others starting to fan out, a practically instinctive move, making themselves less of a cluster target.

Finally, Keith Draper started back toward the group of law enforcement. He had short black hair, a neatly trimmed salt-and-pepper beard, and sharp dark blue eyes. The tux looked like he had been wearing it a while, and the black dress shoes had not seen polish since the Clinton administration.

Draper had taken only two steps toward them when his right hand went into his jacket pocket and their hands all went to their pistols.

"*Freeze,* Keith!" Jacks ordered, his pistol in hand.

Draper took another step.

Jacks's gun barrel leveled at Draper.

"Whoa," Draper said, the hand moving away from the pocket, fingers splayed to indicate that hand was still empty, "Cody! Easy!"

"Then don't move, Keith," Jacks said.

Lopez and Bell each had their pistols drawn now and had fanned out so each had a clean, clear shot. As Jacks kept Draper covered, Lopez and Bell moved in from the sides. While Bell got the man's right hand and swung it behind him, Lopez dipped into the jacket pocket and pulled out a small blue pistol.

"Gun!" the chief said.

Frightened murmurs filled the snack bar.

Bell wasted no time forcing Draper down. "Spread 'em, Keith," he said, his voice high, tense. "You know the drill. . . ."

Draper started to say something, but Sara couldn't make it out.

"*Do* it," Lopez interrupted.

Draper complied, and Bell cuffed him and patted him down.

"Clean," Bell said, helping Draper back to his feet.

"Keith," Lopez said as he holstered his own pistol, "what the hell are you doing with this piece?"

Draper whined, "I *always* carry it."

"Why in the hell did you reach into your goddamn pocket? You got a death wish?"

Draper shrugged. "I . . . I was going to give it to you."

"Oh?"

"The *gun*! Hand over the gun. . . ."

Jacks was shaking his head. "Goddamn . . . you fired it during the gunfight, didn't you, Keith?"

"Well . . . they were all shooting!" Draper pouted. "I was trying to protect the customers, is all."

"Then why were you sneaking out just now?"

No response.

"You were going to ditch the pistol, right?"

Draper said nothing.

Grissom stepped forward and Lopez dropped the pistol into an evidence bag the CSI held out.

"Smith & Wesson 2214," Grissom said. "Quite possibly the same caliber that killed Nick Valpo. And possibly Vanessa Delware, as well."

Every eye in the snack bar had turned to Keith Draper. He was crying now, shaking his head.

"I didn't think I *hit* anyone. . . ."

"Oooh, Keith," Lopez said, "you're in a lotta trouble. You wouldn't have any idea where Tom Price is, would ya?"

Draper shook his head and kept sniffling.

The police chief shook his head. He glanced at his CSI guests, and his gaze settled on Grissom. "I tell you, Doc, sometimes I don't know what's worse— the bikers or the casino employees."

5

WARRICK HAD DEPOSITED TOMAS NUÑEZ at a workstation in a lab office, with the Ames computer hooked up to a flat screen.

Nuñez had a room-filling personality. He was shorter than most people perceived, and older, though the thinning hair should have been a giveaway. The charismatic computer guru projected a bandito vibe in his faded jeans and black T-shirt (emblazoned with the spiked wheel logo of Colombian singer Juanes), and his shoulder-length black hair (slicked back and ponytailed) bore modest, almost stylish streaks of gray; his black mustache seemed more droopy than usual, but late-in-the-day CSI calls like this one weren't SOP.

"You want to know all you can, naturally," Nuñez said.

"Naturally," Warrick said.

"But these things can take time. Fast track or slow?"

"Fast would be cool."

Nuñez said, "I can give you both—from what you've told me, I have a few ideas about where to look. That'll get you *on* track, fast; then I can go through in-depth, so when you go to court, every digital 'i' and 't' will be dotted and crossed."

"No wonder Catherine adores you, man."

"From your lips to her ears. . . . Check back in an hour, *amigo*."

"Office is yours."

A throat cleared and Warrick glanced over at Greg, in the doorway, paperwork in hand.

Warrick slipped out into the corridor with the young CSI. "Got something already?"

"Couple of prints off the note, couple more off the envelope."

"Good start."

Greg gestured with a head nod down the hall. "David told me that Dr. Robbins is ready to go over the autopsy with us—can you get away?"

"Your timing and the doc's are perfect. Tomas says he may have an idea or two about the suicide note in an hour or so."

"Cool."

Warrick stuck his head back into the office and told the computer expert he was heading over to Doc Robbins's domain.

"If you get something before I'm back," Warrick said, "call my cell."

"You really want to wrap this one up quick, don't you, *jefe*?"

"If it's a straight suicide, I want to get out of the bereaved husband's life. But if he's a murderer, I'd like to do his late wife a favor and not have him sleeping in their double bed, enjoying the extra room."

"I hear you," Nuñez said, and turned back to the screen.

Warrick and Greg walked briskly to the coroner's wing, got into blue scrubs, and joined Dr. Albert Robbins in the autopsy room, a sterile chamber, cold in several senses of the word, with tiled walls and floor and metal doors—not Warrick's favorite place to be, but always a vital stop to make on the journey to justice.

The body of Kelly Ames lay nude on the metal table; Dr. Robbins stood on the opposite side as the two CSIs joined him. Graying, with short hair and a full beard, Doc Robbins had warm, crinkly eyes that seemed at odds with these surroundings, not to mention his profession. Warrick had known Doc Robbins for some time now and had never once seen the man lose his professional cool or his personal compassion. The coroner possessed one of the sharpest minds in the department.

"David said you have doubts this is a suicide," Robbins said blandly, leaning over the body, his metal crutch occupying its usual place in the corner while he worked.

Warrick shrugged. "Let's say I've got issues."

"That's good to have, issues," Robbins said. "Because there's no doubt Kelly Ames was murdered."

Greg's eyes tightened. "You know that because her skin isn't red?"

"It was a good indicator," Robbins said, switching to teacher mode now. "Do you know why?"

"Well, I don't claim I knew this before Warrick told me."

"And what did he tell you?"

"That people exposed to lethal doses of carbon monoxide turn that shade."

Smiling gravely, Robbins said, "That's one of the symptoms. If, as in Kelly's case, her skin *hasn't* turned color, what would be the next step?"

Greg knew he was being quizzed, but from what Warrick saw, the kid seemed to be thriving on it.

"I'd come knocking on your door and ask you to do a blood test . . . to tell us if there's CO in Kelly's lungs."

"Good. But you don't have to knock, I can tell you right now—no carbon monoxide in her lungs at all. Which tells us . . . ?"

Greg didn't hesitate at all. "She was dead when somebody put her in that car and staged a suicide."

Warrick said, "Which is likely why she had on the odd combination of colors and a T-shirt on inside out."

Nodding, Greg said, "Someone else dressed her."

Warrick asked the coroner, "What about time of death?"

Robbins also didn't hesitate. "Sometime around noon."

"Which is when Kelly's husband said he was on his way to work." Warrick studied the somber, pretty face belonging to the corpse on the slab. "Did you find anything else?"

"Cotton fibers in her nose and lungs. She was suffocated with a pillow, most likely."

Greg said, "So she was in bed, in pajamas or lingerie or undies or whatever, and the murderer smothered her and then got her into some clothes and into the garage and the car."

"That's a reasonable reconstruction," Warrick said. To Robbins, he said, "Thanks, Doc."

"Sure. Warrick?"

"Yeah?"

Robbins, his face blank and yet infinitely sad, nodded toward his patient. "Let's see if we can't do right by her."

"That's gonna happen," Warrick said with quiet confidence.

He and Greg left the autopsy room, got out of the scrubs, and—in the corridor—Warrick said, "So far, we've got two suspects, the husband and the friend."

"Why the friend?" Greg asked.

"You know the rule, Greg—first on the scene, first suspect. Who called nine-one-one?"

Glumly, Greg said, "The friend."

"That makes you unhappy?"

"Yeah, well, I liked her. She was nice."

"You mean she was a hottie."

Greg frowned. "Hey. That's not fair. I'd just hate to think she's a killer, is all."

Warrick shook his head. "Do you want chapter and verse on how many hotties have torn up chicken coops since I started this job? I don't care if she lives at the Playboy Mansion or she's some little old lady offering us cookies—this is business. Stay objective, and let's check out both the friend and the husband."

"Good idea," Greg said. ". . . I'll take the friend."

Warrick sighed, then laughed. "Oh-kay. Just remember what I said, and meet me where Nuñez is working, in an hour."

They parted ways and Warrick found himself a quiet office where he could try to corroborate Charlie Ames's story.

Tonight's return to graveyard provided him a reminder of why he preferred swing shift. Here he sat in an office just after one A.M., with no one he could call at Cactus Plastics to find out what time Charlie Ames had come into work and no one to question about Megan Voetberg's assertion that Ames was having an affair with a coworker, and that his wife knew about it.

Most of the questions Warrick really wanted answered would have to wait until sunup, toward the tail end of the shift. This was an old pattern, a constant night-shift problem, that he hadn't missed at all. In the meantime, he settled for doing background on Charlie and Kelly Ames, tapping the many data banks, local and national, that didn't care what time it was.

High school sweethearts who went to college together at UNLV, the Ames couple had been married a little over two years. After college, Kelly had worked briefly for an insurance company before taking the job at the postal encoding station that allowed them to work roughly the same hours. Charlie, who had spent college summer internships at Cactus Plastics, had graduated to a decent job there. If something had gone south with their marriage, their online story didn't reveal it.

An hour later, Warrick knew little more than that and was running late to meet Greg. After shutting down his computer, Warrick trotted off and found Greg sitting with Nuñez, both of them wearing headsets, bouncing to two different rhythms, the pair having traded iPods.

"I like this," Nuñez said, too loud. "What is it?"

"The last Garbage CD," Greg said, his voice also rising to where he could hear it over the headphone volume. "Great, isn't it? . . . This is pretty tight, too."

Nuñez said, "That's Molotov. Latin punk."

Normally, this musical detente across cultures and even generations (Nuñez being at least twenty years older than Greg) would have given the music-loving Warrick a warm glow. Tonight, the only glow in him came from a burning desire to capture whoever murdered Kelly Ames.

Greg looked up, saw Warrick, then grinned and jerked the buds out. "You gotta hear this stuff. Tomas, what's this band again?"

"Molotov," Nuñez repeated.

"Molotov," Greg said, slipping the buds back on. "This *rocks*."

Warrick shook his head and Greg grinned sheepishly; the buds came out again.

"Sorry," Greg said.

Warrick tried to soften the blow: "I'll have a listen after we close the case."

But it came out harshly, and the mood in the room changed as abruptly as if Grissom had just walked in and found them using a Bunsen burner to warm up pizza.

While Greg looked chagrined, Nuñez only smiled.

All professionalism now, Greg said, "Megan Voetberg checks out. She's the real deal."

"You already *had* that opinion," Warrick said.

"Hey," Greg said, hurt or pretending to be. "She may be hot, but work is work . . . and her story checked out, and nothing suspicious turned up."

"What about prints from the note and envelope?"

"Just one set," Greg said. "And here's the fun part—they *don't* match Kelly Ames."

Warrick thought about that. "We'll run them through AFIS and—"

"Hey, *amigo*, you want a killer," Nuñez said, his grin growing wider, "I got a killer for you."

"That sounds definitive," Warrick said, and pulled up a chair.

"Your guy Ames is not an idiot," Nuñez said. "He's even kind of smart . . . just not—"

"Smart enough," Warrick said.

"Had enough on the ball to figure out somebody might go poking around in his computer." Nuñez pulled out a printout and handed it to Warrick, keeping a duplicate in hand for himself. "Hubby wrote the suicide note *after* Kelly was gone."

Warrick digested that for a moment, then asked, "How could you know that?"

"Here's how smart Kelly's husband was—smart enough to change the clock, move the file, delete the original, then change the clock back. To the naked eye—the untrained naked eye, anyway—it looked like Kelly typed the suicide note within an hour of her time of death."

"And we know she didn't how?"

"'Cause of the metadata."

"The meta what?" Warrick asked.

"Metadata," Nuñez said. "That's where our smart killer turns very, very dumb."

"Well," Greg admitted, "I never heard of metadata, either."

"Yes," the computer guru said, "but you aren't a

murdering husband faking his wife's suicide. . . .
See, metadata is basically data *about* data. It's embed-
ded in every Word document, Excel spreadsheet,
and PowerPoint presentation. Tells when the original file was created . . . and the metadata for the suicide note? Over an hour *after* Kelly's TOD."

"Whoa," Warrick said. "Never mind Catherine,
Tomas. *I* love your ass."

"Well, I do have my moments," Nuñez grinned.
"But be prepared to love more of me, 'cause that's
not *all* I found."

"Oh?"

"Found a bunch of deleted e-mails coming from . . .
and going *to* . . . the same address—Plasticgirl@nev.isp."

"Which is who?" Warrick asked.

Nuñez shrugged. "And now love fades—afraid I
can't find that out until morning. Get me a court
order, and I'll talk to the internet service provider
and find out."

Greg asked, "*Where* were the deleted e-mails?"

"In unallocated space on the hard drive," Nuñez
said. "When you delete something on your computer, it's not really gone forever."

Warrick said, "I knew that."

Greg said, "Me too," but seemed to be covering.

Nuñez ignored both of them and explained anyway: "Deleted things go to unallocated space on the
hard drive until that space is used by some other
file."

Nodding, Warrick said, "And how many e-mails
did you uncover?"

"Couple hundred."

"Whoa," Warrick said, his mouth dropping open like a trapdoor. "*How* many?"

"A couple hundred," Nuñez repeated, "at least."

Warrick, shaking his head, said, "How is that even *possible*?"

Stroking his mustache, Nuñez asked, "How much memory on your first computer—a meg maybe?"

Warrick shrugged. "Yeah, I think."

Nuñez gestured to the computer tower on the counter. "This puppy has an eighty *gigabyte* hard drive. Takes a lot longer, these days, to start reusing hard drive space . . . unless you're downloading movies or something."

"So," Greg said. "What exactly is in these hundreds of e-mails?"

"Pretty much everything you would want for a motive," Nuñez said. "Both of them saying, 'I love you,' both complaining about Kelly, what an obstacle she is to them, and one from this morning where Charlie said, 'We're not going to have to worry about her anymore.'"

The computer expert had a folder of printed-out e-mails, with significant ones marked with Post-its. This he handed to Warrick, who perused them.

"One more question," Warrick said, sitting forward. "If I didn't want to wait until morning and get a court order . . . how might someone go about finding out who Plasticgirl@nev.isp is?"

Nuñez eyeballed him. "Are you going to use this knowledge before you get a court order?"

Warrick waved that off. "I'm not going to use it in court. Just looking to move forward faster."

"Nothing else?"

Serving up a nasty chuckle, Warrick said, "Well . . . I thought I might whisper it in Charlie Ames's ear. Like a sweet nothing?"

Nuñez seemed to like the sound of that. "Okay, then. . . . If you're not going to mention how you obtained the info, you might just ask me."

"*Ask* you?"

Nuñez grinned again. "I have an old friend at nev.isp who I spoke to just a short time ago. . . . You know—just trying to move forward faster?"

Warrick grinned slowly. "I see . . . and what did your old friend have to say?"

"That things have been going really well at work and she got a promotion."

"That's nice."

"Yeah. Oh, and she also mentioned that Plasticgirl is the user ID of a certain Henderson woman named Paula Ferguson."

"Tomas," Warrick said, "has anyone ever told you you're a genius?"

"First time tonight," Nuñez admitted. "One other little detail you might care to know."

"What's that?"

"Plasticgirl, Paula Ferguson? She works at Cactus Plastics."

Warrick's eyebrows rose. "Tomas—you . . . are . . . the . . . *man.*"

"Second time tonight," Nuñez said with a toothy grin, "for that one. . . ."

Forty minutes later, Warrick and Greg met up with Brass out in front of the Ames house; a black-and-white rolled in seconds later. Throughout the neighborhood, lights were off, the Ames house shrouded in darkness. The only sound was a lone dog squawking at them from down the street, behind a fence.

Brass signaled the uniformed officer from the black-and-white to go around behind the house, and for Greg to back him up.

Warrick and Brass went up to the front door and spread out on either side. The detective's look silently asked Warrick if he was ready, and the CSI nodded.

Then Brass hit the doorbell.

Both men had their pistols unholstered and at their sides. They waited, the night air cool, but not enough to keep sweat from running down Warrick's back beneath the navy blue CSI windbreaker.

Nothing happened.

Brass rang the bell again.

This time a light clicked on inside and they heard someone moving around. Finally, the outside light came on and Charlie Ames peered at them through one of the door's tiny windows.

Shaking his head, Kelly Ames's husband threw open the door, wearing navy blue boxers and nothing else. His chest was pasty white with very little hair, and he had skinny arms and spindly knob-kneed white legs. And yet at least two women had loved this prize specimen.

Ames's voice was a whisper so harsh and loud that the idea behind whispering was nullified. "What the hell do you people want at this hour?"

Several other dogs in the neighborhood picked up the chorus of the first.

"You might want to ask us in," Brass said, "so we can tell you."

"And maybe I might not. Maybe you have something official to show me, like a warrant, if you're gonna bother me again, after what I been through."

Warrick stepped forward and his eyes locked with the husband's. "It has been a rough night, hasn't it, Mr. Ames?"

Brass's sigh was beyond world-weary, though his smile was perfunctory. "We're going to talk, Mr. Ames—out here, in there, it doesn't matter to us. But we *are* going to talk about you and . . . what's her name?"

Warrick said, "Paula Ferguson."

Brass said, "Thanks . . . you and Paula Ferguson, Mr. Ames. And we're going to talk about you and her *right now.*"

Ames's face went whiter than his chest; then another color, a yellowish green, began to spread across his features, and Warrick wondered if the guy might not throw up on the porch.

"Inside," Brass said, and gently nudged Ames back into the house. Ames did not protest. Warrick followed them.

"What do you people think you know, anyway?" the husband asked.

Brass did not answer, and neither did Warrick, as Ames turned on a light and led them into the living room, a tiny area with ratty olive-green carpeting, a sofa, a chair, a cheap coffee table, and a good-sized TV with a DVD player and a game system hooked up to it; no books in the room, only a few magazines (*People, TV Guide, Sports Illustrated*), and a newspaper opened to the sports section.

Their host sat in the chair and gestured to the sofa, but neither Brass nor Warrick took his invitation.

Into his walkie-talkie, Brass said, "We've got him."

"*Ten-four,*" came the uniform's voice through the radio.

"What do you mean," Ames said, ever more alarmed, sitting forward, "'got' me?"

"Before we go any further," Brass said, "I need to tell you something."

Ames was getting testy now. "About time you explained yourselves!"

"You have the right to remain silent . . ."

"What . . . ?"

Brass shook his head. "Don't interrupt, Mr. Ames, and this will go faster. You have the right to an attorney. . . ."

The detective went on a while, finally saying, "Do you understand the rights I have just explained to you?"

Ames nodded numbly.

"Out loud, please."

"I understand."

Warrick sat next to the man on the sofa and Brass hovered over them.

The CSI asked, "You want to tell us why you did it?"

"Did what?"

"Murdered your wife."

The three words seemed to hit Ames like physical blows, and he said nothing for several long moments.

Finally, he managed, "It's an absurd accusation. I loved her. We hit a rough patch. She committed suicide. End of story."

"Not even close to the whole story, Mr. Ames," Warrick said. "We knew this evening this wasn't a suicide."

Ames glared at Warrick as if the CSI were insane.

Warrick said, "Mr. Ames, carbon monoxide will turn your skin red. Kelly's wasn't. She had no carbon monoxide in her lungs and she had cotton fibers in her nose and lungs, indicating she'd been smothered, probably with a pillow. She was murdered. End of story."

"I don't see it," Ames said, obviously stalling for something, anything.

Greg and the uniformed officer came in through the front door to join the party.

Warrick signaled to the hall with a head bob, and Greg headed down toward the bedroom, pulling a roll of large garbage bags out of his jacket pocket as he went. When he returned, Greg had the pillows from the Ames's bedroom in four plastic bags.

"Mr. Ames," Warrick said, "fibers from one of those pillows are going to match the fibers from Kelly's nose, aren't they?"

"I . . . I don't see how."

Brass said, "Let's talk about six months' worth of hot e-mails between you and Paula Ferguson."

Ames's face fell into his hands.

"Charlie," Warrick said, shaking his head, getting familiar for the first time. "Where did you think all those e-mails went when you deleted them? Outer space? Blew off into the ether, maybe? And you certainly couldn't think we wouldn't catch that the 'suicide note' was written well after Kelly died. You may think you know your way around computers, but our guy can make them talk and sing and bark on their hind legs."

Ames did not respond.

"You had a nothing plan, Charlie," Warrick said, "and you carried it out badly, to boot. Let me refresh your memory."

You've finally had enough of Kelly and her bitching and plan to trade her in for a new model—Paula, but you don't want to give up the house or any of your stuff. You've got a nice little nest egg in the bank, too, right? So you catch Kelly while she's still sleeping. You press the pillow over her head and push down. She thrashes as she fights, but she's not strong enough to keep you from smothering the life out of her. It's relatively quick and not that hard on either of you. . . .

You dress her, but you're so jacked up about the whole thing and how smooth it's going, how smart you are, that you don't pay any attention to the colors or the fact that you're putting her shirt on inside out. You place her in the car, then go back in and type the suicide note, change the computer clock so it looks like Kelly wrote it before she died, then you put that in the vehicle, too. Then you turn the key on and leave while clouds of carbon monoxide form.

Never dawns on you that her friend will miss her soon enough to cause trouble, and it never even occurs to you that she won't have carbon monoxide in her lungs. Dead people don't breathe, after all. . . . That's what makes them dead.

Warrick finished with, "My only question is . . . did Paula know? Was she in on this, maybe even this was *her* idea . . . ?"

Ames's head shot up, his gaze burning into Warrick. "Paula had *no* idea—you have *got* to believe me."

"Yeah," Brass said affably, "because you're so well known for your honesty, right, Mr. Ames?" He signaled to the uniformed officer, who got Ames up. "Get him dressed, cuff him, and take him in."

"*Really*," Ames pleaded, his distraught look bouncing from Warrick to Brass and back again. "Paula had *nothing* to do with it. She's innocent!"

Warrick thought, *Innocent isn't the word for those steamy e-mails*, but he said nothing. Besides, the e-mails did not indicate a murder plan, just a motive.

"About . . . about Kelly's clothes," Ames said, hesitating to look back at Warrick.

"Yeah?"

"That . . . that wasn't my fault."

"Oh?"

"I'm . . . I'm color-blind."

Warrick grunted. "Not your *only* blind spot, huh, Charlie?"

He said nothing, head hanging now, and the uniformed guys hustled him away.

With their suspect gone, Brass asked the CSI, "Do you believe him about the girlfriend?"

Warrick shrugged. "Kind of. But we'll check her out just the same. We've already got Kelly Ames's killer, though. Between the evidence and what he gave up even after he'd been Mirandized . . . he's nailed."

"At least we got him quick," Brass said.

"Let's hope quick's the way Kelly died," Warrick said. "Because there's nothing more we can do for her."

They walked outside and, before they'd reached their cars, their cell phones started ringing.

"Brown," Warrick said. He heard Brass answer his as well.

Greg loaded the bagged pillows into the back of the Denali and came around just as Warrick's call ended.

"What is it?" Greg asked.

"Another case. We'll head to the new crime scene from here."

"Where?"

"An apartment house on Paradise Road," Warrick said, "over by the convention center. . . . You drive."

Brass came up. "You get the call for the apartment on Paradise, by any chance?"

Warrick nodded.

"See you there," Brass said, and climbed into his Taurus.

Driving more confidently now, Greg turned off Sweeney, going south on Tenth Street to St. Louis Avenue, then back west to Paradise Road and south again. After crossing Sahara, he passed the Hilton on their left, then the convention center. On the other side of Paradise, the monorail tracks followed the road and beyond that the night sky was spiked with the silhouette of V—Shawn Victor's latest billion-dollar hotel.

Immediately south of the convention center, across Terry Drive, squatted a two-story white stucco apartment house that looked more like a cheap motel. Instead of the usual orange-tile roof, this one bore a grimy green number, guaranteed to hold the heat. Tiny air conditioners stuck through the walls below small picture windows whose only view was the convention center and its parking lot. Cars were parked nose-in toward a building in which only a few lights were on.

Their call was on the second floor, toward the east end of the building.

Not like a motel, Warrick thought, reassessing. *More a minimum security prison. . . . Missing only the fence.*

They went through a central first-floor door and climbed dark stairs to the second floor, where the dimly lit corridor was lined with wood-frame doors on either side. White paint, perhaps intended to make the place seem homey, gave instead an institutional feel.

Halfway to the east end, they found a door ajar, revealing a uniformed officer inside talking to a young woman.

The officer was a tall, slender African-American with a very short-trimmed Afro and wide brown eyes. A thin black mustache trailed across his upper lip and his name plate read CHARLES.

He nodded to them as they came in; Brass trailed by Warrick and Greg.

"This is Tara Donnelly," Charles said.

The young woman, maybe twenty-eight, sat on a large brown sofa. Her hair was long and red, her eyes brown and red-rimmed from tears, her skin pale white. Warrick estimated she weighed maybe one-eighty, and she had a certain well-fed farm-girl attractiveness, wearing a long shiny blue skirt and a black Clash T-shirt while she clutched a tissue. At the mention of her name, she looked up and tried to smile politely, but it didn't come off.

Brass introduced himself, Warrick, and Greg.

"Ms. Donnelly," Brass began, "would you care to tell us what happened?"

She blew her nose into the tissue, took a deep breath, and said, "I went out tonight . . . with a couple of girlfriends?"

Warrick knew Brass wanted to know the girlfriends' names, but that could wait. They let her talk.

"We've been wanting to go to Drizzle. You know, the club?"

The trendy, expensive nightclub inside Las Palmeras Hotel and Casino was the vision of the Mateo brothers, Julio and Enrique, who had grown up in Vegas with the dream of owning the coolest, hippest casino in the city; and now they had it.

Warrick and Brass both nodded for her to continue.

"We'd been there for an hour or so . . . when I met this guy?"

She was an up-talker, Warrick thought, a Valley Girl malady with which CSI Sara Sidle was mildly infected; but this woman seemed terminally afflicted.

"Guy have a name?" Brass asked.

"He said 'Rick.' He was medium tall, with dark hair? Receding hairline, I guess you'd say, brown eyes, and he hardly ever smiled. I thought he was way serious and smart and stuff? Turns out he was psychotic."

"Did your girlfriends see him?" Brass asked.

She thought about that. "No, actually, they'd hooked up with their own guys by then. Jamie had left already with some hunk. And Natalie, she was dancing with this dude, but they were on the other side of the club. With his friends? So I could barely see her."

Brass asked, "What happened next?"

"I told Rick I had to get home. Because I had to work tomorrow. He must have followed me, because the next thing I know, he's in the staircase with me, offering to walk me to my door? I tried to say no, but he just kept, I don't know, easing me toward my apartment. Then we were here, and I unlocked the door and he pushed me inside."

"Did you scream?" Brass asked.

She shook her head. "I was going to, but from out of nowhere, he had this little gun, and he pointed it at me! He said that if I made a sound? He'd shoot me and whoever else came through the door."

Brass nodded. "Then?"

Looking down at her lap now, Tara said, "Then . . . he raped me."

That, Warrick noted, she did *not* phrase as a question.

"Did he hurt you?" Warrick asked.

She gave up another half shrug. "He was rough, but . . . he didn't really hurt me. Not . . . not physically, anyway."

"Did you fight him?" Brass asked.

Shaking her head, she said, "I scratched him once, but he slapped me . . . and I stopped."

"May we scrape under your fingernails?" Warrick asked.

"If you think it will help?"

Greg did the honors, scraping the skin from under her nails into a small cellophane bag that he sealed.

Brass asked, "Would you recognize your attacker if you saw him again?"

"In a heartbeat," Tara said, her jaw set. "I don't drink, Officer—I was dead sober when this happened."

"Did he take anything?"

She thought about that. "No—he just . . . *did* me . . . and then he left."

"Did he wear a condom?"

"Yes! Thank God for small favors. And latex gloves, too."

Warrick frowned. "Really?"

"Yeah! It was weird. It was like he was afraid he'd leave fingerprints on me?"

Brass gestured to Warrick and Greg. "Do you mind if our CSIs have a look around while you and I chat a little more?"

"That's fine," she said. "Anything you want, anything you think'll help."

Warrick and Greg went to work, Greg starting in the kitchen, Warrick in the bedroom. The room was small, a queen-sized bed taking up most of the space. A dresser sat on the wall to Warrick's left, a chest of drawers on the same wall as the door, a small television on top.

The bedspread had been disturbed—obviously where the attack had occurred—but using his alternate light source, Warrick could find no sign that the pair had sex on the bed. He did discover a couple of dark hairs, presumably the attacker's; nothing else.

Greg came in from the kitchen. "Nothing," he reported.

"Not much more in here," Warrick said, showing Greg the bag with the hair. "Let's try the bathroom."

The bathroom was barely big enough for one, let alone both investigators. While Greg fingerprinted the faucets and the sink, Warrick got down on his hands and knees around the toilet.

They found nothing.

They talked to Tara Donnelly a short while longer, then worked on convincing her to go to the hospital with Charles to have a rape kit done.

"Listen," she said, "I'm okay. And he used a condom?"

"Please," Warrick said. "It might not show anything, but better to have it than not. Might really be a help in getting this guy before he date-rapes some other young woman."

Soon, out in front of the apartment complex, when they'd watched a squad car take the victim away, Warrick tapped Greg on the shoulder and said, "Let's go for a walk."

At the far end of the building, set back at the end of the parking lot, barely visible in the dim wash of streetlights, was a Dumpster.

Greg turned up his nose even as his flashlight played over the large metal container. "Oh no. I *hate* this sport. . . ."

Dumpster diving.

"I'll do my part," Warrick said.

"Yeah—what?"

"I'll spot you . . . hold the light."

Shaking his head, Greg said, "Dude, this is so not right. Why do I *always* have to be the one—"

"Rank has its privileges."

"Rank is right!"

Warrick held up a finger for silence. "Neighbors are trying to sleep. Get inside . . . your bitching will have a nice resonance in there."

"Very funny."

Greg took the time to slip a white Tyvek suit over his clothes before he climbed into the Dumpster. He came out less than two minutes later, grinning, a pair of latex gloves in a plastic evidence bag.

"Nice going, Speedy Gonzales," Warrick said, looking at the bag under the beam of his flash.

"Right on top," Greg said, pleased with himself. "Guy must have just pitched them in, then split."

Warrick laughed once. "Why is it that the bad guys always think we're lazy, stupid, or both?"

"They're the lazy, stupid ones, not taking their gloves somewhere else to dispose of."

"Yeah—and not just throw them in the nearest Dumpster, like we won't think of *looking* for 'em there!"

Greg held up a finger before his lips, and Warrick stopped his rant.

Greg said, "Neighbors are trying to sleep. . . ."

6

NICK STOKES ALWAYS DID HIS BEST NOT to make snap judgments about witnesses and suspects; but something about this character Keith Draper rubbed the CSI raw—a little too slick, a little too smarmy in that Mr. Monopoly tuxedo and Wal-Mart cologne, his black hair cut just so (probably had to drive to Vegas to a mall salon), and, finally, the guy's emotions-on-his-sleeve mentality. . . .

As Nick, Grissom, and Catherine sat in the security office of the Four Kings with Draper, Chief Lopez, and casino rep Henry Cippolina, Draper was fidgeting in his chair, first sniffling, then worrying a tissue in his hands into shreds.

Not surprisingly, the Boot Hill crime lab was not exactly the biggest, best-outfitted in the nation; but they had a water tank and a microscope, which meant Sara could do firearms comparisons.

Problem was, the bullet they needed to compare it to was not in the town morgue because Boot Hill didn't have one: instead it resided in the local mortuary, inside the body of Nick Valpo.

And the probable difference between some small-town mortician cutting a bullet out of a murder victim and Clark County Chief Medical Examiner Dr. Albert Robbins doing his version of that procedure was . . . troubling. Robbins, of course, could be counted on to get the slug out without tarnishing or abrading any of the markings. A local mortician would be more adept at running a business than preserving evidence.

Nevertheless, as soon as the Draper interview was over, Nick would be on his way to the mortuary to fetch the bullet (whatever shape it might be in) for Sara to compare to a bullet from Draper's confiscated .22.

The gun-toting pit boss sat in a straight-back chair in front of a metal desk. Chief Lopez had deposited himself behind that desk, properly projecting authority, with floor manager Cippolina standing behind him. The seated CSIs were fanned out behind Draper.

"So, Keith," Lopez said with a smile that wasn't cheerful. "Tell us what happened."

"Pretty busy for that time of day," Draper answered. "Maybe a hundred people scattered through the casino. . . . Generally, that late in the afternoon, traffic should be about *half* that."

"Where were you, exactly?"

"Pit six," Draper said, shredding his third tissue. "I was just, you know, making my rounds—no big whoop."

"Then what?"

Draper's face tightened, as if he'd awoken from a bad dream and was compelled to try to recall it. "Then those slimy bastards came."

"The Predators."

"Predators. Valpo leading his entourage, swaggering around like he owned the goddamn place."

"You knew Valpo?"

"Not well. Not particularly. But I knew him and his type, all right."

Lopez remained conversational in tone, not at all threatening. "A type you hate, Keith?"

"I *do* hate that type, and I hated Valpo, as much as you can hate somebody you hardly know."

"If you hardly knew him, then—"

"Valpo and his breed, they barge into a decent town and people are supposed to bend over and kiss their asses just for *being* here, bringing in a little 'business.' We all lose when their type comes to town. When they aren't scaring off regular law-abiding people, then they're wrecking our machines or trying to get something for nothing, out of sheer . . . intimidation."

Nick glanced at Grissom, who was taking all this in with a deceptively bland expression. Draper was growing more heated with each word.

"You know as well as I do, Chief—there are good, decent people here just trying to make a living . . . and this trash rolls in here like God on wheels and tries to take over . . . like we were only put on this earth for their amusement."

As Draper finally paused for breath, Lopez cut in. "All right, Keith—I believe we've established that you don't like the Predators—"

"Not just them! . . . I can't stand the sight or smell of *any* of those maniacs."

Lopez shrugged a little. "Point taken—all bikers are on your bad side. Okay? Okay. Now, Keith—what happened next?"

"Those bastard Spokes barged in and . . ." He shuddered, and Nick couldn't tell if it was real or theatrics. ". . . all *hell* broke loose."

Like a traffic cop, the chief held up a hand: *stop*. "Slow 'er down, Keith—one thing at a time. I'm not looking for a general take on this—one look at the casino and the general idea becomes pretty clear. Be specific. The Spokes came in, and then . . ."

Draper sighed, tried to settle down. "Then I saw Buck Finch."

Lopez glanced past Draper to the CSIs and explained, "Buck Finch is head honcho of the Rusty Spokes."

Catherine nodded, and so did Nick. Grissom remained motionless and might have been in a catatonic state, although those who knew him well could spot the intensity in his eyes.

The chief was saying, "What happened next, Keith?"

"Spokes started pulling guns outta everywhere, pockets, coats, from in back of their belts, even their boots. I kinda took it all in, in slow motion, like one of those old Westerns? . . . Seemed like it took me a million years to react, but it was probably only two or three seconds. But that was two or three seconds too late. When I reached to hit the panic button, it was already all over but the shooting—literally."

The panic button, Nick knew, was something all

casinos had: when a pit boss hit it, all the security men in the place would swarm to that area.

"With so much gunfire blazing," Draper was saying, "I hit the floor. Then I got my own gun out and tried to return fire, only by then the Predators were firing back . . . so many *guns!* So many *bullets* flying everywhere!"

Grissom asked, "Mr. Draper, how many rounds would you say you fired?"

"I can say exactly—I emptied the clip. Eight rounds."

"All in the same direction?"

Draper sighed heavily and hung his head. "I'd like to say I only shot at the Spokes . . . but the truth is, I freaked . . . panicked. Just started pulling the trigger as fast as I could. I . . . I hope to hell I didn't hurt anybody who didn't deserve it."

Grissom asked, "Did you move your position?"

A little embarrassed, Draper said, "No. I stayed in the pit behind a table. That seemed about as close to 'safe' as I could get."

Lopez took over the interview again, and Catherine gave a sign to Grissom and Nick, who followed her out. They huddled against a concrete wall, the empty hallway affording them privacy.

"What do we think, so far?" Catherine asked.

Grissom said, "If Mr. Draper didn't move from pit six, he *couldn't* have shot Valpo from close range."

Eyes tight, Catherine said, "That's my thinking, too—but the security video should show us the shooter, once Sofia and Archie get through it all."

Nick said, "We're not takin' that clown's story at face value, are we?"

Catherine shook her head. "Still, if Draper's lying, be nice to have the bullet from Valpo's head, to catch him in the act."

With a nod, Nick said, "I'm all over that. I'll get one of the cops to drive me over to the mortuary."

"I'm going to work some more here," Catherine said, indicating the casino.

Grissom's head tilted to one side. "I think Chief Lopez is planning to visit the two gangs. . . . How about I go with him, Catherine?"

"Good idea," Catherine said. Her tiny smile told Nick she appreciated Grissom's unobsequious deference to her supervisor role.

The officer who drove Nick across town was a big, strapping concrete block of a kid in a uniform who didn't seem quite old enough to be carrying that sidearm. He'd introduced himself as Dean Montaine and had a firm but not overbearing handshake. Red-haired with pale skin, the young officer didn't seem to have pulled a lot of traffic duty on sunny days.

When they'd been in the car for a few minutes, Nick asked, "Ever play any ball?"

Montaine nodded. "High school. You?"

Briefly Nick told him about Texas A&M and his knee. They talked football and were properly bonded by the time they reached the darkened mortuary.

"Nobody home?" Nick asked. "Nobody who's still breathing, anyway?"

Montaine said, "Mr. Erickson must be 'round back."

After pulling the car into the parking lot, Montaine circled around to the rear of the dark-brick

two-story with the discreet BOOT HILL MORTUARY sign.
They found a dim light shining through an open
door and, under a weak parking-lot light, a blue
minivan, parked.

"That's Mr. Erickson's," Montaine said, indicating
the van as he pulled up next to it.

They got out and approached the building, feet
scuffing the gravel of the lot; but as they grew closer
to the open door, something got the hair prickling
on Nick's neck.

Nick glanced sideways at the young cop. "Would
Mr. Erickson leave the back door open like that?"

"If he's inside," Montaine said with a shrug, "why
not?"

"You guys ever have *any* crime before today?"

"Yeah, a little. But what's to steal in a stiff hotel?"

Nick could think of something, but said, "You
think it's reasonable a Boot Hill businessman would
have the back door of his business wide open . . . in
the middle of the night?"

Montaine's hand dropped to the nine millimeter
on his hip.

Holding out a hand to keep the young man where
he was, Nick eased forward, hand on his own gun's
butt, the strap of the holster undone.

Nick went in first.

A garage awaited, with a hearse and a limousine
both sitting under a naked hundred-watt bulb in the
center of the ceiling.

"Mr. Erickson?" Nick called.

Only half an echo off cement answered the CSI.

Nick took in the surroundings: garage walls clut-
tered with tools, a lawn mower, a workbench, and

other things blocked by the parked vehicles. Easing his gun from its holster, but keeping the pistol at his side, Nick called out again. "*Mr. Erickson?*"

Still no answer but the echo.

Nick glanced back to see Officer Montaine, all business now, pistol out.

Beyond the workbench, a door stood ajar—to the interior of the mortuary, Nick assumed. He brought his gun up and kept it trained on that door. Behind him, he hoped Montaine had his pistol set to cover them if someone popped up from behind a vehicle.

Though that door was open, Nick could see no light beyond. He got out his mini-flash, turned it on, and used his left wrist to brace the pistol so the light and gun were both pointed into the darkness. With a head motion he summoned the young local cop to follow.

The door opened into a small hallway. To Nick's right, in a corner, were two expandable carts that the coffins sat on during transportation from room to room, or to the back of the hearse. The hall in front of him was lined with doors. To his left, at the other end of the short hallway, was a door on the right. He could see no light coming from beneath. Nodding toward that door, Nick kept his pistol on the main hall while Montaine tried the door.

Locked.

The young officer caught up to Nick and they moved slowly down the corridor to a closed door on the left, where Nick signaled for Montaine to cover the hallway. No light escaped from beneath this door, either; but this one was *not* locked . . .

. . . and swung easily open when Nick turned the knob with the heel of his flashlight hand.

An office.

A quick sweep of the flash told Nick that he was in here alone. Closing the door as he came out, Nick nodded for them to move on.

Montaine went through an open doorway to the right. Nick could see a table and chairs under the beam of the young man's flash, but nothing else. The officer came out and shook his head—safe to move to the next door.

Nick did not like mortuaries. He'd had a bad experience at night in another one, not long ago; and while he did not like to think he was easily creeped out, this excursion was making him progressively edgier. He hoped it didn't show, because the last thing they needed was for the young officer to get spooked. . . .

Nick took a breath, and—with the flashlight hand—tried the next door.

His initial sweep of the light joined with pungent chemical odors to tell him he was in the body preparation chamber.

A metal table, not unlike the one back in Robbins's morgue, sat centrally, and counters and sinks and cupboards lined the walls. An embalming machine sat conspicuously on a counter in the corner. At first, Nick thought he had entered another empty room . . .

. . . then he heard the moan.

Turning the beam toward the sound, the CSI saw a man sprawled on the floor beyond the metal table.

"Montaine!" Nick said. "In here."

Without waiting, Nick went to the man, who was groggy but very much alive.

Montaine entered the room and flicked the light switch.

"Oh hell," the young officer said. "Mr. Erickson, are you all right?"

Erickson was struggling to all fours now, his head toward Nick, a bloody wound in the back of his skull.

"Ambulance," Nick said, "now."

Montaine was on the radio immediately.

"Lay back, Mr. Erickson," Nick said.

The mortician peered up unsteadily through glassy gray eyes—a tall, broad, balding man of perhaps fifty. His glasses had been knocked off and lay askew on the floor nearby.

"Who . . . who are you?" Erickson managed.

"Nick Stokes, sir—Las Vegas Crime Lab."

"Oh. Oh, yes . . . the CSI coming about the dead biker. . . ."

"Yes, sir. Lay back now; rest easy. You've probably got a concussion."

"Damnit!" Erickson snapped, suddenly angry. "I never even saw him."

"Who would that be?" Nick asked, holstering his weapon and flicking off the flashlight. Possibly he should have just told the mortician to remain quiet; but this was a crime scene, and Erickson's words were evidence.

"The SOB that hit me—never even saw him. One moment I was leaning over the body, next you and Dean were here . . . and all I've got to show is . . . ahhhh . . ." Erickson winced in pain.

Nick didn't want to ask the next question—he already had a really bad feeling about the answer. He grabbed a towel off a rack by a sink, ran it under cold water, wrung it out, then knelt next to the mortician and pressed it to his wound. "Mr. Erickson . . ."

"Stan . . . call me . . . call me Stan."

"Stan," Nick said. "Do you know where the body is now?"

Erickson glanced forlornly at the metal table. "Oh, hell. Bloody goddamn hell. They stole it!"

"Valpo didn't walk away," Nick said.

"What's the matter?" Montaine asked.

Nick glanced at the young cop. "Whoever assaulted Mr. Erickson did so in order to steal Valpo's corpse."

Montaine looked at the table. "No way."

"Way," Nick said. "And incidentally, we're standing in the middle of a crime scene. So keep that in mind."

The officer looked around quickly, as if he'd just stepped into a room slithering with snakes.

"I'm sorry, so sorry," the mortician was saying.

"Please, sir," Nick said. "Just take it easy till help comes."

"It's my . . . my first bodysnatching."

Nick almost said *Not mine*, but let the man have his special if humiliating moment.

Hauling his cell phone off his belt, Nick could find solace only in knowing breaking this news to Catherine would be marginally better than doing so to his previous supervisor.

After all, Gris could get cranky when evidence got tampered with. And how could you tamper with murder evidence more than by stealing the victim's body itself?

* * *

As Chief Lopez's Blazer rolled down the highway out of town, Gil Grissom, in the passenger seat, stared out his window, taking in the beauty of the night sky. He found it pleasant to be away from the constant glare of the Las Vegas lights, and commented, "Pretty out here."

"Yeah," Lopez agreed. He was wearing a white Stetson now, perhaps to announce his status as head good guy. "I never get tired of it. Not exactly the big city, is it?"

"Provides a whole new point of reference for 'big,'" Grissom said, gazing deep into the black sky, searching for the farthest star. "Lived here your whole life, Chief?"

"Nah, started in LA. My folks moved the family out here when I was a sophomore in high school."

"Tough time to change," Grissom said.

"Wasn't that tough," Lopez said. "I was all-state in three sports—didn't have to take as much crap as most new kids."

Grissom turned to look at his new ally; small talk was not his forte, but he knew finding common ground with new colleagues was important. "Sounds like you were quite an athlete—why'd you give it up? Get hurt?"

Lopez shook his head. "Nope. I always wanted to be a cop."

"Why?"

"Putting things right appeals to me."

"We do what we can in a chaotic universe."

"Is it really chaotic?"

Grissom smiled thinly. "As long as people are in it, it is. . . . How far?"

"Six, seven miles. The Predators stay at a campground, out in the middle of nowhere."

"Little early in the morning for a visit. Or is that a little late at night?"

Lopez chuckled. "Either way, Doc, these type of people don't sleep by any regular clock, and with what happened today? Won't be in any mood to sleep."

They had already passed the roadblock on the way out of town—two Highway Patrol cars making sure that no one, especially the Predators, entered Boot Hill without authorization. As yet the governor had not called out the depleted National Guard or instituted martial law; but this was the next best thing. The Highway Patrol had the town pretty well locked down.

Lopez had not enforced a curfew but had already told the CSIs that in the case of more trouble, virtually anything this side of jaywalking, he would not hesitate to impose one. Grissom agreed with this attitude. Various chamber of commerce members, however, had contacted the chief to beg him not to enforce a curfew. The Gold Vault, with its captive audience of Rusty Spokes under house arrest, was doing fairly brisk business, and with the Four Kings down, the smaller Boot Hill establishments were doing okay, considering the only potential customers were locals and the few tourists who hadn't bailed after the gun battle.

The Highway Patrol had informed these bikers that none of them could leave; the state's investigation division would question them when the Rusty Spokes back at the Gold Vault had all been interviewed.

Long before the Blazer got to the campground, the glow of the Predators' bonfires lit the dark sky in a blush of orange, like an early threat of dawn. As Lopez and Grissom neared the camp's entrance, they were greeted by the flashing lights of more Highway Patrol cars and a Highway Patrolman held up a hand for them to stop.

The chief lowered his window and offered half a smile to the middle-aged Patrolman.

"Jorge," the officer said, offering up another half. "How're you doing, now that Armageddon's come to Nevada?"

"Hey, Bill, good as can be expected. We're still sorting things out in town, at the casino."

"I heard it was one righteous mess."

"Oh yeah. . . . Still, it could have been worse—by all rights, we should've had a dozen dead bodies littering the place." Lopez pushed his Stetson back farther, dragged a hand across a sweaty brow. "What's the mood out here?"

The Patrolman turned from the Blazer and looked toward the camp. "They're pissed, obviously . . . but so far, at least, they haven't gone completely nuts."

"Well, Bill, we'll see if we can calm them down a little. Doc Grissom here is from Vegas—a crime scene expert."

"Nice to meet you, Doc."

Grissom nodded hello.

"Here's hoping," the Patrolman said to Grissom, "this whole damn campground doesn't become a crime scene. . . . Good luck, fellas."

The Patrolman waved them through the gate.

The campground's main building was a one-story concrete bunker at right. At left was a bivouac of RVs, pickup trucks, tents, pull-along trailers, and thirty-some small campfires aside from the huge bonfires that burned every hundred yards or so. Motorcycles were scattered everywhere, and men and women, most of them in black leather, were—despite the lateness of the hour—still walking around and talking and partying.

"You weren't kidding," Grissom said. "They *don't* sleep."

Lopez tugged his Stetson back down. "Probably more meth per capita in this camp than anywhere else in Nevada, about now."

Grissom eyed the chief, asking a question without saying anything.

"And," Lopez said, answering that question, "now would not be the best time to bust 'em for it."

Grissom had no argument with that.

Two leather-clad bikers, each carrying a shotgun, approached the Blazer on either side. As the one on the driver's side got closer, he racked the slide, pumping a round into the chamber.

"Help you, girls?" he asked, his accent soft and southern.

Lopez lifted his badge on its necklace, the star catching light from a nearby bonfire and winking. "You have a permit for that weapon, son?"

The biker grinned crookedly. "Yeah—but not on me."

Waving a dismissive hand and smiling back, Lopez said, "Just checkin'. Jake around?"

The biker snorted. "Who should I say is calling?"

"Chief of Police Jorge Lopez and Dr. Gil Grissom from Vegas."

Looking past Lopez at Grissom, the biker frowned nastily. "Nobody called for a doctor."

"Nobody called for a chief of police, either," Lopez said, neither threatening nor loud, keeping his eyes on the biker. "Does this have to turn into something, son?"

Grissom watched as the biker and the police chief sized each other up. The CSI could not get a real fix on the biker's eyes as they kept darting from the chief to the entrance where the Highway Patrol sat, to Grissom, then back to Lopez and around and around.

His tone genial but with the faintest edge, Lopez said, "You've got a lot of questions floating in your head, don't you?"

The biker stayed silent, his grip tightening on the shotgun. Working carefully, Grissom unsnapped his holster, hoping no one had noticed his tiny movements.

"You're trying to figure out if you can get away with killing us," the chief was saying. "You're wondering if the good doctor can do anything before you cap him, too. You're wondering what the Highway Patrol will do when you fire that shotgun. You're wondering if Jake will give you a promotion for knocking off a cop, or maybe tear you a new asshole. All these things you wonder, and more."

The biker's knuckles were turning white on the gun and to Grissom, the guy seemed about to make a move. Grissom gripped the butt of his holstered weapon.

"What you didn't consider, son," Lopez continued,

"was where my gun was while your mind was runnin' through all the other possibilities."

Tensing, the biker got the shotgun maybe a half inch higher when Lopez's pistol seemed to blossom from nowhere, his right hand going through the open window, pressing his pistol's snout to the man's forehead.

Grissom's gun came out and the biker on the other side, whose shotgun nose had stayed down throughout the prior exchange, shook his head as if to say *I'm not part of this* and lowered his weapon to the ground and left it there.

"Why don't you stop trying to think about anything," Lopez advised the belligerent biker, whose eyes tried to look up at the gun barrel pressing into his forehead, "and just go get Jake."

The biker's eyes were wide and his mouth hung open. He managed to nod his head with the barest minimum of movement. He drew away from Lopez's gun, a circle in the flesh of his forehead.

Lopez stopped him with, "Leave the shotgun."

Obeying, the biker eased the gun to the ground and took off to get his boss, his pal falling in with him, looking irritated with what the other sentry had nearly initiated.

Holstering his weapon, Grissom said, "By the way, I hate guns."

Lopez grinned. "Me too. That was kinda hairy, for Boot Hill, anyway."

"That would have been 'hairy' in Vegas, too," Grissom said with a relieved smile. "Chief, you handled it well."

"Thanks, Doc," the chief said, almost embarrassed

by the praise. "But that's what the paycheck's for."

Jake Hanson materialized out of the darkness, a group of half a dozen pissed-off Predators moving up behind him, like a posse. Backlit by the firelight, the tall, handsome Hanson—brown hair parted on the left, blue eyes gleaming with anger, chest bare under a Predators leather vest, abs hard and lean—looked almost like a rock star, but the persona worked fine for a leader of men and motorcycles. To Grissom, Hanson's theatrical appearance did not bode well, considering that this man might be the only thing standing between peace and an all-out biker gang war in a tiny desert community.

"Chief Lopez," Hanson called out as he approached. "I hope you're here with news that you've caught Val's killer. . . ."

A series of whoops and shouts went up behind him, the group growing to a dozen, then doubling almost instantaneously.

"The Predators demand *justice*," Hanson said, his voice carrying over the crowd, and he wasn't even shouting.

Lopez jumped out of the Blazer and, fearless, marched toward Hanson. Grissom questioned the strategy of leaving the vehicle in favor of being afoot, but followed, getting out and coming around the Blazer fast, to provide a united front, even though the pair were outnumbered about fifty to two.

"We haven't arrested *anyone* yet!" Lopez announced to the crowd.

Boos cascaded and shouted epithets and calls for the Predators to "burn the whole fucking town down!" burst from the back of the crowd.

Addressing them, but close enough to Hanson to knock heads, Lopez said, "We're doing everything we can, and we will bring the killer to justice."

The response was more boos and shouts of "Kill the pigs," which struck Grissom as a nostalgic but nonetheless sinister touch.

Hanson's upper lip curled back in what was, technically at least, a smile; but the biker chief also held both hands up over his head, not in a surrender fashion, but to silence the crowd.

"We're not animals!" Hanson yelled to his people, his eyes still burning into Lopez. "We'll trust the police to do their job. We are law-abiding citizens who were attacked in a public establishment—we did nothing wrong. We'll give the police a chance to do the right thing."

Some in the crowd muttered, but mostly there was just a sort of stunned silence.

"We need to talk," Lopez said quietly.

Hanson shrugged elaborately. "Feel free."

"Without an audience, Jake."

Signaling for the group to remain behind, Hanson accompanied Lopez and Grissom into the darkness to a spot behind the bunker building. The soil here was sandy, giving slightly under the pressure of their steps, sparse vegetation springing up here and there. A breeze, far warmer than it probably should have been for this hour, swept over them, bringing with it the promise of an impossibly hot day to come.

"Talk about what?" Hanson asked when the crowd was far behind them.

"If you continue inciting your people like that," Lopez said, "a tragic incident will escalate into full-scale tragedy."

Shrugging, Hanson said, "You say inciting—I say I'm consolidating my position."

"Why? Aren't you in line to succeed Valpo?"

"I'm at the head of the line, yeah," Hanson said, still walking slowly, aimlessly. "But there's others behind me, and none of them have my restraint. If I weren't standing here, it'd be a free-for-all."

"Expecting a coup?" Lopez asked.

"If you don't expect that," the biker said with a fatalistic shrug, "you're not ready, if it comes."

This seemed a perfectly reasonable position to Grissom.

Lopez asked, "Did you see who shot Val?"

The abrupt change of subject caused Hanson to stop. "No. Hell no." He sighed, shook his head. "One minute he was there, next he was down."

"And you didn't see—"

"Hey—Chief. It was a little hectic in there."

Grissom asked, "Mr. Hanson, where were you when it started?"

Hanson frowned at Grissom, seemingly assessing him for the first time. "You're Vegas?"

"Yes. Crime lab."

That seemed to satisfy the biker. "I was sitting at a table next to Val, playing blackjack."

"Then you have a problem," Grissom said with a raise of the eyebrows. "You see that, don't you, Mr. Hanson?"

Hanson sneered. "You think *I* capped him? What

are you, high? Val and me were tight! What kinda crap—"

Unfazed, Grissom said, "You had opportunity, means, motive—"

"*I* had motive?" Hanson exploded.

"Who's leading the Predators now?"

The biker's eyes and nostrils flared. "Screw you, man! Nick Valpo was like a father to me."

"Duncan was like a father to MacBeth," Grissom said.

"Maybe," Hanson said, with a dangerous smile, "but I've got no Lady MacBeth pushing me into doing stupid shit."

Grissom smiled, pleased that his instinct was right: Hanson was a literate, intelligent person.

"Anyway," Hanson was saying dismissively, "I told you, man—I loved Val. And I didn't go into that casino looking to kill anybody."

The crackle of bonfires provided percussive punctuation to their conversation, but the partying seemed to have died down to a rumbling murmur.

Grissom said, "But you *were* armed—and you did shoot back, didn't you?"

Hanson didn't reply—he wasn't anxious to cop to anything in front of the Boot Hill chief of police, even on Predator turf.

"Confirm it or not, Mr. Hanson," Grissom said. "We've got video of the whole shoot-out."

Hanson's laughter was a short, mean burst, like machine-gun fire. "Then you haven't seen it, or you'd already know I *didn't* kill Nick." His eyes narrowed, and he lowered his voice. "But if you have that footage . . . you have pictures of whoever did this thing. Why aren't you going after *them*?"

"We're still looking," Grissom said.

A nasty edge undercut Hanson's attempt to sound matter of fact. "Do you know who you're looking for?"

Grissom did not play games with the man. "We have stacks of security cam tapes to review. We do *not* know who we're looking for . . . yet."

Abruptly, Hanson started strolling again and they fell in with him as he changed subjects. "Look, I can keep the lid on this camp, but I need something from you boys."

Lopez asked, "What's that?"

Just as abruptly, Hanson stopped and turned his gaze on the chief. "The Predators want Val's body."

"You can't be serious," Lopez said.

"I'm as serious as a heart attack."

"You can't have it, not yet," Grissom said. "It's still part of a criminal investigation. His body is evidence."

"His body," Hanson said, "deserves a Viking funeral. And some of these Predators think that oughtta be sooner than later."

"When we can release the body," Lopez said, "we will release it to the next of kin or whatever rightful claimant—but in the meantime, you have to calm your people down, Jake."

"Don't know if I can," Hanson said. "Between them wanting their funeral and champin' at the bit to rip the lungs and guts outta every one of those Spokes, well . . . this party's about to turn real ugly."

"'Heavy lies the head that wears the crown,' Jake," Grissom said.

Hanson's features contorted. "What the hell's that supposed to mean?"

Grissom found that amusing, but Lopez seemed singularly unamused, saying, "Doc here's the one telling you, in his own unique way, that you're the *leader* of this outfit . . . so you better start leading, Jake. Somebody's got to talk them down."

The biker spat. "What, for the sake of your two-horse town?"

"Not entirely for the town's sake, no." Lopez leaned toward the biker. "Truth is, Jake, more cops are coming here by the hour, and if the Predators and Rusty Spokes go head to head, plenty will die on both sides. You survived a skirmish in that casino, but a war? The governor is not about to let two motorcycle gangs annihilate one of his towns."

They were all considering that when Grissom heard an unmistakable whirring: a rattlesnake warning them they'd chosen a bad spot to stop and chat.

The other two heard it, too—Hanson froze and Lopez slowly reached for his pistol. Grissom could barely make out the coiled snake, but there it was, under a bush . . . less than a foot from Hanson's left leg.

For the first time in memory, Gil Grissom found himself drawing his weapon for the second time in one night, firing once, next to the snake, kicking up sand . . .

. . . and convincing the reptile to slither off into the night to search for a quieter, friendlier spot.

Hanson let out a nervous chuckle and he grinned wolfishly. "Looks like you missed, Doc."

"Did I?"

Hanson's smile disappeared as Predators came running from every direction, their guns out, dozens of metal fingers pointing accusingly at Grissom and Lopez.

Hanson held up his hands. "It's all right, it's all right! He shot at a rattler—probably saved my sorry ass."

The crowd did not want to buy this answer and milled there, looking surlier than ever.

"No harm, no foul," Hanson insisted. "Go back to your parties. Grab some booze, grab a snooze. . . . Go on, get outta here! These guys won't cause any trouble . . . and they're just about to go, anyway."

Many in the crowd were still eyeballing the two intruders even as the bikers slowly dispersed, seeming to vaporize back into the night.

When the three were alone again, Hanson said to the CSI, "You mean you *deliberately* didn't kill the snake."

"Tell me, Mr. Hanson," Grissom said, his tone light, "what was to be gained by killing that snake?"

"Plenty—would've stopped the threat of us getting fanged and poisoned, and there'd be one less snake in the world. I *hate* snakes!"

Grissom's eyebrows frowned; his lips smiled. "Hate? Certainly that's uncalled for. That creature has an important place in the ecosystem. Just as we *all* have our place, Mr. Hanson."

"Well, when a snake's in *my* place, I kill its scaly ass. Find a place in your ecosystem for *that*, Doc."

Moving a step closer, locking eyes with the biker, Grissom said evenly, "Let me put it another way— just because my presence makes a predator feel threatened, that doesn't mean I have to destroy it."

Hanson was chewing on that when Grissom's cell phone chirped.

Reholstering his pistol first, he yanked the device off his belt. "Grissom," he said.

"It's me," Catherine's voice said.

"How are things?" he asked.

"Weird. Not good."

"Oh?"

A sigh. "Nicky just called—Valpo's body has been stolen from the mortuary."

Grissom shot a look toward Lopez, whose own cell phone was ringing. "It's evidence. We need to find it."

"Tell me about it," she said. "We're working on it. Bullet's still in the body, by the way. Nicky's working the mortuary crime scene, and Sara and I are still here at the Four Kings; but this is not a fun development."

"I concur," Grissom said. "Where do you want me?"

"Can you check on Nick?"

"Yes." He signed off, then turned to see Lopez looking at him and rolling his eyes. Obviously the chief had just gotten the same news that Grissom had.

"What's the matter?" Hanson asked.

Lopez blew out a deep breath. "As long as it's just the three of us out here, I'll tell you. Jake, this is a show of good faith, a vote of confidence in your leadership if I tell you this."

"Tell me *what*?"

Lopez looked to Grissom, who nodded; then the chief told the biker honcho, "Your friend Valpo's body's been stolen from the mortuary."

Grissom had thought Hanson might explode, but instead the guy seemed to sag a little, a hand going to the bridge of his nose. "Aw, hell . . . how does *that* happen?"

"Don't know yet," Lopez said.

"But," Grissom said, "we will."

"My guys find out about this," Hanson said, nodding toward the bonfires, "don't look at *me* to control 'em."

Lopez stepped very near the biker. "That's why, Jake, you have to make sure they don't find out."

His eyes went wild. "How the hell am I going to do *that*? Why did you even *tell* me?"

"Because," Lopez said. "You're the leader, and leaders need to be informed and respected. I could have kept it from you, but it's not that big a town and you'd probably've found out by lunch and figured I kept it from you. Like I said, this is an act of good faith, Jake. I'm trying to make things right . . . for everybody."

Hanson nodded; Lopez seemed to have gotten through to him. "Chief, I'll do what I can."

"I've got your word," Lopez said.

"If the Spokes did this . . ."

"Hey!" Lopez said. "That's just what we *don't* need."

Hanson gave Lopez a sly smile. "Chief—that was for me . . . get it out of my system."

"You're sure that's all it is?"

"Yeah. Yeah." He grunted a sort of laugh, but the biker's eyes were somber. "I heard what you said before, Chief. . . ."

"Just for the record," Grissom said, "what would be the motive for the Spokes to steal Valpo's body?"

"They hated his ass!"

Grissom shook his head. "If they killed him, no need to take the body."

Grasping at straws now, Hanson said, "Maybe to destroy the evidence."

"What evidence?" Grissom asked. "The bullets that killed him? Why not just pitch the gun?"

Hanson had no answer for that, but he did say, "Look, man, they know damn well we'd want Val's body for a Viking funeral, a real blowout to honor his memory. That's reason enough to snatch him."

"Maybe," Grissom admitted. "But we will find your friend's killer—that I promise."

"You're pretty goddamn sure of yourself."

"Thank you. Mind another question?"

"Go."

"How did you Predators know you could get guns into that casino, past the metal detectors?"

Without hesitation, Hanson said, "Val told us the fix was in—those detectors would be off or dead or something."

"How was it managed?"

"Some friend of Val's, on the inside—that's all he ever told us."

Lopez looked unconvinced. "Come on, Jake— you were the number two guy. That's all you knew?"

Hanson shrugged. "You see anybody but me talking to you right now, Chief? Top guy knows things nobody else does. All I know is, Val had somebody inside the casino. He wouldn't tell me, or anybody else, who that was."

The conversation was over. Nods of goodbye were

followed by Grissom and Lopez returning to the Blazer.

The two of them rode back to town, still in the early-morning darkness.

"Why was the body stolen?" Lopez wondered aloud.

"Maybe whoever stole the body," Grissom said, "doesn't want to give up the gun."

"Murder bullet vanishes, then the gun doesn't have to? . . . Well, if that's the case, we better figure out who stole that goddamn corpse, 'cause this town's a powder keg, and I just handed a lit match to the leader of the biggest gang of bikers in the southwest."

Grissom pondered that. "I think you did the right thing, Jorge. If there's an official inquiry, and this comes up, I'll back you all the way."

Lopez glanced sideways at Grissom, wondering if the CSI was kidding. But Grissom's expression gave no clue.

7

THE MICROWAVE PINGED and Warrick Brown withdrew the bowl of soup like a lab sample whose processing was complete, carted it over to a break-room
table, and sat. He was waiting for Mia Dickerson to
finish the DNA testing on the sample he'd given her
from the scraping under Tara Donnelly's fingernails.

An attractive African-American of around thirty,
Mia possessed straight black hair, large brown eyes,
and a formidable IQ. He smiled at the thought of her
as he dipped a spoon into his steaming tomato soup.
The CSI and the lab technician had flirted from time
to time, and she'd alternated ignoring him with giving him a hard time, which he chose to interpret as a
sure sign that she dug him.

A buoyant Greg strolled in, removed a bottle of
juice from the fridge, shook it up, then joined Warrick. This was Greg's normal shift, so the graveyard
hours weren't fazing him. Warrick—who had been
on the swing shift for a while now—was feeling

the hands of his inner clock spinning in confusion.

"Are you tired?" Greg asked, with an impish grin. "Or just laid back?"

"Don't mistake 'cool' for 'beat,' Greg—I'm here for the long haul."

"Don't feel bad. I'm starting to drag, too."

If the young CSI had looked any fresher, Warrick would've had to dump his remaining soup on him.

Warrick asked, "How'd you do with the glove?"

Greg swigged and swallowed, then said, "I did what you told me—turned it inside out, then hung it in the super-glue chamber."

"Raise a print?"

Greg grinned in satisfaction. "Oh yeah—two clear ones: middle finger and index."

Often criminals made their biggest mistakes when thinking they were at their most clever. To avoid leaving fingerprints, a perp would wear gloves—not realizing that cotton gloves had fibers that could be matched, or that leather gloves showed wear in a particular fashion on a particular person and were, therefore, as good as fingerprints.

When criminal masterminds graduated to latex gloves—and once more considered themselves bulletproof (or anyway fingerprint-proof)—they were again proved wrong.

Lawbreaking has a natural tendency to make even the coolest criminal nervous. Sweating, a criminal might wipe his or her brow—then, if touching something at the crime scene, leave a print behind just as if he were wearing no glove at all. The same thing occurs on the inside of the glove; most criminals didn't realize that the inner latex surface is a perfect place for the energetic crime scene investigator to search.

Warrick asked, "How'd you get those prints?"

Greg worked at seeming matter-of-fact, though Warrick could tell the young CSI was proud of himself. "I filled the fingers of the glove with one-inch PVC pipe, then rolled each finger over a black gel lifter. I got clean prints from those two fingers, and various smears from the thumb and other fingers."

"Nice," Warrick said. "Now we've got reverse prints from the inside of the gloves."

"That's pretty slick procedure, 'Rick," Greg said. "Where'd you learn *that* one?"

"Velders and Zonjee—two Dutchmen I saw at the IAI conference last year."

"Who are they, anyway?"

"Theo Velders is a cop from the Netherlands and Jan Zonjee is the research chemist who helped him. They kept trying to find a way to lift prints out of latex gloves, and they came up with this—God bless 'em."

"I'm impressed," Greg said, bright-eyed. "What's next?"

"Go back and photograph the prints you lifted, then reverse them so they're not backward, and run them through AFIS."

Greg chugged the rest of his juice. "What are *you* up to, now?"

"Gonna catch up with you . . . soon as I check on the DNA testing on that skin you got from under Tara's fingernails."

"Oh, really?" Greg said with a smile. "That may take a while."

"What?"

"Nothing." Greg got to the door, dropping his empty juice bottle in the recycling tub on his way by, before saying, "Just, somehow, you seem to spend more time going over DNA evidence with Mia than *I* ever rated."

Greg fired off a grin and was gone before Warrick could throw his soup spoon at him.

Shaking his head but smiling, Warrick cleaned up after himself, then headed for the DNA lab.

Mia, in a neat ponytail, was leaning over a microscope, studying a slide as Warrick sauntered in.

"Hey," he said good-naturedly.

She glanced up at him, eyebrows tense. "Did I call you? Funny, I don't *remember* calling you."

He managed a smile. "People work as well and closely as we do, you can anticipate the other guy."

"You figured just because it was you," she said, giving him a smile that was all sass and challenge, "I'd drop everything and put you at the head of the line?"

"Well . . . yeah. Kinda."

She returned her attention to the slide.

Warrick, who'd felt himself on fairly solid footing when he came in, noticed a shift beneath him and wondered if he was hovering on a precipice. Of a deep hole. "So . . . I should come back later . . . ?"

Mia glanced up from the slide. "Are you still here?"

Warrick could see no way of winning this round, and no way of exiting with even a modicum of grace. "Okay. I'm at your beck and call—lemme know when you have something."

He was halfway out when she said, "You are

gonna have to sharpen up your game, Slugger, if you're gonna play in the big leagues."

She was looking up at him with just a hint of a smile.

He regarded her with suspicion. "I'll keep that in mind."

"Now get out of my lab."

"I can take a hint."

"Oh, and . . . take this with you."

She held out a folder.

He came back and took it, responding like a kid on Christmas morning getting that big gift he'd given up on. "My test results?"

"Was about to call you," she admitted.

Risking no snappy comeback, Warrick merely thanked her and scooted.

In his office, Warrick plopped onto a chair and read the results of the DNA profile; then he punched them into CODIS. The COmbined DNA Index System stored DNA samples from criminals and crime scenes in all fifty states, Puerto Rico, the FBI, and the U.S. Army.

Warrick did not expect much. CODIS worked, sometimes; but nowhere near always. Many offenders were not in the system, and the odds of his getting a match were against him.

Which was why he jumped a little when the ping from the computer went off.

The name staring at him from the screen was Matt David, a convicted sex offender paroled by the state of Nevada less than six months ago.

If convicted of Tara Donnelly's rape, David would be a three-time loser and would go into the system for good and ever. Warrick slow-scanned the material again as he printed the file. If Greg's fingerprints brought up the same name, they were *really* in business.

On his way past the DNA lab, he stuck his head in, acknowledging Mia with "Paydirt—thank you," winning a sincere smile for his trouble.

Greg was staring wide-eyed at the AFIS computer when Warrick rolled in.

"Don't tell me," Warrick said. "A match."

"What are you, a witch? I thought Grissom was the only warlock around this place. . . ."

Warrick leaned over Greg's shoulder. "Didn't take a magician to read the look on your face—anyway, I got a hit, too—on CODIS."

"Matt David," Greg said with a nod toward the screen.

"Matt David," Warrick agreed. "You find an address—I'll call Brass."

"Deal."

Getting the address was not as easy as either CSI had hoped: the CODIS address was a downtown flophouse that had closed over a year ago, and the AFIS address was a house in North Las Vegas that had burned down while David was in prison.

They only had one idea left when Brass joined them.

"Need you to make a phone call," Warrick said to the captain.

"Hey, nice to see you, too," Brass said.

Warrick said, "No, seriously. Our suspect, Matt David—you gotta call his PO."

"His parole officer?" Brass said with a frown, and looked at his watch. "You know, real people are asleep right now. Only criminals and damn fool cops are up."

"Tell me about it. Look, this guy's a serial rapist, Jim, and we need to get him off the street."

Warrick held out a piece of paper with the PO's number; Brass took it and made the call.

"Mr. Tinsley? Sorry about the hour—Captain Jim Brass, LVPD."

A short pause followed, during which Brass shot Warrick a thanks-for-*this*-dirty-job look.

"Yes, sir, I do know what time it is. That's why I said I was sorry about the hour. . . . It *is* 'goddamned important'—about one of your parolees, Matt David."

Another pause.

"We don't know for sure that he's done anything, sir—but evidence in a rape that went down earlier tonight indicates we need to talk to him. May I have his address?"

Another pause, this one longer. Brass cradled the phone against his neck as he got his notepad and pen out, and soon he was scribbling.

"Thanks, Mr. Tinsley, uh, yes—Joe. Yeah, I've got it, thanks."

One last pause.

Brass ended the call and gave Warrick a grin. "Officer Tinsley reminds us to respect the parolee's rights. And *citizen* Joe Tinsley suggests that should Mr. David be guilty of the crime we're investigating him for, one of us might put a foot in Mr. David's ass, with Mr. Tinsley's compliments."

"Always willing to pay reciprocal service to our brothers in law enforcement," Warrick said. "I see you have an address on our sex offender."

"Gold Avenue—not far from MLK Boulevard."

Greg raised an eyebrow. "Always a fun part of town to visit after midnight."

But midnight was a memory, the sun rising over the eastern horizon, when they pulled up in front of the dilapidated one-story stucco house on Gold Avenue, just east of Martin Luther King Boulevard. An old blue Ford in the driveway was the only sign of life as Brass, Warrick, Greg, and two uniformed officers approached.

Brass waved the uniforms around back while Warrick pulled his pistol—Brass already had—and the detective and lead CSI went up to the front door, Greg hanging back near the Denali.

Ringing the doorbell did no good. Nothing happened the second time, either, or the third. But when Brass pounded on the door and yelled, "*LVPD, open up,*" he got a reaction, all right.

Three bullets blasted through the front door . . .

. . . and everybody hit the deck, Greg practically hurling himself under the SUV.

Then, silence.

Silence in which, despite the ear-ringing noise of the gun, Warrick could hear his heart trip-hammering as he struggled to discern the slightest sound from inside the structure.

After a long moment, he heard sounds that were anything but slight—two more gunshots, ripping through the back door, and the uniformed officers returning fire.

On his haunches now, Warrick was just thinking about peeking in a window when the front door swung open and a wild-eyed Matt David burst out wearing nothing but a pair of ragged cutoff jeans and waving a big handgun.

The suspect started to sprint across the yard, apparently having not seen Warrick or Brass, his target clearly Greg and the SUV. Before David was halfway across the dirt yard, Warrick ran and tackled him, the two men rolling to the ground, David's gun seeming to fling itself from the suspect's fingers and skimming across the hard-packed earth.

David scuttled after it, Warrick hanging on to the man's legs as the suspect alternately tried to kick the CSI and pull himself closer to the gun. The guy had just gotten his fingertips on the butt when Brass almost nonchalantly placed the barrel of his pistol against David's temple.

"Pick that up," Brass advised, quiet, confident. "See what happens."

David growled, but his hand drew back from the weapon as if it were white hot.

"Probably a good choice," Brass said, kicking the gun away and handing a hard-breathing Warrick a pair of handcuffs.

"What are you *doing*, harassing me?" David screeched. "I *did* my time! I *paid* for what I did! This is discrim-i-*nation*!"

Shaking his head, Brass said, "Matt, we do apologize for dropping by so early, and we know we probably woke you . . . but even so, it's darn rude of you to fire five rounds at Las Vegas police officers."

"How the hell should *I* know you was cops!" David insisted, twisting his head but stopping when he felt the barrel of Brass's pistol again.

"Well," Brass said reasonably, "out front, we

announced ourselves—and out back, we were in uniform. But we won't sweat that charge, really— it's kinda, you know . . . frosting on the cake."

David's brow knit in confusion. "What are you talking about?"

"The rape charge, Matt. The rape charge."

"What? I didn't *rape* that bitch!" David said, struggling against the cuffs now. "Just 'cause I was inside, that don't mean I can't have normal, consenuating sex, does it?"

Brass lowered his weapon and leaned in close enough to kiss the suspect, though that seemed unlikely to Warrick. "Matt, does the 'bitch' you had 'consenuating sex' with happen to live over on Paradise Road?"

"So what if? It was just a *date*!"

Warrick said, "A date, Matt? A date where you left your hair in her bed, your skin under her nails, and your gloves in her Dumpster?"

David quit talking; he also quit struggling. Something died in his eyes.

Warrick said, "Your 'date' is no bitch, Matt—she's a nice young woman named Tara Donnelly and, thanks to her, you're going back inside for the rest of your unnatural life."

Brass said, "You should feel at home there. And you'll be in the company of your peers. No shortage of rapists in jail, I hear."

The uniformed cops came sprinting around the house and took custody of the prisoner, dragging him off as if his legs and feet had gone limp.

"Well," Warrick said. "Don't you meet the most charming people on graveyard."

Greg had crawled out from under the Denali some time ago; he approached Brass and Warrick with an embarrassed expression.

"Sorry," he said, holstering his sidearm.

Brass patted him on the back. "Nice job, Greg."

"Is that sarcasm?"

"No."

"I mean, damn—I was scared. Nobody shoots at you in the lab."

Warrick grinned slowly and said, "I considered it a couple times."

Grinning himself, Brass said, "Greg—you didn't kill anybody, and you didn't get yourself killed. That's a good day, when we have a crazy trigger-happy asshole like that to bring in."

Greg sighed, but in relief, his chagrin fading. Warrick was pleased with his charge—this kid was going to make it, no problem.

Wiping dirt off his pants, watching the perp being loaded into the squad car, Warrick said, "I got a waffle jones that needs feeding. Anybody up for that? My treat."

Brass shrugged as if to say *Why not?*, while Greg nodded his head eagerly. They had all taken exactly one step toward their vehicles when their cell phones rang—at once.

"Damn," Warrick said. "A man could starve to death in this job."

Brass smirked, patted his stomach, and said, "I don't seem to be," and they answered their phones.

Two minutes later, they were racing up I-15 toward the Speedway Boulevard exit, red lights flashing on both vehicles, Warrick driving the SUV this time, following Brass's Taurus as the detective wove in and out of traffic.

"I don't get this," Greg said, frowning, bracing himself against the dashboard with one hand. "Why are we being called to a traffic accident?"

Warrick glanced at the young CSI. "Didn't you get the same call I did? Who called you?"

Greg shrugged. "Dispatcher. She said she was calling me in case no one got through to you."

Eyes back on the interstate, Warrick said, "Didn't she mention shots were fired?"

"No! . . . She must have figured the other dispatcher got through to you."

"Not good," Warrick said, shaking his head, hands tight on the wheel. "If we weren't in the same car, you wouldn't know what you were getting into. We'll have to tell Gris and Catherine about that."

Greg nodded, but his discomfort was clear, though whether it was over the high speed of their vehicle or that dispatcher screwup remained unclear.

The accident scene was in the northbound lane of I-15 just past the Speedway Boulevard exit. Traffic had slowed to a crawl before Craig Road, with uniformed officers diverting vehicles off the interstate at both Craig and farther north at Speedway. After that exit, the SUV and Taurus were the only traffic as they sped north the last mile to where a squad car sat on the shoulder, its lights flashing, a late-model four-door Cadillac angled crossways in the road. The driver's door and both passenger doors yawned open. Two uniformed officers, the only people visible, stood on the far side of the car.

Brass pulled to an abrupt stop on the left shoulder, while Warrick parked the Denali right in the middle of the road.

The detective and the two CSIs got out of their vehicles simultaneously. While Warrick and Greg fetched their crime scene kits from the back of the SUV, Brass was calling to the officers. "What's this about gunshots?"

The two officers came around the car. One—short, with a shaved head, light blue eyes, and a wrestler's build—wore a nameplate identifying him as KRAMER. His partner's nameplate labeled the blonde female officer as WHITFORD. Her hair in a bun, Whitford wore sunglasses, which was appropriate, because the "night shift" was officially a bright morning now.

As Warrick and Greg trotted up to the small group, Officer Kramer was saying, "This is the weirdest goddamn car accident I ever saw."

"Looks like an abandoned car," Greg said with an openhanded gesture.

"On this side it does," Officer Whitford agreed. "Walk your crime-lab eyeballs around the other side of this bad boy. . . ."

Warrick shared Greg's opinion—from the driver's side, this looked exactly like a hastily abandoned car, with three of the four doors left open—but as the senior CSI crossed in front of the vehicle, his outlook changed.

Something scarlet had been splashed across the bumper and up onto the hood.

Looked like blood.

And Warrick at once wondered if it was human; an animal wandering the highway was a possibility—and a human, say a drunk, might have meandered in front of a moving car . . . not likely but certainly not impossible.

The bumper had been dented, the grill caved in slightly—plus a small dent in the hood, near the blood spot there.

Warrick said, "Most likely, the car had hit an animal . . ."

"And the driver lost control?" Greg offered.

Warrick nodded, as he swabbed the bumper. The lab would tell them if it was human or animal.

Greg continued: "Okay, then—why did the driver abandon his wheels?"

"Stolen, maybe."

Walking on, Warrick spotted something and called to Greg, who was behind him several paces.

"*There's* why," Warrick said.

Well past the vehicle, on the road's shoulder, the view previously blocked by the abandoned Caddy and the squad car, lay Warrick's least favorite form of roadkill: a human body.

From this distance, it appeared to be a male—on his stomach, pants and underwear pulled down around his ankles.

"Oh God," Greg said. "Dead?"

"Looks that way."

Brass shook his head as he approached the apparent corpse. "What have we here?"

Warrick thought he knew, and the closer he got, the more sure he was. The CSI looked back toward the car: the passenger-side door's window had a bullet hole through it.

Now he knew for sure.

The bald officer, Kramer, was just behind the CSI. "Ever see anything like this before?"

"Yeah," Warrick said, and heaved a sigh. "At a forensics convention. Similar case happened on the east coast."

The blonde officer, Whitford, asked, "Is this some sort of . . . gay thing?"

Warrick—who had a clear view of the bare behind of the kid on the ground, baggy jeans gathered around his ankles—shook his head.

"Gang thing," Warrick said at last.

The vic, his face turned toward Warrick, was an African-American no more than twenty, probably closer to seventeen. Kid wore a white T-shirt with a hole in the back, blood leaking around the wound, and two more in the head. Eyes closed, gaping exit wound in his forehead. Someone had dropped him from a distance, probably explaining the bullet hole in the passenger window, then made it personal with a double tap to the back of the skull.

"Damn," the CSI said to no one.

Brass was the only one who did not seem surprised.

"This young man screwed up," Warrick explained. "He offended somebody in his gang, or maybe a rival gang. . . . They weren't just going to kill him—they were going to make an example of him."

"That why his pants are down?" Kramer asked.

"No. His pants are down as a form of restraint."

Whitford blinked. *"Restraint?"*

"It's common among some gangs," Warrick said. "They can't afford handcuffs, and they don't want their prisoners running off whenever they want, so they make them drop trou. Not only makes it harder to run, it's humiliating."

Now Whitford nodded, getting it. "The prisoner becomes more compliant."

"That's the idea. Doesn't always work, of course. Especially if you hit something in the road and lose control of the car—that might make your prisoner think he can roll out and run for it . . . even with his lowriders riding way low. . . ."

Officer Kramer's eyes narrowed. "And that's what you think happened here?"

"That's my first take," Warrick said. "Let's not get ahead of ourselves. . . . Check around for animal roadkill, would you?"

The officers went off to look.

While Greg worked the car, Warrick investigated the scene outside the vehicle, starting with the body. Standing over the corpse—the vic's head at left, body sprawled out perpendicular—Warrick began snapping photos of the three wounds: two in the head—one in the middle of the vic's skull, the next down a little and slightly left—another in the lower back near the left kidney. The scarlet line of bullet holes looked like the jagged line of a falling stock.

The bullet holes were all of pretty good size— probably a nine mil. Uppermost head shot had been a through-and-through that exited centrally in the kid's forehead. The lower one had exited over the right ear, the two wounds turning the victim's skull into a pulpy mess. The torso shot had entered but not exited, meaning the bullet was still in the body somewhere.

After taking pictures of the corpse from various angles, Warrick walked the shoulder of the road, looking for footprints. He found several sneaker prints, which he cast in dental stone. Most appeared to be the victim's, but four more had been made by other shoes—two pairs, as near as Warrick could tell. Both uniformed officers wore rubber-soled police shoes whose tire-tread soles looked like no sneakers in the world and could be ruled out; these prints belonged to the perps.

With the footprint impressions and pictures out of the way, Warrick processed the body, starting by scraping under the victim's fingernails—the left index fingernail was broken off—and ending by scraping something oily off the soles of the vic's expensive tennis shoes.

Officer Whitford trotted up and said, "You want to see something weird?"

Warrick stood. "Do I?"

"I found your roadkill."

She led him across the highway and into the adjacent field where a big shape that could almost be a man lay in tall grass, where it had lumbered off to die.

"Tell me," the blond officer said, her eyes large in a face gone pale, "if that's what I think it is."

"That," Warrick said, "would be a lion. . . ."

A dead lion, with a full mane clotted with darkening blood, two limbs broken, rib cage crushed, a magnificent if not-breathing and somewhat bony specimen right out of a circus or a movie.

Soon everyone had gathered around and had circled the dead beast, as if this were a burial service and someone was going to say a few words.

So Warrick did. "Circus Circus, or any of the other casinos with elaborate animal-act shows, report a missing animal?"

"No," Brass said, dumbfounded. "Or a local zoo, or anybody else."

Greg said, "I think I know where this came from."

All eyes went from the king of the jungle to the prince of CSIs.

"Remember when a certain heavyweight champ lived here in Vegas? Wasn't that long ago. He collected exotic pets. A few were rumored to've gotten away. I think this beauty was prowling at night—there's no people around here to speak of, up north. I bet he's been keeping a low profile in these foothills."

Brass said, "Well, he didn't keep much of a low profile when he got in front of those headlights."

Warrick found himself chuckling. "Brother, would I like to've seen the look on the faces of those kids in that car. . . ."

Before long, as Warrick loaded his evidence into the back of the SUV, Greg came over. They didn't speak for a moment as the coroner's wagon pulled up and the two-man crew climbed down and took out their gurney.

"You guys done?" one asked Warrick.

"Yeah—all yours."

The CSIs watched in silence as the coroner's men loaded the body onto the gurney, wheeled it to their van, and soon were swinging across the median for the trip back to the city. When they were gone, the only signs a body had been lying on the side of the road were a few blood drops and two short wheel tracks where the gurney had momentarily slipped onto the dusty shoulder.

"God, he was young," Greg said.

"Get anything?" Warrick asked.

"Load of fingerprints," Greg said. "Mostly off the steering wheel and gear shift, few off the dashboard and door handle on the passenger side. Two ciggie butts in the ashtray. Possible DNA."

Warrick asked, "What about the car?"

"I got a sample of the blood off the hood. That's the outside. Inside, registration was in the glove box. I gave it to Brass to run. My guess is—"

"Stolen," Brass chimed in, coming over from his car to join them. "Registered to a Clark County couple who reported it missing from the parking lot of the Platinum King."

Warrick asked, "When was it taken?"

"Early last night. Our perps probably grabbed it before they snatched our John Doe."

Greg asked, "Did you happen to ask if either of the owners smokes?"

"Yeah, I asked," Brass said. "I saw those cigarette butts, too. And they're both nonsmokers."

Greg grinned tightly. "Good. Cigarette butts came from our perps then. I'll get those right to the DNA lab."

"Good," Warrick said.

"What about our John Doe?" Brass asked.

"We'll catch up to him in the morgue," Warrick said. "Maybe his prints will turn up in AFIS. He was a kid, but probably a gangbanger. Might be in the system."

"We've got the prints from the car to run, too," Greg reminded them.

"And if none of those match anything?" Brass asked.

Warrick shrugged elaborately. "Then we've pretty much got jack squat."

Greg shook his head. "We've really been rackin' 'em up tonight. We'll crack this one, too."

"Yeah," Warrick said, not having the heart to rain on the young CSI's parade. "Tow truck coming for the car?"

Brass nodded. "Should be here any minute. You want it taken to the lab?"

"You know it. Maybe there's something in or on it we haven't found yet."

"How about the lion carcass?"

"We should collect that, too."

Brass smirked. "You gonna ask Doc Robbins to do an autopsy?"

"I don't think so. Poor creature."

"Oh," Greg said, "something *else* was in that car. . . ." He got out an evidence bag from his crime-scene kit. Within the bag was another bag, a fast-food sack that looked to've been used as a trash receptacle.

"If that belongs to the couple who own the car," Warrick said, "it's nothing."

Brass examined the bag in the early-morning sun. "And if it belongs to the perps?"

Warrick nearly smiled. "Then it might just be a break. And Greg gets another gold star."

"I'm up for that," Greg said cheerfully.

* * *

Back in the lab, while Greg loaded the various fingerprints into AFIS, Warrick went through that bag of garbage the young CSI had scored. He picked the items out one at a time: cup from a large orange soda; smaller cup from a strawberry shake; four double cheeseburger wrappers; two large fry boxes; and—at the very bottom, wadded into a tiny ball—the receipt from Bob's Round-Up Grill on Tropicana.

The computerized receipt offered up more information than Warrick could possibly have hoped for: the exact time of the transaction, just after midnight—less than an hour after the couple had reported their car stolen; the register used; the drive-through; and "Sandy," the name of the employee who had taken the order.

After slipping the receipt into a smaller evidence bag, as well as individually bagging each straw for DNA testing, Warrick took them all with him. He stopped to check on Greg's progress on his way out.

"How you doin'?" Warrick asked.

Greg shrugged. "Blood on the car belonged to that lion. Otherwise, slow going."

"Stick with it. Give Animal Control a call about our lion corpse—they should be informed about this incident, and anyway, they're the ones who can properly dispose of the remains."

"Sure thing."

Warrick handed Greg the bags containing the two straws. "And do me a favor—get these to the DNA lab, too."

"Okay." Realizing this was from the garbage he'd

8

AT A TABLE IN THE FOUR KINGS SNACK BAR, Catherine sat nursing a cup of coffee—enjoying her first lull since taking on the biker/casino shoot-out crime scene.

The last of the witnesses had been cleared out. Two local investigators, Bell and Hamilton, had left for the police station; she'd lost track of the lead investigator, Cody Jacks. For now, she had the place to herself, not counting the two waitresses in a booth near the kitchen door, anyway.

She hadn't pulled a shift this long for some time. At least she didn't have to worry about her daughter, with her mom taking care of Lindsey. Comforting as that was, there remained the aches in her neck and back, the weariness in her legs, and the general exhaustion that came with being up for over twenty-four hours. She was doing all right, she'd make it through fine; but when this case wrapped up, she'd need a day off to collapse and recharge.

Sara ambled up, coffee cup in hand, plopping into

the chair opposite. The younger woman didn't look any more peppy than her supervisor. "Are you as tired as I am?"

"At least."

Sara allowed herself a yawn, covering with a hand. "Long haul. And I was in the laundry room, at my apartment house, when the call came in—just put in a load."

"Washer or dryer?"

"Washer. Had to pull everything out and throw it in the sink in my kitchen." Sara grinned in her appealing way. "Always nice to have a mess waiting, huh?"

Catherine smirked and shook her head in commiseration. "Nature of the job, though."

"Yeah, and I'm not ready to buy a house yet. I've been in an apartment for a long time now, and that's bad enough. Don't know if I could handle all the hassle that comes with a house."

"There is a lot of stuff," Catherine admitted. "But at least you can leave your laundry in the washer when you get called in to clean up somebody *else's* mess." Her cell rang and she picked it up on the second ring. "Catherine Willows."

"Sofia, Catherine. How are things in the wild west?"

"Wild is right. Got something from the home front?"

"The CSI mantra, I'm afraid—good news, bad news."

"I can use the good," Catherine said.

"We're making progress with the videotapes. We've picked out several of the Spokes who opened fire, so we should be able to sort out the perps from the self-defense crowd. . . . We've just been unable to identify them all yet."

"That last part—was that the bad news?"

A long pause was finally broken by, "Sorry. Not really."

Catherine swore silently to herself. "Okay—lemme have the bad."

How bad could the news be? All Sofia was doing was checking security tape. . . .

Sofia said, "We haven't found any footage of Valpo's murder."

That *bad.* . . .

"Impossible," Catherine said. "You obviously haven't gotten through all the tapes yet."

"But we have. And the Valpo murder isn't anywhere."

"Damn."

"We got footage of the shoulder wound taking him down . . . but he falls out of frame and we can't see him after that. And that's when the execution happened. We don't see it, so we can't pinpoint the shooter."

Catherine allowed herself a sigh. "When can we expect you back at Boot Hill?"

Sofia considered that for a moment. "I'm not sure. Archie and I are going through tapes again and again, trying to identify shooters based on file and database photos of Spokes and Predators. And the labs are going all out on the other evidence." She let out her own sigh. "Cath, I'd like to go through the tapes one more time myself. Let's say . . . late afternoon?"

"See you then," Catherine said, and rang off.

"What's the problem?" Sara asked.

Catherine filled Sara in.

"Will they be bringing in the riot wagon," Sara asked, "now that Sofia's getting the shooters I.D.'d?"

"Probably by the end of the day, yeah."

Sara frowned over her coffee. "That could get nasty."

"Yeah—sure be a pity if this turned nasty, huh?"

Sara sipped and swallowed; her grin was MIA. "What are we supposed to do in the meantime?"

Catherine rose. "Keep at it. We can start by finding out one thing."

"Yeah?" Sara asked, getting up.

"Let's talk to casino security and find out why those tapes don't show everything they should."

They asked directions from the waitresses and, on the second floor, found Henry Cippolina in the security suite, a less high-tech affair than just about any comparable Vegas casino setup, taking Catherine back, in fact, to the kind of gear she ran into when she first became a CSI.

A bank of videotape players occupied one wall to the right; three uniformed guards sat at different stations watching monitors, even though there was little to see with the casino closed down for business. One guard was keeping an eye on the hotel screens, since that side of the operation was up and running, on a limited basis, anyway.

Three offices lined the left wall and Cippolina was in the middle one, door open. The floor manager sat behind a massive wooden rectangle of a desk, with an equally large workstation to his left laden with computer equipment. The walls blazed with posters touting getaways to, and performers appearing at, the Four Kings Casino. The office otherwise was a joyless affair, medium-sized, Cippolina's desk and workstation taking up much of the space, a few filing cabinets between posters taking up the rest.

Two visitor's chairs were opposite the fortyish security chief, his receding black hair parted on the left and well-oiled, his mouth a thin, straight, colorless line, his skin tone flat-out cadaverous. On one chair was the security chief's jacket, wrinkled, underarm sweat stains visible, tossed haphazardly there.

Though the air-conditioning was working overtime, Cippolina's shirt looked at least as wrinkled and sweaty as the jacket, and the casino man had rolled the shirt's sleeves up to the elbow. He had dark circles under his eyes that seemed to suggest more than simple exhaustion, rather full-time malaise.

Entering without knocking, Sara on her heels, Catherine said, "We need to talk."

Cippolina started to rise, but Catherine held up a hand for him to remain seated as she and Sara came in and ignored the visitor's chairs, taking a position just inside the door.

"Make yourself at home," he said, with just a hint of sarcasm. "Need to talk about what?"

"For starters, about how your cameras don't cover the whole casino floor."

Cippolina held his hands out. "Why, is that illegal? Look, Ms. Willets—"

"Willows."

"Willows—sorry." He got up, removed his coat from the visitor's chair, and gestured for them to sit.

Sara glanced at Catherine, who nodded, and they

took the chairs while Cippolina got back behind the desk, draping his suit coat over his own chair, and sat.

The security chief did his best to affect a genial expression. "Look—you folks up Vegas way get more visitors to the Strip in one *day* than we get down here in Boot Hill all year. We simply don't have as much money for security as we would like." He spread his hands. "Good God, people—everything in this joint is at least twenty years old. You think *I* don't know our security's subpar?"

The speech had no effect on Catherine. She folded her arms and looked daggers at the man. "Mr. Cippolina, we've been going over your security tapes, searching for a needle in a haystack for hours . . . and now I find out there's no damn haystack. Your cameras didn't catch Valpo's killer."

"What can I say? Nobody's perfect."

She ignored his remark. "If there was a flaw in your system, you had a responsibility to point it out at the start of this inquiry. An investigation this size, with violence all around us ready to erupt any instant . . . I expect *full* cooperation."

"I *have* been cooperating. You people waltz in, take over, and—"

Catherine held up a palm. Then, almost gently, she said, "Just please tell me why and how it happened."

Cippolina leaned on an elbow and his expression was almost painfully earnest. "Look, Ms. Willows . . . Ms. Simon was it?"

"Sidle."

"Ms. Sidle. Like I said, I haven't had enough

money to do proper security in this place since I got
here, what . . . eight years ago. So, I do the best I can
with a . . . not a bad situation, exactly—a limited
one." He shifted in his chair. "That means utilizing
my assets to cover the most territory. There are, ac-
cordingly, blind spots on the floor."

Catherine felt her temper rising again but cur-
tailed it. "How *many* 'blind spots' in that casino?"

"We operate on the principle that the very presence of the video cameras discourages misconduct."

Sara said, "Like a security company sticker on a
homeowner's window . . . when the homeowner
doesn't even have a security system."

"Well . . . not quite that bad, Ms. Sidle, but—"

Catherine tried again: "How many blind spots?"

"Four."

"Four?" Catherine asked, appalled.

He shrugged; he had the expression of a schoolkid
in the principal's office trying to explain after getting
caught cheating. "We cover as much space as we
can."

"Just how big *are* these blind spots?"

Cippolina toyed with a paper clip on his desk.
"Three of them . . . maybe a bit bigger than the size
of this desk . . . the fourth one is about twice that.
There are no slots or poker machines in any of those
areas, although they're all busy traffic sections of the
casino."

Catherine and Sara exchanged glances; each knew
what the other was thinking.

They had been swimming upstream all day
against this crime scene and now they were being
jerked around again, this time by the economics of

trying to secure a casino this size with a convenience-store surveillance system budget.

Sara asked, "Mr. Cippolina—how many people in this casino know about these security-cam blind spots?"

Another embarrassed shrug. "Everyone in upper management—the security department, of course, even some of the floor employees."

Catherine raised an eyebrow. "Who in the casino doesn't know about the blind spots?"

Cippolina swallowed. "The customers."

Shaking her head, Catherine said, "Are you sure about that?"

That took Cippolina by surprise. "What do you mean, Ms. Willows?"

"This is a small town—you're a big employer here, and even the lower-echelon staff seems to know about these security limitations."

"So?"

"Well . . . loose lips sink ships."

He shifted heavily in his chair. "Uh—I suppose you make a valid point. . . ."

"So," Catherine said, quietly seething, "it's conceivable that the only people who *didn't* know about your faulty security would be . . . us?"

Cippolina's head lowered again. "I'd like to be able to say that remark is unfair. But . . . frankly . . . I can't."

The security chief had taken enough of a beating. Catherine shifted gears and asked, "Have you had any luck locating your missing employee—Tom Price?"

"No. He's not on the premises anywhere."

Sara smiled and said, "You might check and see if he's standing in a blind spot."

Catherine gave her a look and Sara backed off. "Well, I do appreciate your frankness and cooperation in this meeting."

"It's the least I can do."

On that, Catherine agreed with him. "I need a picture of Tom Price. Can you provide one? Soon would be good. Now would be better."

Cippolina, as if anticipating the request, had one in a manila folder on his desk. He handed it over. "Thought you might want this."

She studied the face of a bespectacled man bearing wide-set eyes, short brown hair with bangs, and a countenance that appeared not to have smiled since sometime early in childhood.

"Can you e-mail one of these as an attached file?"

"Yeah, we do have the internet here," Cippolina said a little defensively.

Catherine gave him Sofia's e-mail address.

He said, "I'll do it right away," got up, and left them alone in his office.

Catherine punched a number into her cell phone and connected with Sofia.

"This Tom Price character," Catherine told her, "who seems to have made himself scarce—his photo should be showing up in your e-mail any time."

"Okay. I'll check right now. . . ."

"See if you can find this guy in any of the videotape."

"Will do," Sofia said. A short pause followed. Then: "Yeah, it's here . . . I've got the photo just fine. Get back to you when I have something."

Cippolina came back into the office as Catherine returned the cell to her belt.

"That was fast," she said, and gave the security chief a smile and a nod. "Nice job."

"We're not incompetent," he said wearily, "just poorly funded." He resumed his seat behind the desk.

"Thank you, Mr. Cippolina," Catherine said, rising, Sara following suit. "We'll keep that in mind."

Catherine took the manila folder with the picture of Tom Price with her.

Once the two CSIs were in the stairwell, heading back down, Sara said, "He seemed embarrassed by their security shortcomings, but not really, uh . . . broken up about any of this."

"What do you mean?"

"Well, when your workplace gets shot up and your fellow employees get wounded or even killed, doesn't a normal person *feel* it?"

Catherine's father, Sam Braun, was a casino mogul in Vegas. She thought back to her relationship with him, and said, "Casinos are a lot more about making money than friends—it's a guarded world that doesn't usually put strong interpersonal relationships first."

"How odd. And sad."

Catherine nodded. "Our friend Mr. Cippolina's biggest concern might just be that a customer named Valpo died with unbet money in his pocket."

At the bottom of the stairwell, Catherine opened the door and led the way back onto the casino floor. Even hours after the firefight, she could still detect the odor of cordite in the air.

"So," Sara asked, "what's next?"

"Everything with this crime scene has worked against us so far. I'd just like one thing to go our way."

"Maybe one thing has," Sara said.

Catherine shot Sara a curious frown. "Spill."

Sara's half smile held a hint of apology. "That 3D scan of the crime scene Nicky and I did? We got so busy collecting evidence after that, we never got a chance to really study it."

"Well, why don't you, then?"

"Why don't I. Why don't *we*?"

On the way back, Sara picked up her laptop from the cashier's cage that had become a de facto HQ for the team and storage site for their equipment. In the café, she took a seat at a table in the middle of the room and rested the computer on the formica surface before her.

While Sara booted up, Catherine pulled a chair around so she could sit next to her colleague and view the screen easily, rather than hover over Sara's shoulder.

Once Sara had logged on and launched the Delta-Sphere's software, only a second or so passed before they were staring at a 3D rendering of the crime scene as it had appeared hours ago, the wounded already gone but the two deceased victims still in place, the detritus of the firefight not yet collected and bagged and marked.

As they maneuvered through the scene on the screen, Catherine had a feeling similar to when she took Lindsey to the IMAX theater to see James Cameron's documentary on the *Titanic*. Watching his

drone cameras, Jake and Elwood, motor around the
corridors of the world's most famous ghost ship, she
had felt a combination of enormous curiosity and a
weird voyeuristic guilt about sifting through someone else's life so long after death—as if somehow she
were violating someone's privacy in the extreme.

This odd combination of sharp curiosity and near
guilt flowed over her again now, even though she'd
felt no compunction when surveying every inch of the
real scene as she took this 3D tour via Sara's laptop.

The odd sensation almost instantly vanished as Sara
manipulated them through the scene, Catherine now
feeling wrapped up in some hyperreal video game.

These graphics were far better than she'd expected, and she found herself studying the monitor
as if the crime scene on the screen were the real deal
and not the digital reproduction.

Fingers flying, Sara put them in position to study
Valpo's body from one side.

The Predator leader lay on his stomach, his shoulder showing signs of what Catherine now knew for
sure was an exit wound. Though she could see blood
on Valpo's head, she had from this angle no clear
view of the base-of-the-skull entrance wound.

As if reading Catherine's mind, Sara swivelled the
view until they were above and behind Valpo, standing over the biker, so to speak, and looking down
into the bloody wound in the Predator's skull.

"Shooter got up close and personal," Sara said,
even though they both knew that already.

"Yeah," Catherine agreed. "Plenty of GSR on his
neck."

The gunshot residue gave Valpo's neck the appearance that a ghoulish waiter had hand-milled pepper over him after he died, the black pinpoints readily apparent around the wound.

"Let's try something," Sara said, eyes slitted, swivelling the view yet again.

They were still above Valpo's corpse—Catherine was sure they had not moved—but now their view was toward the blackjack table, where the young dealer had died.

From here, the dealer was in plain view, her corpse on the floor, maybe six feet away. The distance between the bodies had seemed greater in the casino; either that, or Catherine had not noticed how close together they were. But she noticed now, all right, from this new vantage point, and had a new thought about this entire matter.

Entire *murder* . . .

"One killer could have shot them both," she said.

Sara nodded. "Grissom speculated that the young woman may have witnessed the 'execution' and been killed for it."

"If so," Catherine said, "she should have had time to scramble out of the way . . . even in that firefight. Why didn't she?"

Everywhere they turned on this case, they got more questions . . . and precious few answers, rolling one snake eyes after another.

Catherine hoped that the other CSIs were having better luck.

When Grissom showed up with Police Chief Jorge Lopez, Nick had been working the mortuary crime scene for the better part of two hours.

The two men climbed out of the Blazer and came over to where Nick was using an electrostatic print-lifter to collect footprints and tire tracks from the mortuary's rear parking lot.

Keeping a proper distance from the evidence-gathering, Grissom called, "Nick—how's it coming?"

"Not bad," Nick said. "Almost done here."

Lopez asked, "How's Mr. Erickson?"

Nick removed his eyes from his work and met the chief's worried gaze. "Paramedics made him get in the ambulance and ride over to Laughlin . . . but I'm guessing it was just a concussion. He seemed less than thrilled about having to walk away—or get *rolled* away—from his business, with it wide open and us poking around."

Lopez chuckled. "Sounds like Erickson. But just the same, you'll get all the help you need from him."

Nick nodded. "Mostly he seemed upset somebody got the drop on him."

"Most of his customers don't sneak up on him," Lopez said dryly. "Where's Officer Montaine?"

Montaine's squad car was still parked at the mortuary.

Nick said, "He had this idea he should go canvassing the neighborhood."

Lopez frowned, shook his head. "Who's to canvass this early on a Saturday in this neighborhood? It's all businesses."

Nick shrugged. "He's been gone over an hour. Can't tell you."

Grissom asked Nick, "What have you got so far?"

"Just that Valpo's body was stolen, still in the body bag. No real trail to follow."

"Fingerprints?"

"On all the doorknobs in the joint, but I'm guessing that once we print Mr. Erickson, that'll be the only match."

The chief asked, "Anything else taken?"

"Not that Mr. Erickson could see," Nick said. "But, then, he was shuffled out of here pretty much right away. He did take a look around the preparation chamber and said everything seemed to be right where it should be. Just that one missing item: the body."

"What about these footprints?" Grissom asked, indicating Nick's current efforts.

Nick said, "That's why I'd like Officer Montaine to get back here. This footprint looks like a Rocky to me."

Lopez frowned again. "Rocky *police* boots?"

"Yeah. What's it look like to you?" He turned over the mylar sheet he had just charged and showed them the electrostatic footprint of a boot tread.

Grissom nodded. "Looks like a Rocky, all right."

"Hell," Lopez said, and turned up the sole of his shoe so the CSIs could see it. "Looks like *my* Rocky."

"On the surface," Grissom said, bending for a look, "it's a match. But you've been doing this long enough to know that every individual boot wears differently. Your wear is up on the toes—you walk on the balls of your feet."

"These boots," Nick said, picking up Grissom's thread, "show more wear along the sides and on the heel. These shoes, whoever's wearing 'em? Uncomfortable."

"So," Lopez said, eyes narrowing. "You think a

cop stole the body . . . or did Officer Montaine happen to step here?"

"Either is a possibility," Nick said.

"Just two of *many* possibilities," Grissom said, obviously trying to prevent anyone from taking a premature path. "A lot of bikers wear Rocky boots these days. So we have any number of potential boots in Boot Hill—only one we seem to have ruled out so far, Chief, is you."

"I better go find Montaine," Lopez said.

"Nick," Grissom said, "how much longer do you think you'll need here?"

"Just finishing up, really. Chief, can you get me to your lab?"

"Sure," Lopez said. "Not much by your standards, but I can provide a computer and some basic lab equipment."

"I'd appreciate that."

The three loaded Nick's gear into the Blazer and drove off to find Officer Montaine, which proved a short search: the young deputy was just around the block, walking out of a café with a Styrofoam cup of coffee.

When they rolled up to him, Montaine smiled and waved.

Lopez, leaning out the window, was in no mood. "Are you canvassing the neighborhood," he exploded, "or on goddamn doughnut duty?"

"What . . . this is just coffee."

"Oh, you're drinking coffee, then? Weren't you supposed to be off canvassing the neighborhood?"

"Chief, I'm really sorry," the kid said, "but Mr. Ross . . . the breakfast cook back there at Racheal's?"

He pointed toward the café, barely twenty feet away. "He insisted I take the coffee. And it wasn't such a bad idea to canvass, 'cause he told me he came in a little after five, to start everything up at the café, and he saw some of those bikers riding by—toward the mortuary."

Grissom's eyes tightened. "I thought all the bikers were quarantined—either at the campground or that other hotel."

Lopez nodded. "Yeah. . . . Dean, did Mr. Ross recognize the bikers?"

"He said there were only three bikers, but that the one nearest the café? When they went roaring by? Had on a vest with 'Rusty Spokes' on the back."

"All right," Lopez said. He worked up a smile. "Sorry I jumped on you, Dean. That's good work you did. Damn good work."

The kid beamed. "Thanks, Chief. . . . Okay if I drink this coffee, then?"

"Go right ahead," Lopez said with a chuckle. "Say, do you know where Sergeant Jacks is? . . . Haven't seen him all night."

Montaine nodded. "Cody said he was heading out to the Price place, to see if he was there. That's the last I heard."

"Hell," Lopez muttered.

Grissom asked, "Why is that a bad thing? Don't we need to talk to Price, and isn't Cody Jacks your top investigator?"

"He is that, Doc," Lopez said. "But we've got more important things to be worried about than Tom Price, who lives way the hell southeast of Cal Nev Ari—almost an hour from here."

"I see."

Lopez glanced in the rearview mirror to catch Nick's eye. "Mr. Stokes, I'm going to drop you off at the station so you can get your lab work going."

"Great."

"I can reach Cody from there," Lopez said, "after which, Doc, you and me, we can go talk with the Rusty Spokes about breaking house arrest."

"Sounds like fun," Grissom said.

Nick asked from the back, "Why don't you just call Detective Jacks on the radio?"

"Cody'll be in the Newberry Mountains, which play hell with cell phone and radio traffic. Never reach him from my car, but the transmitter at the station should do the trick."

The police station was just down Allen Street from the two hotels, a one-story brick-and-glass building smaller than the garage back at CSI. A sign out front proudly proclaimed:

BOOT HILL POLICE DEPARTMENT

and in smaller letters

CHIEF JORGE G. LOPEZ

As he parked, Lopez said, "Doc, you can come in or not—should only take a couple of minutes. I'll set Nick up with his chemistry set, call Cody, then you and me can walk up to the Gold Vault."

"I'll stay out here," Grissom said. "I could use the fresh air. Mind if I start up the street?"

Lopez said, "Sure—I'll catch up. If I'm not right

there, wait in the lobby. Don't take on the Spokes without me, Doc."

"I think you can rest assured of that."

Lopez grinned. "Okay, Nick, come on—I'll get ya set up on the cutting edge of forensics circa 1975. . . ."

Grissom watched as the chief escorted Nick—carting his crime scene kit and evidence—inside the modest station. Part of Grissom wanted to stay with his guy and give him a hand—possibly the senior CSI would have a better handle on using the limited materials at hand—but Nick was a first-rate analyst now and didn't need Grissom looking over his shoulder. Better to stay outside and accompany the chief.

The hotel was two blocks away. Grissom started off at a leisurely pace, enjoying the gentle desert breeze. For a guy who lived in labs, Gil Grissom loved the outdoors. The sun was up but not hot yet, and only a handful of people were out moving around. Whether this was normal Boot Hill Saturday activity or a severe curtailment after the gunplay in the casino, Grissom did not know.

He passed a video rental store, a drugstore, and two restaurants. None were open, not even the restaurant, despite its promise of an all-you-can-eat breakfast buffet and twenty-four-hour service.

A block away from the two casino hotels now, Grissom noticed activity out front of the Four Kings.

As he drew closer, Grissom could see that a makeshift memorial to Nick Valpo had sprung up on a chain-link fence that bordered a casino parking lot. Several Predators were huddling around the area, though Grissom had no idea whether they'd stayed at the Four Kings (the Predators did have some rooms there) or had somehow broken containment from the campground.

Crossing the street, Grissom took a bench opposite and was able to watch without intruding as bikers set down flowers and other mementos under a large elaborate colored-pencil drawing on poster board (leaned against the fence and secured with duct tape) of the fallen Predator leader. Some flowers and other items were wired or otherwise attached to the chain-link. A certain melancholy sweetness was undercut by dark black letters over the somewhat idealized portrait of the dead biker captain: MURDERED IN BOOT HILL!!!

On Grissom's side of the street, light traffic passed in and out of the Gold Vault Casino. From his bench near the curb, the CSI had a clear view as a young woman—maybe twenty, maybe not—wearing a flowered hippie-ish dress, her long blonde hair tied back in a bow, approached the chain-link memorial and carefully positioned a bouquet of twelve red roses, bright as blood amid otherwise pastel flowers.

When she turned away and walked toward Grissom's side of the street, her big light-brown eyes brimmed with tears that caught sunlight and glimmered. She moved with an easy, sensuous grace, passed Grissom, and kept going.

Grissom stopped a brunette, fortyish woman walking by wearing a Gold Vault casino employee vest and asked if she knew the young woman.

Without looking at the receding figure, she said, "No," and moved on.

Then he asked a man about his own age who was

carrying a drugstore sack, just as the young woman was turning a corner and disappearing.

"Yeah, I know who that is," the man said, catching her just in time. "Wendy Sierra's her name."

And he kept on walking.

Grissom glanced toward the police station: still no sign of Chief Lopez.

Crossing the street again, Grissom entered the Four Kings, gave his eyes a moment to adjust to the lighting change, then took a step through the metal detectors, which promptly started screaming.

Uniformed and nonuniformed personnel descended on him, Catherine and Sara rushing up, right in the middle. He flashed his ID, which got the security people to back off, and a guard turned off the metal-detector alarm with a key.

"Sorry, sir," the guard said, recognizing the CSI. "We've got these babies active again."

"Good," Grissom said.

He and Catherine brought each other up to speed on what they had learned.

Then Grissom turned to Sara. "There's a name I want you to run—Wendy Sierra. Local girl. That's all I know."

Sara went off to call Vegas. Grissom figured he could get better information that way than trying to get anything out of anyone in this taciturn town.

"Wendy Sierra?" Catherine asked.

"Just a hunch," he said. "There's a memorial out on the sidewalk. This girl left a dozen roses. And tears."

Catherine said, "That's not a hunch. That's just you being sensitive."

That seemed to puzzle him. "Really? . . . Anyway,

I've got to go—Chief Lopez is meeting me to talk to the Spokes."

Catherine's face turned steely and she said, "Then I'm coming, too. Sofia e-mailed us a partial list of shooters; we can start making arrests."

"Oh?" Grissom asked. "Where are we going to put them? Presidential suites of these hotels?"

"In jail is a start," Catherine said. "The list is the first four shooters—*all* Spokes. We can at least get those four on ice."

"Good. That *is* a start."

They had crossed the street to the Gold Vault lobby when Lopez came in quickly and joined them. Highway Patrolmen, a visible presence outside the building, were in greater number in the lobby.

Business continued here, the slots still open, gambling going on for those guests not unnerved by the possibility of another gunfight breaking out. So much post-9/11 chatter had been in the air about Vegas as a possible terrorist target that many casino players were now simply immune to such fears and went back to playing as they always had. Life itself was a gamble, after all.

The chief's worried expression told Grissom something had not gone well at the station. The CSI decided not to bring up the Sierra girl until later; right now he wanted to know what was troubling Lopez. So he asked him.

Lopez craned his neck around to make sure no one was within earshot besides the two CSIs. "I talked to Cody, and he's out at Tom Price's. Price is dead."

"How?" Grissom asked.

"Suicide. Hanged himself in his house. Cody found ten thousand dollars on the kitchen table . . . and a note."

"Which said?" Grissom asked.

"That he was sorry. He didn't mean for anyone to get hurt. And he left the money to the Delware woman's infant daughter."

Catherine said, "You don't sound very sympathetic."

"At least three people are dead, including that single mother, all because this greedy bastard took a bribe to turn off those metal detectors . . . and now I don't even get the goddamn satisfaction of putting him away for it. Far as I'm concerned, son of a bitch got off easy."

Grissom said, "Is Jacks maintaining the crime scene?"

"No—he's on his way back here. Can't waste one of my few detectives on one dead body with so many live threats. I sent Montaine."

Grissom would have preferred to go straight out there, but with so much crime in this one case, he was feeling as much like an air traffic controller as a CSI.

Catherine was handing Lopez the list Sofia had e-mailed to the security room at the Four Kings. She explained what it was.

Lopez quickly scanned the sheet. "Yeah, I know all these guys—Buck Finch is the Spokes leader . . . he'll be the tricky one. We can get the other three without a lot of trouble; but collaring Finch—the Spokes won't love that."

They huddled with the Highway Patrolmen and, when they broke to get back in the game, the uniforms went straight for the other three Spokes and hustled them out of the hotel. Another larger group of bikers began to gather around Catherine, Grissom, and Lopez. Only two uniformed Patrolmen were left to back them up, but Lopez had already made sure that help was on the way.

But right now the reality was this: the Spokes were closing around them, outnumbering the law thirty or maybe even forty to five, and for the second time in twelve hours, Gil Grissom found himself staring down a massive group that seemed only a heartbeat away from tearing him and his compatriots apart.

With the group growing restless, the Red Sea of Rusty Spokes suddenly parted and a tall, leanly muscular man of forty or so strolled up and took a position in front of Lopez.

Wearing a black T-shirt and black jeans, his blond hair receding slightly, worn just long enough to curl up at the collar, Buck Finch might have been a successful businessman on a weekend getaway.

The only giveaway that something more dangerous might lurk within this rugged, handsome figure was a thick, darker-blond Fu Manchu mustache, large white teeth that appeared and disappeared like those of a growling dog, and cold, hard, dark eyes carrying not the faintest flicker of sympathetic human emotion.

The rival gang might be *called* the Predators, Grissom thought, but standing in front of him now was the real thing. . . .

Lopez didn't beat around the bush. "Why, Buck? Why fire off the first round of a war in a casino filled with civilians?"

Finch merely stared at Lopez.

"You may have gotten the metal detectors shut off," the chief said, "but you didn't stop the video. It's all there—reality TV starring you, Buck."

A tiny, mirthless smile flicked across Finch's face. "Since you haven't read me my rights, Chief, I'll just say—strictly for your benefit—that *if* we were the ones who started the fight, it just might be because those so-called Predators disrespected us for too long, too many times."

Grissom asked, "What did the other casino patrons do to you, Mr. Finch?"

Finch ignored the CSI, keeping his dead eyes on the chief. "Those hot-shit Predators think just because some of us choose to live a straight life, when we're not on the road, that we're only *weekend* warriors—wannabes."

"So," Lopez said. "You were just making a point."

The biker's eyebrows rose, his eyes widening till the whites showed all around. "They don't think we're wannabes *now*, do they? . . . But that's just the opinion, the insight of one concerned citizen, you might say. The Predators could just as easily be the ones that started shooting. You say you have evidence, but this is a casino—lots of bluffing goes on in this place." He grinned, the huge white animal teeth gleaming. "Besides, Chief—to arrest me, you'd still have to get me the hell out of here. And how do you propose doing that?"

Catherine stepped up and said, "The Predators weren't the ones who fired first—you were. You personally, Mr. Finch. Not the, uh, 'weekend warriors' surrounding you . . . who may not be anxious to back you up and trade in their 'straight' lives so they can become accessories after the fact—to murder."

The smile remained, turning slightly glazed. But Finch said, "You know, Chiefie—I like her. She's got balls."

"She's from Vegas," Lopez said. "Crime lab—people who are gonna put your ass away for a long, long time."

"*This* fine little lady?" Finch asked, his eyes wandering over her, inspecting her lasciviously.

She held out her hand and gave him her sexiest smile.

"Catherine Willows," she said.

He laughed and took her hand to shake it, but before he could, she twisted his wrist, spun under his arm, and came up behind him, his right arm in a hammerlock, and snapped on a cuff.

Finch reached for her with his left hand and she got his thumb and bent it back until he howled, and she had control of him. This convinced him to put the other hand behind him, and she put on the second cuff.

The crowd surged but didn't do anything about it, possibly taking Catherine's accessory speech to heart; and anyway, Lopez and the two uniforms had their guns out now.

Everyone froze, Lopez and the Patrolmen each aiming at the nearest of the Spokes, none of whom went for their guns, assuming they had any.

"Just because you've got me cuffed, bitch," Finch snarled, something childish and pathetic about it, "doesn't mean you're gettin' me out of here!"

Catherine had her pistol out now, and spun Finch so he was looking her in the eyes again, his arms locked behind him.

She smiled again—not that sexy this time.

"You might be right, Buck," she said. "But here's the game, and the odds: we don't get out of here, you don't either. You are first in line. Look in my eyes, and tell me you get my drift."

He grinned insolently.

Her voice cold, calm, and low, she said, "Look in my eyes, Buck . . . and *tell* me."

Finch's grin immediately disappeared. He swallowed. "Back off, boys . . . I'm goin' to jail with my new girlfriend here."

But before they hauled Finch out, Grissom saw the man exchange a very meaningful look with one of his cronies.

As if to say *You know what to do. . . .*

9

WARRICK BROWN HAD JOINED Dr. Albert Robbins in the autopsy room when Greg Sanders hurried in. Neither CSI was in scrubs, though Robbins was. The body of their lion-roadkill John Doe lay naked on the metal table, a sheet drawn up to his waist. Under the harsh fluorescent lighting, the corpse looked even younger.

As he crossed the room, Greg announced, "That's *not* John Doe, gentlemen. . . ."

The young CSI took a position beside Warrick, with Dr. Robbins gazing patiently at them from the other side of the table.

"What *is* his name?" Warrick asked.

"DeMarcus Hankins," Greg said, without reading from the piece of paper he held. "Snagged him in AFIS, despite his youth."

"Nice," Warrick said.

Greg beamed. "I ran the vic's prints while you and Brass were making that fast-food run—and thanks for the burrito, by the way. Not exactly delicious, but without it I mighta passed out."

"Two-seventy-five you owe me," Warrick said.

Some of the air went out of Greg, and he started scrounging in his pockets.

With a grin, Warrick said, "You can catch mine next time. Eyes back on the ball."

Greg's smile couldn't have looked more relieved had he just received a presidential pardon.

"Oh-kaay," Warrick said to Greg, then nodded at the corpse. "What do we know about our new best friend DeMarcus Hankins?"

"Member of the Mechas." Greg's eyebrows lifted. "Former member, now. . . ."

The Mechas or Mecha Boys or Mecha Street Boys—sometimes even MSB—was a gang that started (not surprisingly) on Mecha Street in a neighborhood that might best be described as low income, the residents "financially struggling," to quote bureaucrat-speak. Not a happy place for a kid to grow up, with role models including crack dealers, crack whores . . . and members of MSB.

"If he's in AFIS," Warrick said, "he earned his listing."

Greg shrugged. "Only seventeen, so this stuff is all juvie—assault, possession. Even implicated in a couple of B & E's, but never charged."

"Not on his way to becoming a model citizen," Dr. Robbins said evenly. "But you never know—he might've straightened out; certainly didn't have to die like this."

"He'd probably still be alive," Warrick said, "if it hadn't been for that lion on the loose. My take is, he was just being taken out for a dressing down."

"If you define 'dressing down,'" Greg said, "as having your trousers around your ankles."

Robbins said, "By the way, I spoke to Animal Control. I'll know more later, but the king of beasts seems to've been somewhat malnourished."

Warrick said, "Who knows how long it was surviving out in those scrubby hills."

"We could have him brought in for an autopsy," Robbins said, a tightness around his eyes betraying a desire to do anything *but* a procedure on a dead lion. "If you suspect he was drugged and purposely sent out into the highway to spook some motorist as a practical joke, or—"

"I don't see it," Warrick said. "That cat is strictly roadkill—unusual roadkill. That former heavyweight champ *did* lose track of some of his exotic pets."

"If you change your mind," Robbins said, quietly relieved, "let me know."

Warrick asked, "Anything we don't know about our *human* subject?"

Robbins shrugged. "He was fleeing when he got shot in the back. That alone would likely have killed him, given the proximity of decent medical care; but he didn't have to wait to bleed out, did he?"

"You're saying either of the head shots would have been instantly fatal."

"I'm saying that, yes."

"Anything else?"

Robbins held up Hankins's left hand. "Note the index finger."

"Already did, Doc—noticed that when I scraped."

The coroner nodded, gestured to the digit. "Severity

of this tear means the nail was torn off—violently. My guess is, while he was scratching an assailant."

Greg's eyebrows rose. "You think he left a piece of himself in his attacker?"

"Possible," Robbins said.

Their next stop was the DNA lab to see Mia, who was alternating between loading more specimens into the DNA analyzer and poring over reports.

"Just can't stay away, can you?" she asked as they entered, Warrick in the lead.

He risked a grin. "Kinda hoping that you could tell us something about those straws and cigarette butts."

Her smile was wide, but her eyes were tight. "Once again, you assumed I would push Warrick Brown to the front of the line. You figured I'd rush it right through, just so I could see you again, I suppose? You thought that I would just drop everything else and—"

"Actually, we're just on kind of a fast track. No pressure, Mia, just checking. . . ."

"I don't remember calling you."

"Well, you, uh, didn't."

"Actually, if memory serves, I said I'd call you when I had something."

Warrick tasted his words as he said, "Your memory serves you just fine," and didn't much care for the flavor.

Without looking at him, she pointed to the door like the Ghost of Christmas Yet to Come showing Scrooge his gravestone. "Then get your bony butt out of my lab until I call you. Ask your friend, the newbie CSI, there, *he'll* tell you—DNA analysis takes time. In the real world, this would take you a month; you're lucky we've got this kick-ass lab."

"I was just telling Greg that," Warrick said, and eased back into the hall, blowing out air as if narrowly ducking a dire fate.

As they headed down the corridor, Greg glanced back at his old DNA haunts. Admiringly, he said, "Wow—now *that's* attitude. I should've stood up to you like that, back when you used to ride *me* for results!"

"If you had," Warrick said, "you'd still be picking yourself up."

Greg nodded. "Good point."

They went back to their individual tasks, Greg working prints in AFIS, Warrick settling in to watch the Bob's Round-Up Grill security-tape film festival.

The first tape was the parking lot angle. After cruising to three minutes before the time on the receipt, Warrick began looking for the late-model Cadillac (which currently resided in the CSI garage). He didn't spot it at first; then the Caddy rolled through the frame.

Warrick stopped the tape, wound it back, then started the car into the frame again and froze it. Soon he was loading that section of video into his computer, digitizing the material to enable him to enhance it. Even after his best computer tricks, however, all he knew for sure was: A) the car was the correct Cadillac, and B) two men were inside . . . who might, or might not, be African-American.

This did not improve his post-Mia mood.

Back to the tape deck and video monitor, Warrick

loaded the second security-cam vid, an angle courtesy of the underside of a beam that held up a small roof protecting drive-through customers from the dominant desert sun and occasional rain. High enough to avoid the glare of headlights, the camera gave Warrick a direct view down through the windshields of approaching customers. After sunset, though, car interiors were fairly dark, making those inside hard or impossible to make out.

The CSI watched three cars glide through the frame. In two, he could tell a man was driving; third vehicle, he had no idea. In one he could tell the customer was white. In the other two, he couldn't tell whether the customer was black, Latino, or simply a well-tanned Cauc. Fourth car in line was his Caddy, and he strained to see something, anything . . . but the car was too far away, dashboard light too faint. As the car inched closer to the camera . . . *there!*

What was that?

Warrick rewound the tape and played it again.

A burst of light on the driver's side, then it was gone. *What had it been?* He rewound the tape and watched again, this time slowing it way down.

A cigarette lighter.

The driver sparked a lighter, then put his hand over the smoke to light up. *Could he see the guy's face?* Certainly not after the driver's hand came up and obliterated the light source; but in that split second before, could Warrick make him?

The CSI returned to his computer, digitized about ninety seconds of key video, and returned to the frame where the lighter sparked to life. He thought maybe he could distinguish a face, but the distance was so great.

He enhanced the picture, zoomed in, and enhanced some more.

Illuminated for a frozen split second sat one of the kidnappers, lighting a cig. Didn't the guy know smoking was bad for you? Whoever the smoker was, Warrick didn't recognize him, and Warrick had a pretty good handle on the gang scene, for a CSI, having worked dozens of gang-related cases.

Greg rushed in. "AFIS coughed up another name."

"You need to buy a lottery ticket on the way home."

"No, I won't get luckier than this," he said, waving a sheet of paper. "The passenger-side fingerprints belong to Jalon Winsor, a member of the Hoods."

"Where's their territory?"

"Between Lake Mead Boulevard on the north," Greg said, referring to his notes, "and Vegas Drive on the south . . . from MLK west to maybe Simmons Street."

"If they have so much territory," Warrick said, eyes slitting, "why the hell haven't I heard of them?"

"Guess they've been flying under the radar, mostly. Haven't been caught up in anything big . . ."

"Until a lion ran out in front of their stolen car," Warrick said.

"Until then," Greg agreed. The young CSI's eyes locked with his mentor's. "Grissom and I had a crime scene on Beatty a couple weeks ago, 'Rick—right in the middle of Hoods territory. Which is how they got on *my* radar. I even met a couple, watching us work. Lookouts, probably."

"You know *this* guy?" Warrick asked, pointing to the monitor.

Greg glanced at the screen. "Whoa—maybe I will buy a lottery ticket. *That's* one of the guys Grissom and I talked to! Is he involved in this?"

"Seems to be. What's his name?"

"His buddy called him Fleety. Yeah, that's him, lighting the cigarette. I remember that kid smoking like a house on fire."

"Run the nickname," Warrick said, "and see if anything comes up."

"You got it."

"Then we'll call Brass and see if he can get someone to sit on the kid's lookout spot, case he turns up."

"Right away."

"And, Greg?"

"Yeah?"

"Nice memory."

"Thanks."

Twenty minutes later, Warrick found Greg hunkered down at a computer monitor, nose practically pressed to the screen. Warrick pulled up a chair and sat to Greg's right. He ran a hand over his face and wondered when, or if, this shift would ever end.

Not only were Grissom, Catherine, and the others still dealing with the battle aftermath in Boot Hill, day shift had troubles of their own—two CSIs in court and three more working a massive Desert Shores drug bust on the far northwest side. This was one day nobody upstairs would be bitching about overtime.

"Talked to Brass," Warrick told Greg.

"Yeah?" Greg answered, only half interested as he examined the screen.

"No extra *anything* today. If we wanna find a way to track down Fleety, we're on our own."

Greg frowned doubtfully. "Well, is that a CSI's job, really? Is it . . . evidence?"

"It's the best lead, and we're still in the early hours of this murder investigation. And there's nobody else available."

"Okay, then—how about we start with that name you wanted?" Greg said, obviously a little pleased with himself.

Warrick perked. "Got something?"

"Isaiah A. Fleetwood, a.k.a. 'Fleety'—seventeen, Hoods member, small-time brushes with the system . . . but nothing serious enough to ever get him printed. Not violent like some of the other members, at least nothing violent turns up."

"Strictly a lookout, you think?" Warrick asked.

"Could well be . . . but a mouthy one."

"Oh?"

Greg nodded. "Three uniformed officers've had run-ins with him—big talk, but the kid always backed down. Least, that's how the reports are written."

"Anything else?"

"Yeah—lives with his grandmother. Apparently a pretty good kid till his mom died two years ago. Since then, he's a ticking bomb, looking for a place to go off."

"Address on the grandmother?"

Greg held up a slip of paper with something already scrawled on it.

"Good. Then let's go have a talk with Fleety."

"Or Grandma. And we can check out his hangout

corner on the way." Greg slipped the piece of paper into his shirt pocket.

Warrick drove this time, window down, air rushing in, helping him stay alert (and awake).

Warrick cruised the corner of Beatty and Ludwig where Greg had met Fleety before. As they rolled by, Greg thought he saw a surreptitious figure slip hastily into the shadows of a vacant house.

"I think that was him!" Greg said.

"Thought I saw someone, too. Sure it's Fleety?"

"Not sure. But . . . pretty sure."

"Looked nervous . . . We'll go around the block and stop back a ways, then go up on foot. You do have your sidearm, right?"

An acid rumble burned in Greg's stomach. "Yeah. Never without it."

Warrick took four rights and parked the SUV on the same street as the empty house, but at the other end of the block.

"Let's go," the older CSI said.

Though noon neared, the temperature wasn't high for Vegas and a nice cool breeze whispered pleasantly at them. Nonetheless, Greg felt every pore of his body oozing sweat, and some invisible motor had turned over within him, causing every limb to vibrate.

"Stick close," Warrick said.

Instead of walking up the front walk, Warrick led the way around the side, pressing his body against the exterior wall of the house; Greg copied him, trying to control his breathing. As they edged forward, Warrick unholstered his pistol, signaling Greg to do the same.

It took only all of his strength and half an eternity before the younger man could get the damn strap unsnapped and withdraw his Glock nine-millimeter automatic. The pistol seemed unnaturally heavy, a handful of power and terror. His mind raced through every firearms procedure he'd ever learned. His sweaty back pressed against the wall, Greg moved his left hand up, Glock in both hands—surprisingly, the weapon felt even heavier.

Warrick peeked around the corner, then ducked back and shook his head. "Nobody back there," he whispered.

Greg thought, *Good.*

Warrick was saying, "Back door's open, though—we've got to go in."

Greg nodded and felt sweat droplets bounce off his forehead.

Warrick whispered, "You okay?"

Again Greg nodded and with his chin indicated that Warrick should go ahead.

The rear door had no screen and the flimsy wooden thing hung like a loose tooth from one valiant rusty hinge. The house gave off an awful smell—a mingling of must, dust, and urine. Vacant building perhaps, but someone had been using it for something—squatting possibly, or maybe just a look-out for a drug dealer doing business out of a nearby house.

Warrick—his pistol in front of him—stepped through the doorway into the kitchen.

Greg followed him in, ears perked for the slightest sound, vibration, tremor, anything that might signal the presence of others. In the tiny kitchen—cramped even minus any refrigerator or stove—a patina of dust covered the counters and sinks. The dusty floor had so many footprints, however, they might have been made a minute ago or a month or a year. An angry amber light filtered through yellowed, ripped and torn pull shades, and the layer of dirt on the windows provided an art-film soft focus to this dreary, dangerous reality.

Greg stayed on Warrick's heels as he eased through a doorway into what had once been a dining room. The younger CSI, still consciously thinking of his handgun training, wheeled his pistol left, not lowering the barrel until he had cleared his partner.

No furniture in the room, but a couple of sleeping bags snugged flat against the far left wall beneath a row of windows.

The two CSIs moved through a living room with a shaded picture window, under which a boom box and a pile of CDs sat near a card table filled with empty malt-liquor forties and an ashtray overflowing with butts; at the table, two opposing folding chairs (another two leaned against a wall). In here, the same nasty aroma of the kitchen was spiced with the stale sweat smell.

Warrick withdrew his pocket flashlight and, using his left hand, shone it down the hall, his left wrist becoming a brace for his pistol. Greg kept his Glock pointed toward the ceiling in the narrow hallway, where ancient floral wallpaper was peeling itself off. On the left, a closet, then either a bedroom or a bathroom beyond; across the corridor, another open door, and at the end of the hall, another—probably the master bedroom, a term that seemed arcane in this hovel.

Problem was, the closet door would open *toward* the living room—if Warrick passed the door, then came back to open it, the wood would be between Greg and Warrick. If they both passed the door and turned back, they'd have three unchecked rooms at their back.

Sweet, Greg thought bitterly.

They could go down the hallway, back to back; but one would have the closet to cover while the other tried to watch three doors that might hide Fleety or God knew how many of his homies.

Warrick fell back into the living room and, in a barely audible whisper, said, "If we go back and call for backup . . ." and shrugged.

This conveyed to Greg that if the CSIs called for backup from the SUV, any Hoods currently in the house would be gone before anybody got here.

Greg nodded grimly.

Warrick's eyes locked Greg's, and rarely in Greg's experience had anyone looked at him with such intensity. In that same barely audible whisper, Warrick asked, "Up for this?"

Greg wanted to yell, *Hell, no! Let's go call for backup, maybe get SWAT out here, and if they're gone when we get back, well then . . . we'll get 'em next time.* He might even have actually said that if his mouth and tongue had been working and weren't drier than a desert.

Instead, he nodded.

"Stay close," Warrick whispered, and proceeded back to the mouth of the hallway.

Keeping his pistol trained on the closet door, Warrick moved past it. Greg was right on his heels, but before he could pass, the closet door was thrown open, knocking Greg back, and the gun from Warrick's grasp.

When he regained his balance, the door swung lazily shut and Greg found himself staring into the wild brown eyes of a bare-chested, very angry black kid in red sweatpants and a white nylon do-rag with a gun in his left fist.

The young man was trying desperately to find a way to pull the trigger, but Warrick had him by the arms, and the two men wrestled to the end of the hall, where Warrick got the guy down on the floor, the guy's gun hand extended to the left.

Taking one quick step, Greg kicked the gun out of the gang kid's hand and found himself squatting down and pressing his pistol into the kid's skull as Warrick pulled out handcuffs. On the kid's neck were three jagged scratches.

"Freeze!" Greg shouted. "Just hold still!"

The kid's eyes blazed at Greg. "Fuck y'self! Fuck y'self!"

Warrick locked the cuffs and rose off the young man's back. When someone came out of the bedroom in a blur, sweeping up Warrick's gun off the floor, Warrick never saw it coming, his back to the attacker; in half a second, Warrick's own gun was pressed against his temple.

Rising slowly and taking a step back away from the cuffed guy on the floor, Greg leveled his pistol at half the baby face of Isaiah "Fleety" Fleetwood. The other half of the young man's face remained hidden behind Warrick.

Fleety yelled, "Drop the motherfuckin' gun, you five-oh prick!"

Greg felt the gun shaking in his hand as he pointed it at Warrick and the shorter man hiding behind him.

"Can't do that," Greg said.

"Drop the gun or I drop your bud!"

"Make him let me go," the kid in cuffs whined from below.

"Jalon, man," Fleety said, "I *got* this."

So, the guy on the floor was Jalon Winsor—the scratches on Jalon's neck should have told him that. That meant they had both the guys they had come for: now all they had to do was defuse this little situation and walk them out.

"Isaiah," Greg said, amazed at how steady his voice sounded, "you need to put the gun down."

"How you know my name, blondie?" Fleety asked, obviously agitated.

"Let's keep to what's important, Isaiah," Greg said, outwardly calm. "You need to put the gun down."

From the floor, Jalon yelled, "Just *smoke* his white ass, Fleety!"

Fleetwood thumbed back the hammer on Warrick's Glock; the click was a tiny sound that registered to Greg as the loudest he'd ever heard.

Fleety was yelling, "*You* put the gun down, *you* put the gun down!"

Greg suddenly had an intense urge to urinate, but fought it. Slowly, he lowered the barrel of his pistol.

Warrick gave Greg a look that said, *Greg, you put that gun down, we're both dead. . . .*

And Greg gave Warrick a look that said, *Trust me*.

Warrick's eyes closed and Greg couldn't tell if that meant his fellow CSI understood his unspoken message and accepted it, or was making peace within himself before he died.

Fleety's eyes remained wild, but he seemed more scared than angry as he held the gun to Warrick's head. Greg lowered his pistol to his side.

Instantly, Fleety calmed, his eyes narrowing, his breathing slowing.

"Now," Fleety said, his voice still loud but less strident. "Let my man Jalon go."

Greg shook his head. "Can't do it."

"*Your* man's about to get—"

Greg cut him off. "What *happened* to you, Isaiah?"

"What?" Fleety asked, taken aback.

"What happened to you? Until your mom died—"

Fleety snarled, "Hell *d'you* know about my moms!"

"I know she loved you," Greg said, the gun a thousand-pound weight at the end of his arm. "You pulled a B average when she was alive."

"Yeah, well, she gone."

Jalon butted in again. "Fleety, just *smoke* them, and let's get the hell outta here!"

Fleety twitched . . . but didn't pull the trigger.

Greg looked down at Jalon. "You need to be quiet," he said firmly, not believing how calm his voice sounded. He wondered if at any moment a bullet would explode through him and that would be the end.

"*Fuck* you!" Jalon screamed.

"You kill us," Greg said, somehow keeping his

voice matter of fact, "you 'smoke' us five-ohs, this place'll be crawling with blue uniforms. Then SWAT will swarm in here. Twenty-four hours, Hoods'll be history. Every Hood in town will be in jail or dead. Want *that* on your head, Isaiah?"

Jalon's eyes danced with fear.

Was Fleety wavering?

"Isaiah, you have a chance here to do the right thing. Let my partner go, and we'll talk you through this trouble you're in."

"No trouble *I'm* in," Fleety blurted. "*I* got the gun."

Greg could feel the situation slipping away. "Your mother gave you a name that meant something— Isaiah. Very biblical."

"Think I don't know that?" Fleety said, defensive, and shoved the snout of the gun against Warrick's temple. Warrick's eyes widened.

Fleety was staring at Greg now, and Jalon had the good sense to keep a low profile—especially since whenever he looked up, he now stared into the barrel of Greg's gun.

Fleety said nothing.

Greg asked, "What are you doing with the Hoods, anyway? That's the life your mother worked so hard for you to have?"

The gun inched away from Warrick's head.

Greg said, "Maybe that was divine intervention last night . . . maybe that lion *meant* something. . . ."

Fleety, startled by this—eyes flaring as he likely relived that lion leaping in front of their stolen car last night—flinched.

Not waiting for Greg to talk the kid down further, Warrick dropped a shoulder, spun, and punched the gun out of Fleety's hand. Surprised, the kid took a quick step back and slipped, then Warrick had a hold of him and was twisting one hand behind his back.

Then Isaiah was on his knees, as if praying.

Greg yanked out his handcuffs and passed them to Warrick, who bound Fleety up.

"Isaiah Fleetwood and Jalon Winsor," Warrick said, "you are under arrest for the murder of DeMarcus Hankins. You have the right to remain silent . . ."

He went on, but Greg stopped listening. God, he had to pee. . . .

"We didn't do *shit*," Jalon was whining.

Warrick gave him a little smile. "Those scratches on your neck tell a different story—like, the skin we got from under DeMarcus's fingernails is going to match your DNA."

"Hell you say," Jalon said.

"If I'm lyin'," Warrick said through his nastiest grin, "I'm dyin'."

Standing in that cramped hallway, the crisis over, his guts churning, his bladder about to burst, Greg felt an urge to barf, thanks to the smell of stale sweat and fresh fear. The tongue-on-a-battery metallic taste of terror that still clung to his mouth only served to heighten his nausea.

Outside, they called for a squad car and, while they waited with the two young black men, Greg said, "You got this, 'Rick, for a minute?"

"Yeah. Sure."

Greg paused, nodded toward the house. "Is that a crime scene in there?"

"Well . . . not exactly. Sort of."

"I mean . . . can I take a leak in there? I got in trouble for that one time."

Warrick laughed. "Yeah. . . . Yeah. I wouldn't touch anything, though."

"Evidence?"

"Germs."

Greg felt much better when he came back out, but then something inside him sent him running to the farthest back corner of the property, where he threw up.

When he returned to Warrick's side, a squad car was out front, lights flashing, as two uniforms loaded the Hoods in. A small crowd was gathering, some there to bitch, some to demonize the police; most just came to watch.

"If this *is* a crime scene," a pale Greg said to Warrick, with a head bob toward the side of the house, "I hope *we* don't process it."

Innocently, Warrick asked, "You know what Bob's Round-Up Grill's slogan is, don't you?"

"No, I don't."

"One breakfast burrito, comin' right up."

"Oh man. *Please. . . .*"

They climbed into the Denali, Warrick again getting behind the wheel. Warrick turned the key, slipped the SUV into drive, and rolled slowly away from the curb.

"Remind me to thank you, sometime," Warrick said.

Greg was looking out the window.

"That was a hell of a thing, Greg. That may be the single bravest thing I've ever seen."

Smiling, Greg said, "Or the dumbest."

Warrick shrugged. "Right up there for that, too."

"You know me," Greg said, his hands shaking in his lap, "sometimes I just can't stop talking."

"You stayed cool and didn't panic. That's what you do in a situation like that. You stay calm and let the rest come naturally."

"Hope so. Hope I'm never *in* a situation like that again. But could you slow down a little, 'Rick? . . . You know how easily I get scared."

Warrick glanced at his partner, laughed gently, and eased off the accelerator.

10

IN THE BOOT HILL POLICE STATION, Gil Grissom and Catherine Willows were as much prisoners, in a way, as the quartet of Spokes the Patrolmen were in the process of locking up.

The CSIs headed not to a cell, however, but to the mostly glass enclosure of Chief Lopez's office that looked out on a small, empty bullpen for detectives and officers, all of whom were out and about, dealing with the biker dilemma.

Grissom wondered idly why these small-town police chief or sheriff offices were always so similar and bereft of personality. A basic rule of crime scene investigation was broken by such offices: a CSI always viewed personal domains (offices, bedrooms, dens, and kitchens) as windows into the character of their inhabitants, whether victim, suspect, or even witness.

His own office back in Vegas—with all its mysteries and treats scattered around, from the two-headed snake to pickled pig parts, various things in jars, all the insects on display—certainly fit that pattern.

On the other hand, perhaps an impersonal office like Lopez's—with its handful of framed diplomas and commendations, its bulletin board of work-oriented snapshots and circulars, even its police association calendar—spoke of the chief's professionalism. Not that Grissom considered himself any less a complete professional simply because he chose to put a few of his obsessions on display. For a man who spent so much of his life at work, Grissom could hardly keep his own character out of his quarters.

"What was that old Western," Lopez said as he positioned himself behind a metal desk, the CSIs taking visitor's chairs opposite, "the one with John Wayne?"

Catherine blinked at their host. "I'm a good investigator, Chief, but you'll have to narrow that down a little."

"*Rio Bravo*," Grissom said.

Now Catherine looked at Grissom; she did not blink.

"What?" Grissom said to her. "It's a classic—lawmen holed up in a little sheriff's office, while the bad guys converge outside in the town they've taken over. Wonderful film. Howard Hawks."

"Let's hope we survive," she said pleasantly, "so we can rent that some time."

"Fine," Grissom said, and smiled.

Catherine squinted at him, as if not quite sure Grissom were really there.

Lopez said, "Well, this thing started out like the OK Corral or maybe Custer's last stand; but *Rio Bravo* is what it feels like it's turning into."

"We have Highway Patrol support," Grissom said.

"Not enough, I'm afraid," Lopez said.

"You need to call the governor now," Catherine said firmly. "We need help here."

Grissom offered an open palm. "We might be able to cool down the Predators."

"How?" the other two asked at once.

"By catching their fallen leader's killer. On the other hand, as long as Finch is in here, the Spokes will remain a threat."

A dispatcher, a short, thin woman of fifty with trim blonde hair, stuck her head in the glass enclosure. "Chief, the Highway Patrol just called—Predators've run the roadblock. . . . They're on their way into town."

Lopez kept his voice calm, even as he rose from his desk. "Get everyone inside *now*, Gloria. Blow the horn."

"Horn?" Catherine asked.

"Emergency horn for foul weather," Lopez explained. "But everybody in Boot Hill knows, they hear that, they get their butts inside."

"Might keep some innocents from getting hurt," Grissom said.

Catherine rolled her eyes. "I won't be offended if the guilty stay indoors, too."

"Where's Cody?" Lopez yelled, but Gloria was gone.

The tall, paunchy, fiftyish detective, in jeans, boots, and a blue short-sleeved shirt with western pocket trim, swung into his chief's office.

"Right here, boss," Jacks said, thumb in a loop of a belt that included his holstered sidearm. "Just got back. What's up?"

Sara seemed to materialize, her hair slightly mussed as if she'd come on the run; perhaps she had. As she entered the small office, her expression grave, she first noticed Jacks.

After a beat, she said to her fellow CSIs, "Guys, can we talk a sec?"

Sara gestured with her head, arcs of hair swinging, that she wanted to do so in private.

Catherine frowned, but Grissom said, "Sure."

And they joined her in a hallway just off the bullpen.

The trio gathered in a tight little circle, Sara's voice as soft as her expression was grave.

She said, "Sofia just called. Grissom, you gave me a name to run earlier . . . a local girl."

"Right," he said. "Wendy Sierra. What about her?"

"She's that cop's daughter."

Catherine, startled, said, "Lopez?"

But Grissom, who'd seen the girl in question and now put a faint family resemblance together, said, "Jacks. Cody Jacks."

Catherine turned to Grissom. "Remind me why you wanted her name checked?"

Grissom did so, painting a quick picture of the makeshift memorial at the chain-link fence of the Four Kings, and Wendy Sierra's tearful delivery of roses in memory of Nick Valpo.

"So Wendy is Cody's daughter," Catherine said. "It's a small town. Does this tell us anything?"

Nobody seemed to know for sure. Nick came down the hall from the modest crime lab and fell in with his colleagues.

"The Rocky boots from the mortuary are *not* Officer Montaine's," he said.

Sara asked, "Did we suspect him?"

"Not really," Nick said. "But he's eliminated as far as this line of evidence goes."

A piercing electronic scream made the CSIs jump—
the emergency horn . . . three long blasts.

Lopez appeared at the mouth of the hall and said,
"Would you folks step back in my office for a moment?"

They did, standing with their backs to the window-
wall on the bullpen. Jacks was seated behind Lopez's
desk.

"We clearly have a situation here," the chief said, approaching the CSIs. "I know you're all pros, but I don't
want you on the front lines. With my own people, and
the Highway Patrol, I think we can hold on."

"You need to call the governor," Catherine said.

"I have. He says he'll do what he can."

"Specifically . . . ?"

"He wasn't specific. He's getting back to me, ASAP."

Catherine shook her head. "What the hell kind
of—"

"I don't mean to be rude, Ms. Willows, but I do have
to get out there."

"Which leaves us where?" Catherine asked.

Lopez pointed a finger at the floor. "Right here.
Cody'll stay with you guys."

"Chief," Grissom said, "we're all proficient in
firearms. It's part of the job."

"I'm aware of that, Doc—and have full confidence in
your abilities. Remember *Rio Bravo*?"

Nick and Sara exchanged looks: *what the . . . ?*

The chief was saying, "I need you here to keep an
eye on these locked-up Spokes. We may have a mob—
hell, two mobs—on our doorstep any time. One'll want
to spring and save the prisoners; the other'll want them
made dead, in a hurry. At least in the old days, they

took time to find a tree and string up a rope; it'll be quicker now, and probably even uglier."

The CSIs passed glances around; they were being kept off the front line only to guard a beleaguered fort.

Lopez nodded to Jacks, then returned his gaze to his guests. "I need the five of you to make sure that nothing happens to our 'guests,' either way, while I'm out there trying to keep the lid on this sucker. With the exception of Detective Jacks, and the dispatcher down the hall in her cubbyhole, you'll be on your own. Ms. Willows—you're supervisor. You up for this?"

Catherine said, "Yes."

Lopez said, "Thank you, ma'am. Good luck."

He tipped his Stetson and went off to lead his tiny contingent, twenty or twenty-five strong . . . to hold off ten times that many.

Nonetheless, Nick offered Catherine a smile. "Did he just call you *'ma'am'*?"

Catherine said, "Be quiet," through a smile, albeit a troubled one.

Sara said, "I'm pretty sure he called you 'ma'am.'"

"Sara . . ."

Grissom faced Catherine. "We could phone Sheriff Burdick . . ."

"No," she said, with one shake of the head, "this is Lopez's judgment call."

Nick said, "On the other hand, it's *our* butts."

Jacks was up from behind the desk and parting venetian blind blades to look out at the street through one of three windows side by side that formed a sort of picture window, though each had individual blinds.

With his gray sideburns, gray eyes, and vaguely wolfish countenance, Jacks evoked the image of an old

Western sheriff, which was underscored when he drew his sidearm, a Glock, checked the clip, then reholstered the weapon.

"We should be safe enough here," he said, turning his head toward them but maintaining sentry. "But if things gets hairy, you *do* all know the way back to the cells, right?"

Nods all around.

The detective went back to looking out the window, waiting for trouble that seemed ever more inevitable.

Grissom and Catherine took the visitor's chairs, while Nick and Sara kept their own watch out the wall of windows onto the vacant bullpen and on a door that they all hoped would open only when Chief Lopez returned.

"Did you see this coming?" Grissom asked Jacks.

"Damn bikers'll likely do anything," Jacks said. "Normal humans don't shoot up a casino like that and endanger civilians."

"That type might do about any evil thing," Grissom said.

Catherine frowned at him.

Jacks, rather absently, eyes on the street, said, "Might at that."

"Even seduce an innocent girl away from her family," Grissom said.

Now Jacks spun his whole beefy body away from the window. His eyes were hooded, his complexion pale. "What do you know about Wendy?"

Grissom said, "I know she shed tears for Valpo. I know she put a dozen roses under his picture at that improvised memorial."

Lopez's top sergeant heaved a sigh. Then he returned to the window, fingers prying open blinds; but his glazed expression indicated he wasn't looking at the street . . .

. . . perhaps just into his past.

"Her mom, Nancy, and me," he said in that resonant radio announcer's voice, "we got divorced over what happened to that girl."

Jacks's fingers dropped from the blinds, no longer holding them open. Now he stared directly into the metal slats.

"Two years ago," he said, "this bastard Valpo managed to seduce four underage girls into having sex with him . . . four!"

"Roofies?" Catherine asked.

He shrugged. "Some kind of goddamn drugs. Wendy . . . was one of them. In retrospect, we probably sheltered her. Casino trade or not, this is a small town— church and school and family. She was sixteen then, and'd just . . . developed, kind of overnight; went from being a flat-chested little girl to a . . . looked like she was twenty, or even twenty-one . . . and all of sudden, she started to dress like it. Real . . . trampy."

His eyes closed.

"I tried to put my foot down about that slutty crap, but . . . that girl has a way she can look at you and melt you . . . if you're her dad, anyway. Hell, and me, supposed to be so goddamn tough. But her and her mom? I couldn't never say no to them about nothing. Nancy . . . wasn't that upset about how Wendy dressed . . . least, not until the thing with Valpo, and the drugs."

"If it was date rape," Catherine said, "you could have brought him in—"

"It wasn't roofies! It was . . . weed and pills and . . . stuff Wendy *liked* to use. She got into that lifestyle, not every day, but when the bikers rolled in, it was something . . . *rebellious* she could do."

"Sixteen's the age of consent in Nevada," Grissom said. "So a statutory rape charge was out."

"You are unfortunately dead right on that one, Doc . . . and then she started disappearing weekends—going to Vegas and Phoenix and God knows where."

Catherine asked, "Meeting Valpo?"

"I don't know. I don't know. Wherever it was, she got her drugs there—weed mostly, but still. . . . And when I couldn't get our daughter off the stuff and straightened around, my wife took it out on *me*—blamed me for babying the girl, divorced my sorry ass, went back to her maiden name, Sierra. Wendy went with her and took her mom's name, too. My name—they didn't even want *that* no more."

His expression and his tone bland as a glass of cold milk, Grissom asked, "Is that when a daydream started evolving into a plan?"

Jacks's wolfish eyes narrowed and a faint smile formed. "What the hell you talkin' about, Doc?"

"Your plan to execute Nick Valpo."

Jacks grunted a laugh. "Somebody spike your chaw with peyote, Doc?"

"I don't use 'chaw,'" Grissom said softly. "And I don't mind when my friend Chief Lopez calls me 'Doc,' but I'd prefer you didn't."

Thumbs looped in his belt, Jacks said, "If that, before, was some kind of serious accusation, you better have something to back it up."

"Oh, I'll be able to prove it by the end of business

today, if we're not too distracted by another shoot-out. That can provide a real distraction—don't you think, Sergeant Jacks?"

"I think you're on thin ice."

Grissom smiled gently. "Not a terribly apt analogy, in this climate. By sundown, everything will be clear, and you'll be—"

Jacks's lip curled. "On the stage out of town?"

Grissom nodded in the lockup's direction. "No. Behind bars."

Jacks tilted his head toward the street. "You don't think that biker rabble'll have something to say about *that*?"

Shrugging, Grissom said, "I hope not. A lynching in any form I find distasteful."

The eyes of the other CSIs were glued to these two men now as they batted each other the ball. . . .

"And what makes you so sure you've got this figured . . . Doc?"

"Same thing that always convinces me I've got it 'figured,'" Grissom said. "The evidence."

The detective snorted a harsh laugh. "You don't have anything on me."

"I'd say we have plenty."

Jacks frowned. "Like what?"

Grissom shrugged. "Well, there's your boot print at the mortuary, where you stole Valpo's body. You do wear *Rocky* boots, don't you?"

"Who doesn't around here?" Jacks said with a dismissive wave. "Department policy."

"But no two pairs of boots wear the same—they indicate the feet that trod in them . . . kind of like leather and rubber fingerprints. Plus, there's a tire print that Nick lifted. That's going to match your car, too."

The gray eyes grew cold. "What makes you think *I* was at the mortuary?"

"Because you couldn't get rid of the murder weapon without raising suspicion," Grissom answered. "So you had to get rid of the bullet—that meant getting rid of Valpo's body."

Jacks looked as though he were trying to follow a foreign film, minus subtitles. "Back up—*what* murder weapon?"

"Small-caliber pistol," Grissom said. "A twenty-two. You got a hideout piece—maybe on your left ankle?"

Catherine jumped in. "Maybe you wouldn't mind showing us your left ankle, Sergeant?"

Jacks shrugged, said, "Sure, why the hell not?"

And he lifted his right leg up onto the chief's desk, baring his hairy ankle as his pants rode up . . .

. . . showing them an S&W model 2214 automatic pistol.

From behind Grissom, Nick said slowly, "Just like Keith Draper's."

Jacks returned his foot to the floor and said, "So what? It's a typical backup piece. What in hell does that prove?" A wolfish smile bared yellow teeth. "Anyway, my esteemed colleagues from the big-time Vegas crime lab . . . without the bullet, who's to say *what* gun fired the shot that killed that animal?"

Grissom ignored the question. "Just to satisfy my curiosity—why didn't you just pitch the gun? Would've been considerably simpler than body-snatching."

Jacks's lupine grin contained not a hint of humor. "Since I didn't kill him, I don't need to dump *any* gun. . . . Besides, it was a gift—from my wife and daughter." He waved this off, literally. "And, hell—*everybody* in the department knows I have that little gun. I've had it for years!"

"Years?" Grissom asked.

"Wendy's mom bought it for my thirtieth—gave it to me in both their names. Little something extra to make sure Daddy . . . Daddy made it home every night."

Grissom noted the emotion the detective had betrayed and said, "Well, keepsake or not, we'll need to test if it's been fired."

"Why bother? I'll tell you it has—I was out at the range yesterday before work . . . which I can prove, easy. Both my guns were fired there; and so, yes, I'll check positive for GSR—so what?"

Gunshot residue would tell them if Jacks had fired a gun recently and tended to hang around even if the shooter washed his hands; but Jacks's admission was meant to make that go away. In Grissom's view, it didn't, not entirely.

Jacks returned to his window. Easily, not looking at them, as if it were part of his guard duty, Jacks withdrew the Glock from its holster and held it loosely at his side, the barrel pointed toward the floor. "Maybe that pit-boss sleaze Draper took Valpo out. He hates bikers like poison."

The weapon in the suspect's hand stiffened every CSI spine; but no one moved.

"We won't know," Grissom said calmly, "until we match bullets from both guns against the ones that killed Valpo."

Still smiling, Jacks said, "Gonna be kind of tough to match bullets without the body, isn't it?"

Grissom smiled as well. "I don't have the body . . . but I know where it is."

Again Jacks faced them, the venetian blinds at his back. "Really? Well, surprise me—where *are* the earthly remains of that prick?"

"Here's what happened," Grissom said.

You hated Valpo for what he did to your daughter, and whether that wrong was real or imagined, you decided you had to take him out for it—like a diseased branch that had to be pruned from society's tree.

Valpo would come into town, but with you being a cop, he'd be a frustratingly inaccessible target, always surrounded by company—a social breed, bikers. You couldn't get close enough to execute him without some sort of diversion. So you recruited Tom Price. All Price had to do was not change the metal-detector batteries one day during the Biker Blowout . . . and you made sure Finch and the Spokes knew when that would happen.

All they had to do was come in, fire off a few shots, and you would take care of Valpo, making the Spokes' biggest problem disappear. Perhaps Finch knew about the execution you planned, or maybe he just thought you were helping them out in order to get back at Valpo and the Predators for what they'd done to your daughter.

You of course knew where the blind spots were in the Four Kings video security system, and when the shooting started, you waited for your chance . . . and pounced. The safest place to commit a murder, after all, is a battlefield. And when Valpo got wounded, you had the perfect opportunity to finish him off. He was even magnanimous enough to fall into a blind spot for you. In all the commotion, the act was practically invisible—what were a couple more gunshots when there were over a hundred others going off, and where most everyone was ducking for cover?

So you had your revenge . . . and the Spokes had made their "statement" to the Predators, who'd dismissed them as weekend warriors. The perfect solution—almost. You still had that precious gun, with its nostalgic family ties, that you couldn't bring yourself to give up . . . and there was Tom Price to deal with. But as lead investigator in the case (a predictable turn of events) you had the freedom to deal with both those loose ends.

You hit the mortician, Mr. Erickson, over the back of the head and whisked Valpo's body away. Of course, you hadn't thought about the footprints and tire prints you were leaving in a dusty parking lot . . . maybe that was the small-town cop in you.

Under the pretext of searching for the missing Tom Price, you went out to his place in the mountains to clip off your only remaining loose end. You probably got him to stay there by promising to bring the money out as soon as the deed was done. Or perhaps Price had second thoughts—he might not even have known why you wanted the metal detectors tampered with. Price might have wanted more money or perhaps suffered true remorse—maybe that suicide note was a confession he'd already written up, which you utilized for the occasion. At any rate, you went out, dealt with him—that is, killed him—making it look like a suicide.

Price lived in a remote area, far out of town, and you were necessarily gone so long, and out of touch, that nobody would notice the extra time it took for you to bury Nick Valpo's body on Price's property. With the murder victim buried, and the other loose end on the books as a suicide, the only possible problem left for you is Buck Finch. After all, in your eyes, you weren't murdering anyone, just a drug-dealing biker renegade—you were dispensing frontier justice.

"Conjecture," Jacks said.

"When we've had some time at the scene of Price's 'suicide,' we'll see about conjecture," Grissom said. "Anyway, there's some key evidence you didn't consider, which I've already taken steps to secure."

"Such as?"

"The other body."

A harsh laugh tried to dismiss that, but panic in the gray eyes betrayed the suspect's real feelings. "What *other* body?"

"The young woman's. The card dealer. It's under lock and key at the mortuary right now—I quietly took care of that, after I realized the killer had neglected to think through that bullets were in both bodies. And I don't think anybody'll be sneaking up on that particular mortician again."

Jacks's face was as white as the underbelly of a fish. "Young woman . . ."

"The witness you shot. That wasn't part of the plan, was it, Sergeant? A pity—I understand you knew her. Had even been a kind of father figure to her. . . . Horrible irony for you to have to live with . . . and her to die with."

"Shut up, Grissom. . . ."

"You mean to revenge your daughter's honor and, along the way, you have to protect yourself by killing your *other*, surrogate daughter . . . leaving a child motherless. Who's the predator now, Sergeant?"

Silence shrouded the office.

Then Cody Jacks spoke, the rich voice cracking.

"I . . . I thought the world of that girl. Vanessa. Vanessa." Tears glistened in his gray eyes, but his expression remained feral. "But you know how it is for us cops—shit happens."

Grissom shrugged. "Only this isn't police work, is it, Sergeant? By the way—how *do* you plan to keep Buck Finch from ratting you out?"

The gun no longer hung loosely at the suspect's side—Jacks had brought it up, to aim it directly at Grissom's chest.

"Anybody moves, the know-it-all dies first," Jacks said, indicating Grissom. His eyes traveled around the faces of the three other CSIs. "Drop the pistols in that garbage can—*now*. One at a time, ladies first . . . touch only the butt with two fingers or your boss dies."

Slowly, the others did as they were told, their weapons clunking into the garbage can next to Lopez's desk.

"Now *you*, Doc," Jacks said.

Grissom complied and pitched his pistol on top of the others.

Catherine had an amazed smile and was shaking her head. "Sergeant Jacks—you *can't* think you can get away with this."

Jacks laughed once. He gestured with the Glock. "If any of you had been looking outside, you'da seen that the Predators and Spokes have gathered out in the street and're about to go at it full tilt. There's gonna be a hell of a firefight that'll make last night look like a paintball match. Dust clears, a lot of people won't be alive no more . . . including you four fucking busybodies . . . and some lowlife bikers."

"Including Buck Finch," Grissom said.

"Another Kewpie doll to you, Doc—and what a sad goddamn tragedy it'll be, can't you just see it? Be all over cable news. And Chief Lopez will put his best man—me—in charge of the investigation . . . to figure out how this coulda all gone so very, very wrong."

"We were killed during the riot," Grissom said.

"That'd be my best guess," Jacks said. He shook his head. "Helluva story you come up with, Grissom—mostly on the nose. I don't like the way this has gone, entirely—I certainly meant little Vanessa no harm. But you can't imagine what Valpo did to demean and degrade my little girl . . . used her, raped her, got her hooked on drugs. We had her in and out of detox . . . that scumbag ruined my life and my daughter's."

Outside there was a gunshot, and everyone flinched, including Jacks.

"All of you," Jacks said, his voice hard now, "up against the windows." He did not mean the glass walls onto the empty bullpen, rather the three behind the chief's desk, where minutes ago, centuries ago, Jacks had stood watch.

He was saying, "Hate to have a stray shot come through the window here and not get one of you."

They lined up against the windows, facing the closed blinds—all except Grissom. At the end of the CSI lineup, he remained facing Jacks.

"Show me your back, Grissom," Jacks said, waving the Glock irritably. "I'm sick of that face of yours."

Grissom ignored him. "So many people have to die, all to avenge a daughter who's still *alive*?"

"You call that living?" Jacks snorted, eyes and nostrils flaring. "She's a goddamn shell of herself—Valpo destroyed her. She may be breathin', but she hasn't been 'alive' since he got his filthy hands on her."

"What about Price?"

The smile seemed almost inhuman now. "Poor

Tommy—a gambling problem hardly anybody knew of. Worked at the Four Kings, but played in the casino in Cal Nev Ari. Owed some money to some very bad people and needed ten grand real bad . . . I just happened to know where to get it. Buck Finch hated Valpo and the Predators practically as much as I did. Ten thousand was nothing to those assholes, and they had their pride to think about. After all, the Predators thumbed their noses at the Spokes every chance they got."

"Finch knew you intended to kill Valpo."

"He knew. But he wouldn't have talked—couldn't've, without implicating himself. Only now, I think it's better if he goes to that big Biker Blowout in hell."

Another gunshot from outside made everyone flinch again—except Catherine, who stood before blinds only partly shut.

"They're just shooting in the air," Catherine said.

Grissom turned and pried open two venetian blind slats to look out at the crowd of bikers gathered in the street. Local cops and Highway Patrol stood guard, their backs to the police station, others in a line dividing the biker groups; but the lawmen looked edgy—the least little thing might turn this confrontation into a full-fledged melee.

Grissom swivelled to face Jacks again. The suspect did not see the door opening from the street onto the bullpen.

Catherine was saying, over her shoulder, "Is this how you hope to make your daughter proud?"

"Spare me—I been a cop too long."

"Yes," Grissom said, "you have."

Chief Lopez was coming in the outer office, his gun in his hand.

"Have what?" Jacks snarled at Grissom.

"Been a cop too long," the CSI said.

Jacks sneered and raised his weapon, taking a bead on Grissom's head.

Grissom barely flinched when glass broke, carrying the explosion from Lopez's pistol as he fired, the bullet catching Jacks in the back of the head. The detective's eyes widened in surprise in a final instant of consciousness.

The Glock dropped from Jacks's dead fingers to the floor, his body pitching facedown onto the chief's desk. For a split second Grissom thought Jacks's last act had been to spit in the CSI's face; then Grissom realized he had been sprayed with blood and bits of Jacks's skull and brains.

Looking at the body of the man who'd been just about to kill them all, Grissom said, "On the other hand, frontier justice has its merits."

Lopez rushed in, and the CSIs gladly left their spot at the window to gather near the doorway around the chief.

"My God," Lopez said, aghast, "I had to do it—couldn't risk anything but a head shot. I could see he was going to shoot you, Doc! What in God's name . . ."

Grissom took him gently by the arm. "You saved our lives—let's step out into your bullpen. That glass may give way . . ."

Indeed, the large pane of glass in the office wall had spiderwebbed around the bullet hole.

". . . and anyway, that's a crime scene in there now."

The blond fiftyish dispatcher, Gloria, came in, gun in hand. "Chief . . . I heard a shot. Is everything—"

"Get back to your post," Lopez said, patting the air and holstering his weapon.

The woman's eyes were doubtful, particularly as she saw the cracked glass and Cody Jacks's corpse sprawled on the desk.

She said, "That's Cody . . . Sweet Jesus, that's—"

Grissom said, "He was a murderer. You'd have been his next victim, after he took care of us."

The dispatcher, mouth agape, stood frozen.

Lopez said, "Get to your post, Gloria—now."

Finally, moving backward, staggering, her face white with terror, the dispatcher exited the bullpen.

11

WARRICK BROWN LIKED TO THINK he was in tune with his body.

As a musician, melody was important to him, and the tune his exhausted, aching muscles were playing now was a dirge. He and Greg should both have been home and in their own beds by now; but Ecklie had come in, on a Saturday no less, to personally ask them to hang around.

"I don't have to tell you, Brown," Ecklie said, "how shorthanded we are with this Boot Hill shooting."

Plus, two of the day-shift analysts were in the middle of two-week vacations and a third, Bob Halpern, was undergoing yet another round of chemo treatments; Halpern obviously had issues that made Warrick feel guilty about wanting to go home over something as trivial as complete physical exhaustion.

So, now he was bearing down on a full twenty-four-hour shift, as was Greg, with nothing left to do about it but try to hang in there and be ready to be awake and alert when the next call came in. Toward that end, Greg had sacked out on a couch in Catherine's office and Warrick had commandeered one of the holding cells, so he could crash on one of the crappy cots.

Warrick had notified both the dispatcher and Ecklie as to where the pair of CSIs would be, with the hope that they could both catch an hour or two's nap. They were, after all, only here in case of an emergency; and since the Boot Hill shoot-out had already been the biggest emergency in months, how many could there be . . . ?

Don't ask stupid questions, Warrick told himself. *Not even stupid rhetorical ones.*

On his side on the bunk, Warrick closed his eyes and immediately felt a thick, dark curtain sweep over him. Before long he was with his new friend, at home, the two of them on the sofa, she drawing close to him, warm in his arms. . . .

Her hand touched his shoulder, shook it gently.

"Tina," he cooed.

"Tina?" a decidedly male voice asked. "Do I look like a Tina?"

Warrick's eyes flapped open and he found himself staring up at Greg Sanders. "What?"

"Tina who?" Greg asked innocently, though his eyes had a glitter of mischief.

Sitting up, reorienting himself, Warrick wiped a quick hand across his eyes. "Tina None-of-your-damn-business."

Greg kept up the innocent act. "What is that, a German name?"

"I just woke up, bro. Don't push it. . . ."

"Does Mia know?"

"Mia who?"

"Mia Who-you're-always-hitting on, Mia."

Warrick blinked, damn near fully awake. "Uh, no. Anyway, Mia's just a friend."

"Riiiight."

"Tina is . . . I don't know . . . maybe something more."

Now Greg seemed really interested, and the kidding dropped away. "Really? Something more?"

Warrick shook his head. "I don't know, we just met recently. She's a nurse."

"I like a woman in uniform."

"Let it go, Greg. . . . Why did you wake me up, anyway? Did I look too restful?"

"Ecklie," Greg said almost sheepishly. "Got a call."

Rising now, stretching, Warrick asked, "Where's everybody else?"

"No sign of our Boot Hill buddies yet. The day-shift crew caught a bunch of primo stuff—a domestic disturbance turned murder/suicide, two robberies, one burglary, and patrol found a stolen car that Williams is dusting for prints."

"Glad I was asleep. So, what did *we* draw?"

"Bank robbery."

"What about the Feds?"

Greg shrugged. "They've been called and agents are on the scene . . . but they only have one available crime scene analyst, so we got elected to volunteer to help out Uncle Sam."

Warrick admired Greg's enthusiasm, though at the moment he was having a hard time matching it. "Your first bank robbery, right?"

Greg nodded. "Yeah. I won't lie to you—I'm jacked."

Wanting to settle his partner down some, Warrick said, "Don't blame ya, but hey—let the Feds take the lead. Not only is it their case, they're easier to get along with if you let them think they're in charge."

"Roger that."

The Green Valley branch office of the Mountain Creek Bank was a single-story adobe building with a red-tile roof on the outskirts of a mall on Warm Springs Road. Even though the Saturday closing time of noon had come and gone, the parking lot was full.

As they pulled in, Warrick behind the wheel, he saw only a couple of cars out front that looked like they might belong to customers. The rest were a mixture of patrol cars and unmarked Crown Victorias. Toward the back of the lot, on the right, away from the building, sat three cars that probably belonged to bank employees.

Warrick parked and they climbed down. Greg started to open the back door to unload their equipment, but Warrick stopped him. "Let's get the lay of the land first."

They did take a moment to slip into their LVPD Crime Lab windbreakers before approaching the bank.

Crime scene tape had been set up around the front entrance; a uniformed officer stood just behind it with his arms crossed. He was a bruiser with flattop, wide chest, stovepipe arms, and hands the size of frying pans, sausage fingers poking out. His name was Tucker and Warrick knew, fearsome looks or not, the guy was a real softie.

"Hey, Tuck, what's up?"

The big cop gave Warrick a grin as he stepped out of their way and let them step under the tape. "Brand-new day, same old shit."

Warrick nodded. "Who's the Special-Agent-in-Charge?"

"Jamal Reese."

The officer opened one of the double glass doors for the CSIs, and it took a second for Warrick's eyes to adjust to the light in the lobby.

Despite plenty of windows and fluorescent lighting, the bank interior still seemed dark compared to the early-afternoon's brilliant sunshine. With his vision clearing, he glanced around.

To his left, a waiting area was tucked back in the corner next to a counter running down the wall, three teller windows available. A group of people gathered in the waiting area, along with several men in suits who were obviously FBI.

"Looking for Special Agent Jamal Reese?" Warrick called out. One of the agents pointed past Warrick.

Warrick glanced over to his right and saw a slender white man seated behind a desk, talking to a black man seated opposite, his back to them. The African-American had to be Reese.

He walked over to the pair, Greg trailing behind, and came up on Reese's right. Behind the desk, the other man, presumably the branch manager, seemed to be wondering if he should rise as Warrick and Greg approached. Poor guy seemed flummoxed, as would any bank employee after a robbery.

Seeing that, Reese rose himself, his head swivelling toward them.

"Special Agent Jamal Reese," he said, extending a hand.

Warrick shook it. "I'm Warrick Brown; this is Greg Sanders. Las Vegas Crime Lab."

"Thanks for the help," Reese said, offering an easy smile. "We're kinda shorthanded in the CSI department today."

"Tell me about it."

Reese nodded, eyes narrowing. "Ah, that Boot Hill thing—that depleted you but good, I bet."

"Safest bet in Vegas."

Warrick was pleased to see Reese showing none of the arrogance Warrick sometimes encountered in FBI agents.

A couple of inches taller than Warrick, Reese wore a charcoal suit so well-tailored that the armament bulge on his hip barely registered. He had close-cropped hair and a thick, dark mustache with just a pinch of salt, which was also visible at his temples.

"Single armed robber," Reese began, crisply businesslike. "Came in around ten minutes before closing, carrying a large manila envelope. Only a couple customers inside, along with the guard, two tellers . . . and, of course, Mr. Warner, the manager."

Reese nodded toward the man behind the desk, who had stood up by now.

Timidly, Warner nodded to Warrick, who nodded back. The manager wore wire-frame glasses and his sandy hair was combed over in a failed attempt to disguise a sizable bald spot. His suit seemed almost as expensive as Agent Reese's.

Reese said, "Once he's inside, UNSUB jerks a pistol out of the envelope, cold-cocks the guard, yells for the customers to hit the floor, makes the tellers empty the drawers into a bag, then splits."

"Where's the guard?" Greg asked, at Warrick's side now.

"Office in the back. Got an ice bag on a bump on his

head. I suggested he take a ride to the ER, but he doesn't want to leave. Point of pride—more pissed than hurt."

Warrick frowned. "I'd *make* him take that ride."

Reese nodded. "I'll let him hang out a while longer, then I'll see that he goes and gets checked out; but the bump doesn't look like much."

"Who's your crime scene analyst?" Warrick asked.

Reese pointed across the lobby to a man in a business suit; the CSA had the customers and tellers gathered in a small waiting area. The victims sat on sofas and chairs as the analyst talked to them.

"Mark Bynum, one of our best."

"Never met him," Warrick said, "but his name's come up. In a good way."

"You'll be happy with him. Check in with Mark, and he'll tell you what he needs."

Warrick nodded.

He and Greg went over and introduced themselves to Bynum. Tall, thin, wearing a gray suit with a white shirt and red-and-blue striped tie, he was the prototypical Fibbie with the firm handshake and death-glare eyelock issued to all agents with their badges and guns.

"I'm going to print the vics," Bynum said. "We want to be able to eliminate them."

Warrick ignored being told the obvious and asked, "Do we know what he touched while he was here?"

"You guys can dust the whole front counter," Bynum said, with a nod in that direction. "All the vics agree he touched it in several places."

"No gloves?" Greg asked.

"No gloves."

"Nice break."

"Could be," Bynum admitted. Addressing both CSIs,

he said, "You can also collect any physical evidence you can find. I'll probably start by processing the evidence at your lab, just for the sake of speed."

"We're on it," Warrick said.

They retrieved their crime scene kits, and while Warrick dusted the counter, Greg collected evidence.

After printing the victims, Bynum slipped behind the counter and searched for evidence back there. Warrick knew Reese would be talking to the manager, Mr. Warner, about dye packs and marked bills as bait money the robber might have taken. Greg bagged several items from the front side of the counter, then headed to the rear to retrieve the security video with the help of the bank manager.

Meanwhile, Reese and his fellow agents interviewed the vics in separate areas of the lobby so they would not contaminate each other's memories.

When the CSIs were finished, they had scant evidence to go on.

Tons of fingerprints from the counters, but it would take a good while to sort them out. Greg had bagged the manila envelope that had hidden the robber's gun, as well as some hairs he had found, and had photographed the guard's head wound in case there might be a clue about the gunman's pistol.

Along with the security videos, that was pretty much everything.

Bynum told them to take what they had to the lab, adding that he'd catch up as soon as he could.

"Huh. You do all the work, we'll take all the glory," Warrick muttered.

If there *was* any, Warrick reminded himself. Should the evidence lead to a dead end, the FBI would simply move on to the next case, no skin off their collective nose. Warrick and Greg, on the other hand, were working a twenty-four-hour shift . . . and would end it by doing somebody else's dirty work. . . .

"Get anything from the witnesses?" Warrick asked the FBI analyst.

Bynum shrugged. "Not a whole hell of a lot. One customer thought she saw the UNSUB get into a cab in the parking lot. That's about it."

Back at the lab, Warrick told Greg to get the hairs to the trace evidence lab, then use ninhydrin to find fingerprints, which he would then load into AFIS. In the meantime, Warrick would settle in to study the security videos.

He had been at it for over an hour and had seen all the tapes at least once from the time of the robbery, and now he was doing a more in-depth search, since none had given him a good view of the robber.

The problem with banks was the same all over: though they certainly had high-end money, they notoriously tended to buy the lowest-end video security equipment, depending on the well-known fact that they had cameras as a deterrent.

This meant looking through more blurry, scratchy images searching for one frame that might hold a clear shot of the UNSUB's face. . . .

Greg came in carrying the envelope in a metal tray. "In the mood for good news?" he asked.

Warrick looked up, his eyes burning with fatigue. "Always. Anyway, I need a boost to keep me going."

"Took the hairs to trace."

"And?"

"Composed of Dynel and konekolen."

Warrick didn't even have to think. "A synthetic wig, and a cheap one at that."

"And now for the bad news."

Feeling a little deflated, Warrick asked, "You didn't say there was good news *and* bad news."

"Couldn't. You looked too pitiful."

Warrick sighed. "Hit me with it."

"No prints with the ninhydrin."

And sighed again. "Okay. So we have to try something else."

Greg looked perplexed. "What?"

Warrick said nothing, rose, and left his office for the lab. Greg trailed behind.

"You sprayed on the ninhydrin," Warrick said as they walked, "then heated the envelope in the oven, right?"

"Yeah," Greg said as they strode down the hall. "Of course. Mother Sanders raised no idiot pups, y'know."

"Good to hear. And you got nothing?"

"Right."

They turned into the lab, where Warrick tapped the counter for Greg to set down the tray.

"There's this new thing the Canadians have been doing. Hasn't even been in the JFI yet, but they asked Grissom to verify their tests . . . and he did. Gris says it works great, even showed me how to do it."

"So," Greg said, honestly and openly impressed, "you got this process before it was even in *The Journal of Forensic Investigation*?"

Warrick smiled. "Sometimes it's not what you know, but who you know . . . and Grissom? Guy knows everybody. Like Anissa Rawji at the University of Toronto and Alexandre Beaudoin from the Sûreté du Québec."

Greg frowned in interest. "Who are . . . ?"

"The guys who came up with this solution called Red Oil O. It's better on white or thermal paper than this brown stuff, but it's worth a try."

Greg hovered nearby. "How does it work?"

"Instead of all the steps and mess of physical developer, Red Oil O only involves three steps."

Greg squinted. "Uh . . . what is Red Oil O again?"

"A lysochrome used in biology for staining lipoproteins," Warrick said, "recovered after electrophoresis separation. Sometimes it's used in electron microscopy as well. Didn't you ever use it to stain lip prints on a porous surface before?"

Greg shook his head.

"Well, with fingerprints it's the same theory as with lip prints. The ROO stains the lipids, and we're left with a red print on a pink background. That is, if we get anything at all."

Warrick walked Greg through the process; but, when they got through soaking the envelope and drying it, they still had nothing.

"Another dead end," Greg muttered.

Shaking his head, Warrick held the envelope up to the light. "There's just nothing here. . . ."

"At least we tried," Greg said.

"Wait a minute," Warrick said, turning the envelope in the light. "What's that little rectangle at the bottom?"

Greg peeked over his shoulder. "What?"

"Did you look *inside* the envelope?"

"Yeah, of course. There was nothing."

Warrick opened the envelope and, using tweezers, gently withdrew a slim rectangle of thermal paper. "No, there's something—a receipt."

The paper had turned pink; a beautiful red finger-print showed up right in the middle of it.

"Beautiful," Warrick said as he pressed the receipt out flat. "The wig! He bought it at a dollar store at a mall."

"Maybe *they* have security video," Greg said. "A buck's worth, anyway. . . ."

"You contact them, I'll photograph the print and get it into AFIS."

The partners met two hours later in the break room to mainline coffee and compare results, sitting across a table from each other.

"What'd you get?" Warrick asked.

Greg pushed a photo across the table. "Beautiful head shot of our perp from the dollar store's security system. All digital, very cool."

"I'll see your head shot," Warrick said, "and raise you a fingerprint match from AFIS. . . ." He opened a file folder and compared the security photo to the mug shot inside. "Craig Rogers, real piece of crap character."

"Do tell."

"Assault, aggravated assault, robbery, burglary—just got out of the joint two weeks ago."

Greg grunted a little laugh. "Our new best friend Craig also left a nice mark on the guard's head and drew blood. We can probably match the pistol if he's still got it."

Warrick said, "Judging from his rap sheet, Craig's just too damn dumb to dump it. I went back to the bank security tapes and—though I didn't get a better picture of Rogers—I did find a shot through the lobby that showed him climbing into a black-and-yellow striped cab."

"Sunburst Taxi," Greg said. "Easy trace."

"Better tell Reese," Warrick said, getting out his cell phone.

He caught the FBI agent in his office and filled him in.

"Nice work, Mr. Brown," Reese said in a genuine manner. "I'll get back to you."

Warrick ended the call, expecting to never hear the FBI agent's voice again.

But half an hour later, as Warrick finished bagging up the bank robbery evidence, his cell phone chirped. He pulled it off his belt and hit the talk button. "Brown."

"Jamal Reese."

"Special Agent Reese, what can I do for you?"

"We tracked down Rogers. He's at a fleabag hotel downtown. I'm getting ready to go bust down his door and ruin his day . . . thought you and your partner might want the pleasure of joining in. You earned it."

Warrick smiled. "Appreciate the gesture, Special Agent—"

"Jamal," Reese interrupted. "You can call me Jamal."

"I appreciate the gesture, Jamal, and the name is Warrick . . . but to tell you the truth, we're just too tired. We are running on fumes right now, after the shift from hell."

Reese chuckled. "I hear you."

"Anyway, he's your bust—put him away. Shut the door on his cell hard enough, maybe we'll hear it over here."

"All right. Give it my best shot."

"Really, thanks. Mention the crime lab if you get a

chance at the press conference—my boss, Ecklie, would like that—but Greg and I were just doing our job."

There was a short pause, then Reese said, "And you do it very well, Warrick. Both of you. Thanks again."

Warrick ended the call and reported the FBI agent's words to Greg, emphasizing the "both of you" part.

Greg obviously liked hearing that.

"Is this shift finally over?" Greg asked.

From the break-room doorway, looking half asleep, Captain Jim Brass said, "No."

Within minutes, Warrick and Brass sat across the table from Isaiah "Fleety" Fleetwood in an interrogation room.

After so many hours on the job, Warrick felt like death warmed over; but Fleety looked like it. The kid was obviously terrified after spending hours in a holding tank, waiting to find out just how screwed he was.

Brass drummed his fingers on the table, adding to the kid's anxiety. "Look, Fleety—here's the deal. Jalon's going down for murder. Right now, you're going with him."

"But, man, I didn't kill nobody!"

Warrick said coldly, "You damn near killed me."

"No, man, I was jus' talkin'—I woulda never—"

"Knock it off, Fleety. Now," Warrick said, and he sent his hardest, iciest gaze across the table to Fleety.

Who ducked those laser beams, hanging his head.

Brass said, "You do have a chance here. You can tell us what happened—how and why Jalon murdered De-Marcus Hankins. That way, you can avoid death row."

The kid's eyes looked everywhere but at Brass and Warrick. "I ain't no rat."

Warrick said, "Fleety, we've got both Jalon's and your footprints at the murder scene. We've got Jalon's gun with his prints on it, *and* his bullets in DeMarcus. We have both your fingerprints in the car. We have both your DNA on the straws from Bob's Round-Up Grill. Jalon's DNA matches the skin under DeMarcus's nails. We even have a dead lion you fellas ran down. Truth is, Fleety, we don't need you. Jalon goes down, or you both go down—you choose."

With the evidence laid out that way, Fleety needed little time to make a decision. "Damn straight Jalon did it! But it wasn't supposed to be no murder. Hell, I didn't even want to go out on that party, anyway. But Jalon, he told me, if I didn't drive? Then I was a punk-ass bitch, and he'd make sure that all the Hoods knew it."

"What was the party *supposed* to be?" Brass asked.

Fleety shook his head. "Jalon jus' wanted to knock this chump down to size. We grabbed him in a parking lot? He been, you know, soldierin' through our neighborhood like he own the damn place. Jalon said, 'Fuck that,' and we grab him. Jalon say we had to teach the MSB a lesson, that we ain't no pushovers whose turf don't need respecting."

Tears streamed now, and Warrick decided that Brass could finish this interview without him.

The CSI had had enough of this gang stuff for one shift. Hell, enough for every future shift, too; enough of watching strong young brothers going down this weak old path that ruined so many lives.

Maybe it was exhaustion from a twenty-four-hour shift, but Warrick felt sick to his stomach. He made his way to the break room, where he grabbed a bottle of juice, dropped into a chair, and held the cold bottle to his forehead.

Greg came bounding in like the shift had just started. "That oily substance on DeMarcus Hankins's shoes was motor oil."

Warrick nodded. "They snatched him in a parking lot. He probably stepped in somebody's oil leak. Puts him in that car, too, though."

Greg sat across from Warrick, leaned forward. "How bad will it go on Fleety?"

"He's cooperating. That'll help. But you don't draw down on cops and not do some major time. Felony murder, too, though his age may help him."

Greg shifted in his chair. "I talked to Paula Ferguson—Charlie Ames's mistress?"

Again, Warrick nodded. His head felt heavy. The Ames case seemed like a thousand years ago. . . .

Greg was saying, "She said she was getting ready to dump Charlie's behind, next time she saw him. She'd already figured out he wasn't playing with a full deck."

"Oh, he was playing with a full deck, all right—all jokers. You believe her story, Greg? Or is she an accessory, backpedaling?"

Greg considered that. "No—it rang true."

"Got any evidence against her?"

Greg shook his head. "No."

"She's probably in the clear, then."

Greg yawned and rested his head on his folded arms, like a kid catching a nap at a school desk.

And it looked so damned restful, Warrick did the same.

12

THE EMOTIONALLY EXHAUSTED CSIs and the stunned Boot Hill police chief took chairs at the empty desks in the bullpen and sat facing each other. Grissom, tired of talking, nodded to Catherine, who filled Lopez in.

When she'd finished—a concise and accurate account that Grissom admired—Lopez, shaking his head, his eyes rather dazed, muttered, "I was . . . I was just coming in to call the governor again and tell him that we were about to be overrun."

And the chief reached for a phone.

Catherine raised a hand. "No—get Finch out of his cell."

"What?" Lopez said, astonished. "Why?"

Her colleagues gazed at her in bewilderment—all but Grissom, that is.

Quietly she said, "What does that mob want?"

"Half of them want Finch free," Lopez said. "Half want his head."

"Get him," she repeated. "And I'll need a bull-horn. . . . Chief, you have to trust me on this."

Lopez looked searchingly at Grissom. "Doc . . . ?"

"Do what she says, Chief," Grissom said. "I think I know where she's going, and it's our best chance."

Less than two minutes later, Chief Lopez and the cuffed prisoner, Finch, emerged onto the front stoop of the station, several steps above the crowd of several hundred agitated faces. Catherine, Grissom, Sara, and Nick came out right behind them.

Before them milled two distinct groups, the Spokes and the Predators, a thin line of Highway Patrolmen and Boot Hill cops between the two groups in riot squad formation; another line of lawmen stood behind some flimsy barricades in front of the station.

The two biker contingents had been shouting each other down, but a hush of surprise fell across both camps at the sight of the cops and the prisoner at the top of the short flight of cement steps.

To Catherine Willows, the bullhorn in her hands felt heavier than any weapon she had ever held. Her stomach was doing a fluttery dance and she knew that if she botched this, if her instincts were wrong, they all might die.

She took a deep breath and raised the bullhorn.

"*Everybody please listen,*" she said.

This prompted the shouting to resume, but now instead of each other, screams and yells and obscenities were directed at the front of the police station, in defiance of Catherine's request.

She pressed on: "*No one has to die here today!*"

These words—she would never quite be sure why—caused the crowd noise to dissipate. They were looking up at her, bikers and cops alike, with the same bewilderment that her colleagues had when she first suggested Buck Finch be brought from his cell.

"We know who killed Nick Valpo."

With the Spokes leader there in custody, on public view, the Predators assumed Catherine meant Finch and began to cheer. And the Spokes roared their disapproval.

Catherine put a quick stop to this: *"The killer was not Buck Finch! Not any of the Rusty Spokes!"*

And now the Spokes whooped and hollered, while the Predators booed and catcalled, the small presence of cops below looking uneasy as hell, and Catherine knew the scene was as close to erupting into violence as it had ever been.

"Sergeant Cody Jacks, a Boot Hill police officer with a grudge, killed Valpo. Minutes ago, Jacks was taken down by Chief Lopez inside the station."

The crowd fell eerily silent as it absorbed these words.

Every face, Predator or Spoke or police, froze; so many wide eyes and gaping mouths—it might have seemed comic to Catherine had she not been so terrified.

"You had to have heard the shot. . . . Valpo's killer is dead. Not a result of your feud, but of Cody Jacks wanting revenge."

Murmuring rippled through the crowd, building, building . . . she hoped it would not build into a full-throttle riot. . . .

Then, in the distance, so far away she didn't know if she really perceived it or if it was just wishful thinking, Catherine heard a familiar electronic wail . . .

. . . the swell of sirens.

The crowd heard it, too, and looked behind them, then back at her as she continued on the bullhorn.

"The four Spokes now in custody—including Buck Finch—will remain with us to answer for their crimes."

On the Spokes side of the police line, the bikers began to shout threats and obscenities again. They seemed about to surge forward. . . .

Lopez leaned in where only the CSIs—and Finch—could hear him and see what he was up to. Easing his pistol out of his holster, behind Finch's back, he pressed the barrel into Finch's spine and said, "You care to defuse this for us, Buck? Because if we have any more fatalities here today, I'd say you're first on the firing line."

Finch craned his neck to look into the dangerously placid face of the police chief.

Catherine held the bullhorn toward the biker honcho. "Anything you'd like to say to the Spokes, Mr. Finch?"

He sighed.

And nodded.

Catherine held the bullhorn up.

"Enough killing," he said in a voice that would have been loud and commanding without the amplification. *"You Spokes—all of you! Back down."*

Some of Finch's gang appeared confused by this order, and a few seemed outright angry, but scattered booing was cut off by their leader's voice.

"Goddamnit! I still run the Spokes, and I say back down! Now!"

Both gangs backed off a little, but they did not disperse. The sirens in the distance seemed very real to Catherine now, growing ever closer.

Lopez, who had holstered his pistol without the crowd ever seeing it, held out his hand for the bull-horn; Finch gave it to him.

The chief asked Finch, "Who's your second in command?"

"Eddy," Finch said. All of the air was out of him. "Eddy Prentice."

Using the bullhorn, Lopez called Prentice of the Spokes and Jake Hanson of the Predators to join the group on the stairs. As they waited for the two to make their way up, Lopez called a uniformed officer over and had him take Finch back inside.

"But just inside—out of sight, in case we need to play this card again."

The two high-ranking reps from either gang came up the short flight of steps simultaneously, never taking their eyes off each other.

Prentice was maybe six feet tall, skinny but muscular, with curly black hair, cool dark eyes, and a black soul patch; he had tattoos on either hand and wore tight black jeans and a faded black T-shirt.

The brown-haired, ripped, rock-star-ish Hanson wore a frayed white Harley T-shirt and blue jeans.

Neither man spoke to his counterpart. Catherine could tell that was fine with Lopez, who had plenty to say.

"First thing," the chief said quietly to the new leaders, "is I want you to both look at the roof of the building across the street."

Lopez waved and—out of view for most of the crowd, but plainly visible from the steps of the police station—a Boot Hill police officer wielding a sniper's rifle waved back.

The chief said, "Any questions?"

Prentice shook his head.

Hanson said, "No."

"Eddy," Lopez said to the Spokes rep, "Buck's being charged with inciting a riot and attempted murder. You try to break him out"—he glanced toward the sniper—"let's just say, we *all* know you're top dog with Finch in jail."

Prentice said, "Spare me the threats, Jorge—Buck says it's done . . . it's done."

Hanson nodded. "Yeah. Done. Hell . . . sometimes, both sides lose."

"Town lost, too," Lopez put in.

"What d'you want from us?" Hanson asked.

"I want you gone," Lopez said. "Now. The state police have names and addresses from all of you; we'll know where to find you. Get your people out of here—both of you. This was the last Biker Blowout in Boot Hill—ever."

The Spokes rep nodded and started down the stairs; but he stopped when Hanson didn't move to go, too.

Hanson's eyes locked with Lopez's. "We'll go. This is done. But Chief—we still want Val's body."

Grissom stepped forward. "We don't have it, but we know where to look. We'll get it back, do what we need to, then you can have the body . . . tomorrow, next day at the latest."

Lopez said, "You can stay in town, Jake—send your crew away, and you can stay and collect your leader. I'll need next-of-kin sanction, understand?"

Hanson considered all that; then he slowly nodded. Finally, they both went down the steps, side by side, parting to lead their respective gangs away. The officers on the street—Boot Hill cops and Highway Patrolmen alike—watched the bikers file away; but none of the officers relaxed their stance an iota.

As the stragglers filtered off and the sirens grew steadily louder, Lopez asked, "Doc, can we really find Valpo's body?"

Grissom said, "We'll need a thermal imager, but yes."

"He's been dead for over a day."

"Disturbed soil from where Jacks buried him will give off a different heat signature than the surrounding ground. We'll find him."

"And what about Tom Price, Doc? That's a murder, not a suicide."

"Another crime scene in a very long day," Grissom said.

"How about I call Sheriff Burdick," Catherine said, "and get a fresh team out for that one?"

Grissom smiled. "You're the boss."

Lopez shook hands all around. "I can't thank you people enough." His eyes lingered on Grissom and then even longer on Catherine. "You saved our town—literally."

"Don't know about that, Chief," Grissom said. "You did a pretty good job of staying on top of this yourself. We'll have Valpo's body sent out as soon as possible."

"Appreciate that." Lopez rubbed his forehead. "I just wish . . . hell, wish it hadn't been one of my own."

"He wasn't," Catherine said.

Lopez looked confused.

Grissom said, "Catherine's right—Cody Jacks stopped

being a police officer the day he decided to seek revenge, not justice . . . frontier or otherwise."

Last thing Warrick Brown knew, he was just resting his head on the break-room table for a second. . . .

Something was banging on that table and he sat up with a start, eyes bleary. He rubbed them and saw Nick, Sara, Grissom, and Catherine standing there, like he was Dorothy woken from Oz to find the farmhands gathered at her bedside.

"Sleeping?" Catherine asked, leaning a hand on the table. She was smiling but, for Catherine Willows anyway, looked terrible. "We work our butts off all night, processing the biggest crime scene ever, in the middle of a biker war—and you three are napping?"

Three? Warrick looked around, and Jim Brass and Greg were both groggily waking up, having fallen asleep at the same break-room table.

"Long night," Warrick said.

"Tell us about it," Nick said with a snort.

"Solved three murders," Brass said, trying out the taste in his mouth and obviously not caring for it.

Nick waved that off. "We spilled more than that."

Greg said helpfully, "We had a lion—king of the jungle?—turn up as roadkill at a gang killing."

"Sure you did," Sara said.

"Caught a bank robber," Greg said, only suddenly it sounded kind of lame.

Unimpresed, Nick said, "All *we* did was stare down a couple hundred drugged-out bikers brandishing tire irons and chains."

Brass's eyebrows rose. " 'Brandishing'?"

Somehow Warrick grinned. "Yeah, but did any of you guys have a gun pointed at your head while another of you talked the perp down? And saved your damn *life*?"

Nick said, "Who did that, 'Rick? Jim?"

"Greg."

Grissom said, "Greg—I'm proud of you."

Greg shrugged and tried not to blush.

Catherine said, "Oh, and Greg? Word to the wise. Tip from a pro?"

"Yes?"

"Careful how you sleep on hair with that much product in it. You look a little like a cactus something nasty happened to."

Greg was still processing that remark as if it were a particularly puzzling piece of evidence, when just about everybody else began to laugh. Exhaustion hysteria made Catherine's comment, and Greg's hair sticking up, seem funnier than they really were, causing tears of laughter to flow at an unusual rate for a crime lab.

The only one not laughing was Grissom, who merely smiled—his eyes on Greg, pleased.

A TIP OF THE
TEST TUBE

My ASSISTANT, MATTHEW CLEMENS, HELPED me develop the plot of *Snake Eyes* and worked up a lengthy story treatment, which included all of his considerable forensic research, from which I could work. Matthew—an accomplished true-crime writer who has collaborated with me on numerous published short stories—does most of the on-site Vegas research and is largely responsible for any sense of the real city that might be found herein.

On occasion, however, I accompany him on these trips, as when we spent the better part of two days with the real CSIs of Las Vegas, who told us of a case that inspired, loosely, the casino shoot-out in *Snake Eyes*. Doing so, they won the dedication of this novel, and our gratitude. We also note, however, that the inspiration was of a basic nature and the crimes detailed in this book are wholly fictional.

We would once again like to acknowledge criminalist Lieutenant Chris Kauffman CLPE—the Gil Grissom of the Bettendorf, Iowa, Police Department—who provided comments, insights, and information; Chris has been an important member of our

CSI team since the first novel and remains vital to our efforts. Thank you, too, to another major contributor to our research, Lieutenant Paul Van Steenhuyse, Scott County Sheriff's Office; and also Sergeant Jeff Swanson, Scott County Sheriff's Office (for autopsy and crime scene assistance). Thanks also go to Gary L. Johansen, crime lab supervisor, Salt Lake City Police Department, for sharing the anecdote from which the bank robbery chapter was developed.

Books consulted include two works by Vernon J. Geberth: *Practical Homicide Investigation: Checklist and Field Guide* (1996) and *Practical Homicide Investigation: Tactics, Procedures, and Forensic Techniques* (1996). Also helpful were *Crime Scene: The Ultimate Guide to Forensic Science* by Richard Platt; and *Scene of the Crime: A Writer's Guide to Crime-Scene Investigations* (1992) by Anne Wingate, Ph.D. We also cite the *Journal of Forensic Identification*, Volume 56, No. 1, Jan/Feb 2006, and thank Anissa Rawji and Alexandre Beaudoin for their article about Red Oil O. Any inaccuracies, however, are my own.

At Pocket Books, Ed Schlesinger, our gracious editor, provided his usual keen eye and solid support. The producers of *CSI: Crime Scene Investigation* sent along scripts, background material (including show bibles), and episode tapes. As before, we wish to especially thank Corinne Marrinan, coauthor (with Mike Flaherty) of the indispensible Pocket Books publication *CSI: Crime Scene Investigation Companion*.

Anthony E. Zuiker is gratefully acknowledged as the creator of this concept and these characters; and the cast must be applauded for vivid, memorable characterizations. Our thanks, too, to various *CSI* writers for their inventive and well-documented scripts, which we draw upon for backstory.

Finally, thanks to the fans of the show who have extended their enthusiasm into following these novels. We have a fairly specific continuity in this series of prose "episodes," which tends to lag behind that of the show itself, and we thank our readers for grasping and understanding that reality of production (and difference between mediums) as we have attempted to explore these familiar characters from within.

ABOUT THE AUTHOR

MAX ALLAN COLLINS, a Mystery Writers of America Edgar Award nominee in both fiction and non-fiction categories, was hailed in 2004 by *Publishers Weekly* as "a new breed of writer." He has earned an unprecedented fifteen Private Eye Writers of America Shamus nominations for his historical thrillers, winning twice for his Nathan Heller novels *True Detective* (1983) and *Stolen Away* (1991).

His other credits include film criticism, short fiction, songwriting, trading-card sets, and movie/TV tie-in novels, including *Air Force One*, *In the Line of Fire*, and the *New York Times* bestseller *Saving Private Ryan*.

His graphic novel *Road to Perdition* is the basis of the Academy Award–winning DreamWorks 2002 feature film starring Tom Hanks, Paul Newman, and Jude Law, directed by Sam Mendes. His many comics credits include the *Dick Tracy* syndicated strip; his own *Ms. Tree*; *Batman*; and *CSI: Crime Scene Investigation*, based on the hit TV series for which he has also written video games, jigsaw puzzles, and a *USA Today* bestselling series of novels.

An independent filmmaker in his native Iowa, he

wrote and directed *Mommy*, which premiered on Lifetime in 1996, as well as a 1997 sequel, *Mommy's Day*. The screenwriter of *The Expert*, a 1995 HBO world premiere, he also wrote and directed the innovative made-for-DVD feature *Real Time: Siege at Lucas Street Market* (2000). *Shades of Noir* (2004)—an anthology of his short films, including his award-winning documentary *Mike Hammer's Mickey Spillane*—is included in the recent DVD boxed set of Collins's indie films, *The Black Box*. He recently completed a documentary, *Caveman: V.T. Hamlin and Alley Oop*, and another feature, *Eliot Ness: An Untouchable Life*, based on his Edgar-nominated play.

Collins lives in Muscatine, Iowa, with his wife, writer Barbara Collins; their son, Nathan, is a recent graduate in computer science and Japanese at the University of Iowa and is currently pursuing post-grad studies in Japan.

There's more forensic mystery and drama with

CRIME SCENE INVESTIGATION™

BINDING TIES

by *New York Times* bestselling author
Max Allan Collins

An original novel based on the critically
acclaimed hit CBS series—available now
wherever books are sold!

Turn the page for an electrifying excerpt . . .

WHEN GRISSOM HAD COMPLETED his initial pass at the body, he withdrew his cell phone and punched the speed dial.

On the second ring, a brusque voice answered: "Jim Brass."

"I've got something you need to see," Grissom said, without identifying himself. "It's not in your jurisdiction, but it's right up your alley."

"Cute, Gil. But haven't you heard? I'm on vacation."

"Really kicking back, are you?"

Silence; no, not silence: Grissom, detective that he was, could detect a sigh.

"You know as well as I do," Brass said. "I'm bored out of my mind."

"You know, people who live for their work should seek other outlets."

"What, like collecting bugs? Gil—what have you got?"

"An oldie but baddie—I wasn't with you on it . . . kind of before our time together."

"What are you *talking* about?"

"The one you never forget—your first case."

The long pause that followed contained no sigh. Not even a breath. Just stony silence.

Then Brass said, "You're not talking about my first case back in Jersey, are you?"

"No. I've got a killing out here in North Las Vegas that shares a distinctive M.O. with your *other* first case."

"Christ. Where are you exactly?"

"Just getting started."

"I mean the address!"

"Oh," Grissom said, and gave it to him.

"Twenty minutes," Brass said and broke the connection.

The homicide captain made it in fifteen.

From the open doorway, Grissom watched Brass's car pull up and the detective get out, and cross the lawn like a man on a mission. Which, Grissom supposed, he was.

The compact, mournful-eyed Brass—always one to wear a jacket and tie, no matter the weather—had showed up in jeans and a blue shirt open at the neck.

The uniformed officer, Logan, went out to catch Brass at the front stoop, thinking a relative or other civilian had arrived. The detective flashed his badge, but Logan seemed unimpressed.

"What brings you to our neck of the woods, Captain?"

Leaning out the doorway, Grissom called, "He's with me, Officer. It's all right."

Logan, apparently not wishing to tangle with Grissom again, sighed and nodded, and let Brass pass.

"You could've told him I was coming," Brass complained.

"Yeah, well I'm still working on my social skills," Grissom said.

"Really? How's that coming along?"

Shrugging, Grissom stepped back inside and got out of the way so Brass could see the body.

The detective took one look and shook his head.

The blood had drained from his face and his eyes were large and unblinking. "Well, son of a—"

"*Is* it CASt?" Grissom asked.

Catherine came back in from the kitchen, kit in one latex-gloved hand, gesturing behind her with the other. "I didn't find anything except dirty dishes. . . ."

Seeing Brass, she froze and blinked. "Aren't you on vacation?"

Brass nodded to her. "I was." His sad gaze fixed on Grissom. "Well, it sure *looks* like CASt's handiwork. . . ."

"Cast?" Catherine asked, joining them. The three had the corpse surrounded—he wasn't going anywhere.

Closing his eyes, Brass touched the thumb and middle finger of his right hand to the bridge of his nose. "You didn't work that case . . . you might even have been a lab tech still. I dunno."

Catherine looked at Grissom and tightened her eyes in a signal of *Help me out here?* Grissom, of course, merely shrugged.

Brass was saying, "I know you've heard me talk

about it—my first case here. Never solved? Lot of play in the press? Worst serial killer in Vegas history? Cop in charge an incompetent New Jersey jackass? Sound familiar?"

"Taunted the PD in the papers," Catherine said, nodding, thinking out loud. "Used the initials . . . C period A period S period tee."

"'Capture,'" Grissom said, "'Afflict, and Strangle.'"

"I did a little lab work on the case," Catherine said. "I was nightshift then, too. And wasn't it a dayshift case?"

"Yes. This was ten, eleven years ago." Brass rubbed his forehead. "I had just transferred in, from back East. Still shell-shocked from my . . . my divorce. Not exactly on top of the Vegas scene, yet. . . ."

"All I remember about the case is pretty vague," Catherine admitted. "More from TV and the papers than anything in-house. . . ."

Grissom said, "Lots of media, but we were able to control it better in those days. And fortunately it never caught wide national play."

Brass said, "Yeah, we kept as much out as we could. My partner, Vince Champlain, didn't want to muddy the waters."

"Good call," Catherine said. "Wish we had better luck with that, these days."

Brass continued: "Vince was the senior detective. He figured, more we put in the paper, more crackpots we'd have to deal with. S.O.P. And yet, of course, there were plenty just the same. We must've had twenty different whack jobs try to claim those crimes."

"None of the wrongos looked right?" Catherine asked.

Brass shook his head. "Nah, standard issue nutcases. Serial confessors."

Catherine said, "What *did* you have?"

With a dark, defeated smile, Brass looked at her and said, "Victims—we had victims. Five—all male, all white, all in late middle-age, and all on the heavy side . . ."

As if it had been choreographed, the detective and the two CSIs looked as one at the dead body.

". . . and all strangled with a reverse-eight noose."

Catherine frowned. "Which is what, exactly?"

"A knot—a 'wrong' running noose," Grissom said. "It's about which end of the rope you pull to tighten the noose. This knot's backward . . . and other than yo-yos, you never see it used."

Turning back to Brass, Catherine asked, "Any real suspects back then?"

"We started with a slew, but we narrowed it to three," Brass said. "I had a guy I liked, Vince had a guy *he* liked, and there was a third one that looked good, only neither of us thought he did the killings."

Pointing at the body, Grissom said, "Here's how we do this: Run it like we would any other homicide investigation."

Brass nodded, then asked, "You want me to start with looking into our old suspects?"

Grissom gave him a long, appraising look. "First, a question."

"Second, an answer."

"Should you be working on this?"

"Shouldn't I?" Brass said, his voice rising slightly.

"Jim," Catherine said. "You've carried this one around for a long time. Objectivity—"

"Can kiss my ass," he blurted, then immediately seemed embarrassed about it.

Grissom studied his friend. "So you're Captain Ahab on this one?"

"Let's just say," Brass said, "I'm gonna catch the dick."

"Ah," Grissom said ambiguously.

"And," Brass said, swallowing, his tone softening, "we will, as you say, work it like any other homicide."

Grissom's eyes met Catherine's. Her skepticism was etched in an open-mouthed smile.

Apologetically, Brass said, "Come on, you two— you'll keep me honest on this. You'll keep me—"

"Objective?" Catherine offered. "You really think this is a good idea, Jim?" But her question was obviously intended for Grissom.

Grissom ignored that and said to Brass, "Do you see any reasonable way this could be a coincidence, looking so much like a CASt-off?"

Catherine added, "Which is what the press called his victims, right?"

"Yeah, and it's no coincidence." Brass indicated the corpse. "If this isn't the guy's real signature, it's sure as hell a copycat who knows how to commit a hell of a forgery."

Catherine asked, "How so?"

Brass shrugged. "Well, if it's a copycat, he or she knows way more than was ever in the media."

Nodding, Catherine said, "You kept things back, so you could sort through the false confessions. Of course . . ."

Grissom said, "Whether this is a blast from the past or a latter-day cover artist . . . we're going to need all the help we can get."

Catherine drew in a deep breath and let it out. "New or old—this is one vicious killer."

Grissom was watching the homicide captain. "See anything here, Jim? You're the veteran of the CASt-off crime scenes."

Brass moved closer, squatted next to the dead man, then finally rose and faced Grissom.

"Much as I'd like to have a crack at the original CASt," he said measuredly, "I think this may be a copycat."

Grissom and Catherine traded a look.

"Why?" Grissom asked.

"Appears staged. For one thing, there's not enough blood."

Catherine stared at the coagulating puddle on the rug. "How so?"

"Those five original murder scenes," Brass said, and his eyes took on a haunted cast, "spray was everywhere. Here, there's none of that."

"Blood spatter," she said with satisfaction; after all, it was her specialty. "In the other cases, were the fingers cut off *before* the victims were killed?"

Brass, pleased she was following him, said, "Yes."

"Here it would seem to be postmortem. A living victim would have considerable spray, and might wave his mutilated hand around, further spreading the blood."

"Right," Brass said with a nod. "And there's something that isn't right about how the semen is pooled on his back. . . ."

Grissom fielded that one, explaining his theory,

and concluding with, "It's always hard to tell with ejaculate at a crime scene—configuration of the victim's body, and how the perp's body functions; but this looks almost—poured on."

"B.Y.O.S.," Catherine said.

Brass and Grissom frowned at her in confusion.

Her eyebrows rose. "Bring your own semen? The killer brought his specimen from home. Or maybe it was a woman, who *had* to bring a specimen. . . ."

"Makes sense either way," Brass said. "A copycat is coldly staging a crime; the real crimes were driven by passion, by a killer really . . . *into* it."

"Exactly my point," Grissom said. "Still, this crime scene is close to the originals, right?"

"Yeah," Brass said. "Other than these details we've discussed . . . oh, yeah."

"With a copycat, our lines of inquiry become nicely narrowed." Grissom gestured toward the body. "Who *did* know this much information about those murders?"

Thought clouded the detective's face. Then: "Well, the killer, of course . . . the cops on the case, ourselves . . . and a couple of newspaper guys."

Catherine asked, "Who, specifically?"

"Two crime beat reporters for the Las Vegas *Banner*—Perry Bell and David Paquette. They received the original taunting letters from CASt. And they even did a quickie paperback, about the case."

"Isn't Paquette an editor at the *Banner*?" Catherine asked.

"*Now* he is—Paquette seemed to get the better end of the book notoriety. Paquette got the editor's post, but then Bell *did* get his own column."

Both CSIs nodded. Most LVPD personnel knew of Bell and his column, *The Bell Beat*. Grissom didn't think the guy was much of a writer, but then neither were Walter Winchell or Larry King. However, the columnist did have a reputation for honesty, and it was said he never betrayed a source or any kind of trust, which was a big part of how he'd been successful for so long. When a cop shared something with Bell in confidence, it stayed that way until the officer told him he could print it.

"Guess I better go have a chat with the Fourth Estate," Brass said.

Catherine gestured to the grotesque corpse. "You think either Paquette or Bell might be capable of . . . this?"

Brass shrugged. "Gacy was a clown, Bundy a law student, Juan Corona a labor contractor who killed two dozen for fun and profit. Who's to say *what* people are capable of? One thing I do know—if we're treating this like a normal homicide, then Perry Bell and Dave Paquette are suspects . . . and I'm going to go have a talk with them."

They met with the other cops and CSIs in the yard while paramedics went inside to deal with the body.

Damon looked annoyed as he eyeballed Brass. "What are you doing here, Jim?"

Brass started to say something, but Grissom stepped up like a referee.

"I called him in," Grissom said. "As an advisor. He worked a case very similar to this years ago."

"Similar how?" Damon asked.

"Similar," Grissom said, "exactly."

"Another murder?"

"Murders," Brass said. "A serial killer."

"Oh, come on," Damon said. "What is this, the movies?"

Catherine said, "Why, do you get a lot of d.b.'s out here in North Las Vegas, men with lipstick smiles and semen on their backs?"

Damon's mouth opened but no words came out.

Grissom said, "It's a perp called CASt."

That really got Damon's attention; he took a long pause and swallowed and said, "Holy shit . . . I remember him. It was in the papers when I was in college! Damn . . . you think *he* did this?"

Grissom and Brass exchanged glances; then the CSI supervisor shrugged. "We don't know. He's been inactive for something like eleven years. We'll see."

"You'll be working with me, of course," Damon said. "I mean, it is my case."

Again, Brass started to say something and Grissom cut him off. "Certainly."

"Well . . . then . . . good." Damon nodded, put his hands on his hips and puffed up a little bit. "Glad that's understood. Good."

Turning his attention to his team, Grissom asked, "Well?"

Nick said, "Nothing that seems related in the backyard."

"Front yard looks clean too," Warrick said. "Got a partial footprint, but it could be nothing."

"Or something," Grissom said.

"Or something," Warrick said with a humorless smirk.

"I got a sample of the neighbor's prints," Sara said. "But she claims she never touched the bell or the knob. She says she just looked inside, saw the 'horrible thing,' and called 911."

Grissom began to smile—just a little. "Possible fingerprints, possible footprints, DNA evidence. . . . We've started with less. And we have an M.O. match to past crimes. What do you say, gang? Shall we cast out our line, and reel in a killer?"

Don't Miss

CSI:
CRIME SCENE INVESTIGATION™

BINDING TIES